THE 16TH ACADEMY

THE 16TH ACADEMY

SPENCER YACOS

SWEETWATER
BOOKS

An Imprint of Cedar Fort, Inc.
Springville, Utah

ISBN 13: 978-1-4621-1934-9

Published by Sweetwater Books, an imprint of Cedar Fort, Inc.
2373 W. 700 S., Springville, UT 84663
Distributed by Cedar Fort, Inc. www.cedarfort.com

LIBRARY OF CONGRESS CATALOGING-IN-PUBLICATION DATA

Names: Yacos, Spencer, 1998- author.
Title: The 16th academy / Spencer Yacos.
Other titles: Sixteenth academy
Description: Springville, Utah : Sweet Water Books, an imprint of Cedar Fort, Inc., [2016]
Identifiers: LCCN 2016041816 (print) | LCCN 2016043846 (ebook) | ISBN 9781462119349 (perfect bound : alk. paper) | ISBN 9781462127122 (epub, pdf, and mobi)
Subjects: LCSH: Juvenile delinquents--Education--Fiction. | New York (State), setting. | LCGFT: Thrillers (Fiction) | Novels.
Classification: LCC PS3625.A34 A614 2016 (print) | LCC PS3625.A34 (ebook) | DDC 813/.6--dc23
LC record available at https://lccn.loc.gov/2016041816

Cover design by Priscilla Chaves
Cover design © 2016 Cedar Fort, Inc.
Edited and typeset by Jennifer Johnson

Printed in the United States of America

10 9 8 7 6 5 4 3 2 1

Printed on acid-free paper

To my grandfather, the best storyteller I ever knew.

PROLOGUE

Camelot is ready. The operation is a go," a voice crackled through the transceiver in my ear. The mission was being initiated and a part of me was annoyed. Only halfway through my fried chicken, I was still pretty hungry. I hadn't eaten since the night before, since the plane ride down that morning served no breakfast. Given that I was going to meet with a drug kingpin in a few minutes, the last thing I wanted was for my stomach to be growling.

I sat in the first-floor food court of the Franklin Building, El Paso's premier commercial block and the headquarters of the global fast-food chain Beef 'n' Wings. It was just after noon and the area stirred with visitors eager for their lunch. From my position I could see two other field agents, the only other two in the building. Far off to my right, just outside the crowds and colorful cacophony of restaurants, a hulking teenage boy seemed to have the same idea I had as he snacked on a beef hot dog from one of the stands. He wore a blue hard hat with matching blue overalls and heavy-looking harnesses that clung to his body. At his side, he loosely held a squeegee as well as some napkins, presumably for his meal. After taking a big gulp, his lips began to move. It was much too noisy in the food court to pick up any word he was saying naturally, but on the transceiver I could hear him perfectly. *"Percival is ready. Let's get this over with."*

At the booming sound of Leon's voice, I covered my ear nervously, realizing that there was an elderly couple the next table over. There was a good chance they heard nothing, and an even greater chance that they wouldn't have cared anyway, but one could never be too careful, especially with jobs in public areas. Far off to my right, near the elevators, a small boy lay crouched in the corner, trying his best to stealthily fiddle with an air vent grate next to him. I was only two years his senior, but people often mistook him for being far younger. He had long, greasy hair and pale skin, products of his indoorsy lifestyle. Out of the three of us in the building, his T-shirt and shorts were probably the most appropriate for the balmy weather outside. His high-pitched voice rang up in my ear, *"Kay's ready. The grate's off."*

"Proceed with caution," a young female voice ordered. It belonged to Mabel, one half of this mission's 'Camelot,' or control center. She and another operative, Charlie, gave orders from a different, undisclosed part of town. On their computers, they watched live feeds of the Franklin Building and the surrounding area taken from security cameras and other hacked equipment.

With the go-ahead, Ozzy checked the area directly around him carefully. Then, he swiftly slipped into the air duct, replacing the grate once inside. I made sure not to look at him directly while he did this, as I didn't want him to attract unwanted attention. It was at this point that I realized that it was my turn to check in. Taking one last swig of soda, I said, "Galahad's ready. Looking for a visual on the target."

Our target today was Garret Beauregard, the CEO of Beef 'n' Wings himself, whose products I was currently sampling. Since the Academy's clients are allowed to stay anonymous, we almost never know whom we're working for or for what reason.

As I scanned the first floor for our very special guest, one final voice rang over the transceiver. This one was female like Mabel's but much deeper, as well as much more mature, practically adult. *"Lancelot is ready. I have a visual of the office,"* she said. It was Johanna, who, at eighteen, was the oldest member of our team. As our sniper, if and when things got ugly, she was the first one to pull the trigger. Even on a crackling transceiver, one could still detect the soft, yet ambiguous, tone of voice. It was very hard to tell if in the next sentence she was going to compliment you or warn you of your imminent death. *"Galahad, the Fisher King's car was just sent down to the parking lot,"* she continued. *"He should be in there."*

"Just a sec," I insisted, practically standing on my seat, trying to look through the ocean of people before me. Then, like the Red Sea obeying Moses, the crowd seemed to thin just long enough for me to spot a bigger-looking man with a white cowboy hat. He, along with a couple of men next to him, wore an expensive-looking suit, not unlike the one I donned that day. "I see him. I have a visual on the Fisher King," I whispered into my transceiver. "He's with . . . three other guys. They armed?"

"This is Texas, man," Charlie replied. *"What do you think?"*

"Lovely," I sighed, standing up and throwing away my half-eaten lunch. "He's headed to the elevator. Permission to pursue?"

"*Granted*," Mabel said. Her voice became higher, as it usually did when she knew danger was afoot. "*Now hurry up; five men can't fit in that elevator.*"

"Roger," I responded. Speeding across the food court, I wove my way through the people until I found myself by the shiny elevator doors, standing next to Beauregard and his well-dressed friends. As I waited for the doors to open, I tried my best to avoid eye contact. Beauregard, on an impulse of hospitality, said, "You're pretty dressed up, sonny. On a hot date?"

I gave one last silent mental grimace before lighting up my face with a bright smile, turning to the wealthy gentleman. Enthusiastically, I spouted, "Haha! Very funny, sir. I'm starting an internship upstairs, so obviously I have to look my very best."

"Internship? Where?" the CEO pressed.

I produced a crumpled slip of paper from my pocket and read, "Floor thirty-five, room three. It's with Beef 'n' Wings. You know them? The super-famous-surprisingly-nutritious fast-food chain? I love all their meals."

"Huh," the president gave a tentative smile. He extended his hand, "Well isn't this your lucky day? Garret Beauregard, president of Beef 'n' Wings, at your service."

I sucked in, trying to contain all my feigned excitement, "*The* Garret Beauregard? Founder of Beef 'n' Wings? Inventor of the $1.50 menu? *Restaurant Monthly*'s ninth most powerful man in fast food? David Jones, I'm, like, your biggest fan!" I shook his hand fervently.

Beauregard chuckled, maybe amused by my antics. "I didn't even know I had fans! Pleasure to meet you, boy."

"*We're going radio silent on Galahad*," Charlie buzzed in my ear. "*Keep on his good side and look for an opening.*"

I absentmindedly scratched my ear, switching off my transceiver. My only connection with the rest of my operatives was severed. Now, I was all alone.

The elevator to the right gave a faint *ding* and the doors quietly spread open. Beauregard, two men from his entourage, and I crammed into the elevator. Just as Mabel had predicted, one of the gentlemen volunteered to stay outside, promising to take the next lift up. Right before the doors shut, I managed to spot Leon, squeegee in hand, breaking from the crowd and departing the building.

As I felt the elevator lift us, there was a twinge of anxiety, realizing that I was now stuck in an enclosed space with three armed men. I was allowed to be nervous. A little nervousness was fine; I was pretending to be a student on his first day as an intern.

"This your first time in the city, blondie?" Beauregard asked me, reminding me that I was wearing a blond wig in addition to thick-rimmed glasses to hide my identity.

"You bet!" I said, keeping my enthusiasm high. I brushed my artificial bangs to the side. Out of all the wigs I'd worn over the course of hundreds of missions, this was my least favorite. It was long, got in my eyes, never fit my head right, and suspiciously smelled of cottage cheese. Regardless, wig selection at the Academy was limited, and every one had to be worn once in a while.

"So, you're from the country, then? Don't look like much of a country fella . . . which town?"

"Um, it's a real small town, south of here," I said, trying my best to stay vague.

"South of El Paso?" Beauregard gave me a very confused look.

"I mean north! Just a little north," I corrected myself, rubbing my head. "Sorry, my mind's not working straight today. Still trying to process the fact that I got to meet you."

"Right, right," Beauregard nodded understandingly. "Yeah, it's pretty easy to tell that you're not south of the border. Be able to smell you a mile away!"

The three men laughed heartily. I forced a light chuckle while the hunger in the pit of my stomach changed to disgust. With another *ding* we arrived on floor thirty-five and stepped off. For an extravagant fast-food brand, their headquarters looked pretty ordinary. The walls and carpets were white, and the faint but stinging odor of hand sanitizer wafted through the air. "Welcome to where the magic happens!" Beauregard extended his arm toward the lobby, looking like an artist revealing their magnum opus.

"Gee whiz!" I exclaimed.

The president, still flanked by his two men, who I presumed were his bodyguards, approached the front desk and rang the bell, getting the secretary's attention. "Yes, Mr. Beauregard?"

"Got an intern with me, Marcy," the man declared. "His name's David Jones. I was wondering where I could put him."

"Intern? Sir, new internships don't begin until the summer."

My heart skipped a beat. The moment of truth had arrived. "They said I was a special case when they drove me over here," I said, injecting myself into the conversation. "Please, just check your computer."

Marcy shifted her mouse around, making a quick series of clicks. "Okay . . . here it is. David Jones, intern, arriving today . . . " She looked up at me and then back down to her screen. I whispered a silent prayer to Charlie, the master hacker. A few clicks later, the secretary looked up again. "Yeah, everything looks good. Funny, I don't remember—"

"Well, everything checks out!" I interrupted. "Where should I go?"

Beauregard gestured to one of his guards. "Samson here will take good care of you, kid. Now, I've got a little meeting to go to, but I'll see you around, okay?"

Not counting on it. "Okay!" I cheerfully chirped. "Oh my gosh, this is all so exciting!"

I followed Samson down a hallway, away from Beauregard and the lobby. He directed me through a door, into a room darker than the hallway. Chairs lined the walls and a vacant table with a picnic cloth sat in the center of the room. "Um, this is where we usually bring interns in the summer. There'd be, like, food on the tables and we'd get someone to give you an introduction. Usually it's this hot brunette from marketing."

"Uh-huh," I absentmindedly nodded, no longer bothering to keep up my fake excitement. As the door closed behind us, I began to fiddle through my suit pockets.

Samson, clearly unsure of what to do, continued to ramble. "Yeah, I actually used to be an intern here, once. I was raised right up in Anthony. Wait, where did you say you were from again? Cuz I remember—"

Samson's sentence was cut off as I stabbed a syringe into the side of his throat—one swift and precise movement. As I injected him, the man managed to make a few gargled sounds before collapsing to the floor. I immediately checked for a pulse. Toxins were always difficult, because they needed to be the perfect amount. Too little would have no effect. Too much and you kill the poor guy. After confirming a heartbeat under my fingertips, I quietly dragged him under the table and switched my transceiver back on. "Galahad here. I'm in."

"*Excellent*," I heard Charlie say. "*Kay? Do you copy? Time to shine.*"

"*Roger.*" Just as Ozzy's voice registered in my ear, the already dark room went pitch black. I heard the gentle hum of the air conditioning die, leaving a vacuum of silence.

The power to the floor had been cut.

I stepped back into the hallway, listening to the murmurs of confusion in some of the office rooms as I made my way back to the lobby. Beauregard's office was down the opposite hallway to the right, just out of the view of the befuddled secretary.

"*Security cameras are now running on reserve power. We have a visual of you, Galahad. The conference was supposed to last until one thirty, but who knows how Beauregard will react to a blackout. Just get in and get out.*"

"Roger, Camelot." The room itself differed greatly from the rest of what I'd seen from the floor. Looking beyond the expensive chairs and enormous desk you'd expect from an egocentric executive, an array of mounted cattle heads dominated the wall to my right while a single enormous painting was to my left. I thought the latter was actually a pretty nice picture until I realized it depicted a native getting clubbed to death by a settler with the stock of his shotgun. The wall opposing me filtered noon sunlight into the otherwise dark office, making the "art" that occupied the walls cast eerie shadows. I stood for a moment, dumbfounded.

"*Galahad, we see you in the office. What's your status?*"

"I'm fine," I assured, trying to collect myself. "This guy . . . he's really something, isn't he?" Trying to ignore the Texan stereotypes around me, I approached Beauregard's desk and rummaged through the papers left on top of it.

"*Find anything?*" Mabel asked.

"What do you think?" I said, now making my way to the cabinets. "Why would he just leave it on his desk?"

"*I don't know, maybe he has a bit before going to his conferences,*" Charlie suggested. "*I mean, have you seen the new*

Beef 'n' Wings commercials? The person who conceived those was clearly high."

Allowing myself a small chuckle, I furiously tore open every cabinet under and around the desk. All were unlocked and all contained meaningless folders and files; nothing I was concerned with. "The Grail's not anywhere near the desk," I said. "Are you sure it's in here?"

"The intel's good, I swear," Mabel retorted, her voice getting excited. *"I have the transaction data right in front of me. The pickup isn't until tomorrow, and it definitely entered that room. Where else could it be?"*

Feeling a knot grow in my stomach, I meticulously scanned the room, trying to look with a new perspective as I stood behind the desk. The painting was still horrible, the carpet was the same, and the ceiling was the same. The mounted busts, now to my right, were a different story. As my eyes studied the vacant expressions on the cattle's faces, it became evident that something was wrong. "One of the heads is crooked."

"What?"

"One of the cattle heads is crooked," I repeated, advancing toward the busts. The more I focused and the closer I got, the clearer it was that my hunch was correct. "The white bull in the center. It must be . . ." Firmly grasping the horns of the trophy, I began to pull. It was much heavier than I had imagined—causing me to pause to catch my breath at one point while it was halfway out of the wall—but I managed to have the head at my feet within a minute. In its place, I was greeted with a pleasant new surprise. A black, open hole; a gaping wound in the wall. "Can you guys see from your camera what I see?"

"I see it!" Mabel said excitedly, now for the right reasons. *"What's inside?"*

My hand reached into the newly opened gap. It wasn't a built-in compartment, rather a crude cavity created by someone smashing the wall open. As my hand wrapped around an object, I felt my heartbeat quicken. "I have something. Heavy. Leather. Maybe rectangular."

"Sounds like the Grail to me . . ."

My arm was now almost out of the hole, awkwardly handling the package that had been lodged in the wall. With one final tug, a briefcase slid out of the wall and fell with a soft *thud* on the carpet. A tepid smile growing on my lips, I brought it over to the desk for a closer inspection in the light. Looking near the handle, my small grin immediately dissipated. "It's got a lock on it. I repeat, the briefcase has a lock."

"Cuz hiding it in the freaking wall wasn't secure enough for this guy," Charlie remarked, irritated.

"Yep, there's a latch here. It needs a three-number code," I confirmed, examining the mechanism closely.

"Okay, let's think this through," Mabel said, now practically panting. *"I can . . . I can access old security archives! Yeah! Yeah, maybe one of them has him with the briefcase, and we can zoom in on the numbers . . ."*

Mabel's thoughts came to an abrupt end when I smashed the briefcase into the corner of the desk, shattering the lock.

" . . . Or you can do that."

Taking a deep breath, I opened the case. I was greeted by what we were calling in this mission the Holy Grail, all twenty kilos of it, packed together in six different plastic bags.

"Do we have confirmation?"

"Well, pretty sure this isn't chicken seasoning," I commented. "Percival, are you there? It's time to go."

Just as I spoke, the office door opened. I turned around, realizing it was Beauregard. The two of us stared at each other, shocked. The room was now dead silent, so quiet that

Beauregard could probably hear Mabel buzz, "*Green Plan AA-01 has been compromised. Initiate Green Plan AA-07.*"

Beauregard was the first to recover from the initial shock. He peeked back into the hallway and, making sure everything was clear, shut the door. "I don't believe you're supposed to be in this wing, boy."

I remained silent, seemingly speechless. Inside I had regained focus, but chose not to show it on the outside. Waiting for him to make his move, I observed his hands and facial expressions, trying to get a read on what he was going to do next.

"*Galahad,*" Johanna softly crackled on the transceiver. "*Get down so I can take a shot. I believe it's time for the Fisher King to exit our fable.*"

"Roger," I muttered under my breath.

"Well son," Beauregard sighed, reaching into his coat and pulling out a white pistol. "Sorry 'bout this. Some things are best left secret, hm?"

"Couldn't agree more," I said, dropping to my knees.

Just as the president readjusted his aim down at me, the window behind us broke. A dash of crimson burst onto Beauregard's chest and the man shifted awkwardly. There was a slight pause and a light groan before he collapsed to the floor. Hearing a commotion begin outside from the noise, I hastily grabbed a chair and blocked the door before grabbing the briefcase and waiting by the now-shattered office window. Leon—still dressed as a window washer—descended in a cradle.

"Going down?" he asked, his voice echoing through the transceiver.

"Right," I nodded. Then I gave one last look around the ransacked room. From the angle I was standing at, only the soles of Beauregard's expensive shoes were visible as he lay dead on the floor. "Think we've done enough here. Let's go home."

Clutching the Holy Grail and braving the urban winds outside the building, I descended down to the street, and with it, the promise of escape and safety.

CHAPTER ONE

Eastway Academy was located outside Twin Lakes township, deep in an unfortunate part of rural New York. You knew you were close to home when, no matter where you looked, you either saw the green forest hills of the Appalachians or some forsaken highway leading to nowhere. Nevertheless, the environment had a clean, serene vibe to it, similar to the one you get during a clear night farther up north on the New England coast.

As far as quaint towns go, Twin Lakes was the perfect place for Eastway to plant its roots. The townsfolk were simple and aloof, far less dangerous than the intellectuals you might meet if you went south or east. According to the Twin Lakers, the Academy had over fifty students—which may be a questionably small number, but considering that there were really only six of us, we could live with it. Everyone in town knew that the Eastway kids were the best at what they did. The Academy handpicked its students from across the country, judging them on their academic standards, athletic performance, and even their charisma and attitude. None of us had an IQ lower than 130. In sports, we were the captains. There were also hidden qualifications the Academy always looked for, of course. For instance, hardly any of us had a living family member close, meaning we'd all probably be wards of the state had Eastway not swooped in and "rescued" us.

The drive back from the airport was a quiet one. It was very near midnight as two black limousines carried us home. Mabel, Johanna, and Charlie (ever the ladies' man) opted for one car, leaving me stuck with Ozzy and Leon in the other. I had made the unfortunate decision to sleep on the afternoon plane ride and was now wide awake. Ozzy sat to my right. He must have done the same thing, as he spent most of the ride furiously working on his laptop. I took a peek and saw that he had a colorful video game running. When he saw my interest, he proudly pointed out that his orc named Ida had reached level 100, and he was one of the strongest in the server. Leon slept in the seats behind us, still dressed in his washer attire. Pretending to clean windows must have taken a toll on him, as he had been out cold since the beginning of the flight back.

Gradually, we took a few familiar turns and made our way down equally familiar roads until we finally drove up to the prestigious black gates of Eastway Academy. A minute passed. The gates themselves let out a low rumble, quietly opening. The two limos, now side by side, drove in. In the nearly pitch-black evening, all that could be clearly seen was the moon's reflection on Lake Pavus. The Academy compound had been designed around the lake, with the roads and buildings encircling it. The only time we actually made use of the lake was mid-summer, when maritime exercises were held. It basically boiled down to, as Charlie had once put it, "stabbing and shooting things underwater" class. Of course we needed the experience—we had to be ready for any mission in any environment—but the muck from the lake had a special way of clinging to your skin and was resistant to all but the most meticulous scrubbing, leading me to deeply resent the course.

On the far side of the lake, a faint glow of light could be seen. It was from the Central Building, the house where Professor Weiss lived and worked. The light told me that he was awake even at that late hour, eagerly expecting our return. One student sometimes met with him directly after we got done with a job, when it was a dire situation. Usually, though, a student would meet with him a couple hours after we returned or, in cases of late-night arrivals, in the morning to give him the full official report. There was a fork in the road ahead due to the lake, and the limos veered off to the left. After a few more seconds of driving, passing various buildings and paths, we arrived at the school dormitory.

All buildings on campus had been renovated and redecorated many times over. The dorm was among those that had been most recently updated. The porch got new furniture and the white Corinthian columns that supported the reshingled roof were touched up to look even whiter. All buildings on the compound were composed of red brick, but only the dorm, Central Building, and Hall of Science, which housed the school archives, had columns.

Ozzy volunteered for the dangerous endeavor of waking Leon up, leaving me to click open the door and step out, greeting the lush forest air. I caught up with Charlie, Johanna, and Mabel as they walked up the steps into the dorm.

We stumbled our way through the first floor, which was just as dark as the night outside. Mabel turned on the light over the staircases and the four of us ascended together. As we walked, Charlie asked, "Who drove you this time?"

"The lady with the hoop earrings," I responded. "How 'bout you guys?"

"Ugh, lucky," Charlie whined. "We got the blond guy. Swear to God he's trying to get us killed. Seemed incapable of staying in the same lane for more than twenty seconds."

"Wasn't *that* bad!" Mabel loudly objected. All the energy she had from the mission had clearly not fully dispersed. She was the most fully awake out of all of us, climbing up the stairs with a spring in her step.

"It was bad enough that I couldn't get any sleep," Charlie yawned, adjusting his glasses. "Welp, I'm exhausted. Can't wait to settle down in my own bed, stretch out, sleep in . . ."

The fact that Charlie was so sleepy almost made me angry. Still not feeling the least bit drowsy, I would most likely spend most of the night blankly staring at the ceiling. When we reached the second floor, the girls continued up the staircase, up to the third floor and up to their bedrooms. Charlie and I went our separate ways. He went to his bedroom farther down the hall, while I retired to mine, directly to my right.

The nights after missions ranged from tedious to unbearable, especially if someone was in the hospital. This was often the case with particularly dangerous jobs, often involving organized crime. Our rooms at the Academy were incredibly small, considering how few of us there were, and how large and generally luxurious the campus was. Because of that, furniture was sparse, with only a small desk to work on and a bed in the corner, as well as a window dominating the wall above it. I kept my walls poster-free, for the most part. I had seen how clutter plagued the rooms of Charlie and Ozzy, and I understood that colorful artwork and posters plastered haphazardly to my walls could make a tight room feel even more enclosed. Instead, I had one single item hanging in my room: a map of the world, which had an assortment of red push pins pressed into it. There were over fifty. I walked over to my desk and took another pin from my drawer. I pressed it down carefully on the map, right on the border between Texas, Arizona, and Mexico. With that business taken care of, I turned my attention to the letter on my bed, something I always expected when I completed a mission.

It was heavy. On the front, in big bold letters, it read "Report." The letters were always sealed, which I considered an unnecessary pain. Producing a small razor I had tucked in my sleeve, I sliced the letter open. Inside, there was a folded-up packet of papers. On the front, there was a cutout newspaper article, with the date reading tomorrow. It told of the tragic death of the founder and executive of Beef 'n' Wings, as well as a state senate investigation beginning on shady funds the company was receiving. There was a brief statement from the sheriff and the spokesperson for Beef 'n' Wings, but that was it. Nothing about an intern, or an unaccounted-for window washer, or any explicit details about the homicide. I had always held the firm belief that the Academy somehow had more power than we thought. The news articles always told the sides of the story we wanted to stress. Police investigations always went cold. Johanna and Leon firmly believed that the Academy was run by the United States government, but I wasn't so sure. Ambiguity was the name of the game at Eastway, and I knew any speculation we had about anything we shouldn't know was a wild guess.

The second page of the letter was tinted blue. It was the full transcript of all conversations that occurred over our transceivers on the day of the operation. The print was tiny and my eyes strained to read it, but I could tell it was (as always) perfectly accurate, right down to the *uh*'s and *um*'s. As with any mission, a copy of the transcript would be filed away in the Academy archives.

The last page was always my least favorite. It was colored pink and read "Casualties" at the top. There was a chart of the human body, with a single black dot on his left pectoral, where Johanna had struck Beauregard. There was data saying how he died, how his death was instantaneous, and how the lethal wounds had come from high-quality ammunition fired from a skilled shooter. At the bottom, they had attached a picture of the body, looking the same way I had left him: face-up on the floor, with a blank expression on his face.

I gazed at the picture studiously, feeling my throat tighten. I crumpled up the report and tossed it into the trash by my desk. I sat on my bed, unsure of what to do with myself, as a wave of nausea passed through my stomach. I clenched my bed sheets tightly, realizing my hands were shaking. My throat was dry.

I took a big swallow, letting out a deep breath. The terrible discomfort I had felt passed, and Beauregard's face was now out of my mind. *I shouldn't have looked*, I thought. *Why do I always look?* This was the normal reaction to what I had seen, I had been told. If I didn't react like that—if my brief shock was instead casual indifference—that would mean that I was a psychopath. I was glad I wasn't, but somehow I always thought it would be easier. No matter their age, psychopaths could kill a man on a mission and sleep well that night. I imagined they would have a lot less pain in their lives.

Still carrying a great uneasiness, I picked myself up from my bed and changed, settling down for a long, sleepless night.

CHAPTER TWO

I was thirteen the first time I stepped into Weiss's office. Going through what I was, I certainly was not a doe-eyed innocent child, but I also wasn't the unstable wreck I was two years later. At that point, I was starting to get really good at pretending. I was someone who liked to pretend things were still going right for me, even though deep down I knew they weren't. I pretended not to hear what the grown-ups said about me and my "potential." I pretended to smile, even after my family was gone. I also pretended not to be utterly terrified when I looked Professor Weiss in the eyes for the first time.

He had a laid-back aura to him. His larger, somewhat bloated body didn't sit back in his chair, but lounged in it. It never seemed like he was giving orders to us, but more like helpful bits of advice we were required to follow. His sunken-in eyes held no gleam, and his face was hardly ever tense or tight. I initially thought he was just a naturally lazy, carefree person who ignored his worries, but later I knew that he really had no troubles to worry about. Everything always went according to his plan, so there never seemed to be a reason for him to be excited or angry.

"Have a seat, Davy. What's up?" he gave a polite, mild smile. He ran his thick fingers through his silvery blond hair, perhaps trying to adjust it. "I'm Auric Weiss, pleasure to meet you. I like that name, 'Davy.' My third favorite Monkee. We've had a couple Davids here before, had a Dave—a real jerk, that one—but never Davy. Welcome to Eastway."

"Um, thanks," I said, briefly forgetting my fears. So many questions swirled in my mind that I didn't know where to start. "Are you the principal?"

"Heh," Weiss let out a quick chuckle. When he finished, I realized that his icy blue eyes were glaring at me, reinstating all the terror I had before walking into the room. "Kids around here call me the professor. I'm basically just the director of things around here. You know, like, I direct things onto the right path and make sure the students stay on it."

"What path is that, exactly?" I asked.

Weiss didn't answer. Instead, he picked up a thick, yellow folder that was in the center of his desk and flipped through it. "You've got a very nice record, Davy. As I hope you know, Eastway is very selective of its student body. We try to make our pupils feel as comfortable as possible on campus. We're talking a bowling alley, arcade, and private cinema stocked with all the newest releases. You also can drive to town any time you like too. Can't give you your license right now, but I'm sure the older students would be happy to take you. They're real sweet kids, most of them."

As I listened to Weiss, lingering uncertainty from what I had heard before began to rear its ugly head in my mind. "Um, sir—"

"After you have finished your five years here, you will be accepted to the college or university of your choice. We'll watch over your career path from behind the scenes and make sure it's just as successful as you want it to be. Here at Eastway, we believe connection is key. We have an extensive network of—"

"Sir!" I interjected, immediately regretting the decision.

Weiss frowned. His mild eyes studied me intensely before he said, "Don't interrupt me, Davy. It's common etiquette."

"I'm sorry," I sighed. "It's just . . . I heard we have to do . . . things here."

"Things?" Weiss gave another light chuckle. "Use your words, boy. All schools make you do 'things.' Sure, ours doesn't perfectly fall in the academic variety . . ."

"Yeah, *that*," I said. My heart pounded, awaiting his response.

Weiss opened his mouth to speak and then closed it again. "I suppose the appropriate thing to ask, then, is how much do you know?"

I recalled what the tall boy with the glasses had told me. "This really isn't a school, is it? Here, you go after people and . . . *take them down*."

"'Take them down,'" Weiss repeated to himself. "Yeah, guess that's an appropriate way of putting it. Davy . . . do you know what justice is? It's when a bad guy does something bad, and he's prevented from doing it again." He spoke to me as though he were talking to an infant.

"Bad guys?" I asked with strong skepticism in my voice. I had no idea where this conversation was going, and I didn't like it.

"We're not talking about the mad scientist on your Saturday morning cartoon," Weiss countered. "Evil people. Drug dealers. Mobsters. Crime lords. Mighty and corrupt people the police can't lay a finger on. At least, not without a little help. Help from people like us."

"So you kill the guys? Are you serious?"

"It usually doesn't come down to killing when we play our cards right. C'mon!" Weiss urged, "This is the opportunity of a lifetime! What person your age doesn't want to be the hero, fighting the good fight, taking down the high-and-mighty who think they're above the law?"

"What can you people do here that the police can't?"

"Well . . . ," the professor shrugged innocently. "We're an independent organization that works for private investors. Let's just say our reach extends a little bit further than the arm of the law. Some of our tactics may not exactly be 'legal' if you want to be stringent about it . . ."

"No," I said definitively, standing up from my chair. "I'm not getting into any more trouble. Thank you, 'Professor,' but I don't think Eastway is the right fit for me."

"Sit back down." Weiss's voice dropped lower, and his smile weakened. Something in his voice had changed, and I detected the first hints of emotion, different from his laid-back coos. One look into his icy eyes was enough for me to obey. "We're trying to protect you," he elaborated, pulling out another file from his desk. "Half the kids in here are in the same boat you are. There's a criminal *homicide* case out there against you."

"I didn't do it," I hissed. I had said that sentence at least a thousand times the previous day.

"It isn't a matter of whether you're guilty or not," Weiss stated flatly, tapping the file. "There's enough evidence there—fingerprints, DNA, phone records—to get a pretty clean conviction. Once you're guilty, you'll be put away for the rest of your life. I can't stand that, though. Your IQ might be twice as high as your usual juvenile delinquent. You're twice as articulate and had a future twice as bright as any other kid in your school. We want to give you that future back, Davy. Give you the life someone of your genius is entitled to. We can protect you behind these walls, but not in some state courtroom, exposed to the world. All we ask is that you use your talents for us and our noble cause."

"I don't want to hurt anybody," I muttered, feeling my choices disappear. Now I knew how this conversation was going to end. The office walls around me seemed to get smaller, almost confining me. "No matter how bad they are, crime shouldn't be solved with more crime."

Instead of a smirk, Weiss smiled pleasantly, seemingly amused by my remark. "That's very cute, Davy, but open your eyes. What separates us from them is that we're willing to protect the innocents that they are willing to harm. I'll gladly sacrifice a few of the moral fibers I have left if I can go to sleep knowing that guiltless lives have been saved at the cost of some of the guilty. The bad guys out there need to be brought to justice somehow, whether it's through a jury, some words, or a bullet. I'm willing to take that extra step."

"No," I said, biting my lip. "I don't want this, please . . ."

"Davy," Weiss urged, almost frustrated, "sacrifice today for us, and we'll give you the brightest tomorrow we can."

At that point, I didn't want or care about a bright future. All I wanted to do was go back home with my family and go to sleep in my own bed. Wake up from the nightmare I was living—one with police officers and reporters and men in funny coats who looked at me like I was some sort of zoo animal. I knew that that was reality, though, and even if it meant that I was escaping one hell to be condemned to another, I knew that the Academy was the better choice. "Fine," I said. It was a quiet, suppressed word, as if my body was hoping the professor wouldn't hear it.

"Excellent!" Weiss exploded, clearly pleased. The tension that caked the air seemed to disappear as the grown-up extended his hand for me to shake. "You'll make a fine addition to the Sixteenth Academy, Mr. Prince. Be smart, pay your dues, and you'll be off to college before you know it. Enraptured by the future we're giving you here!"

"Yes, thank you," I said. Now that the deal had been struck, the more compliant I was the faster I could get out of that office.

"You wait downstairs and I'll send some of the kids down to get you acquainted. Today, just relax and get comfortable with the campus. We can start training tomorrow."

"Yes, sir," I said, feeling increasingly obsequious. I stood up once again and turned toward the door, only to turn back once a new thought struck me. "Sir, what kind of training are you talking about?"

"Well, we'll start off with the basics, I guess," Weiss explained. "I mean, do you know how to shoot a gun?"

● ● ●

We have speculated that the first class of the Academy was established sometime during World War II. The students were of varying ages in their teens, known as the First Academy. Every year when one turned eighteen and graduated, a younger teen, usually thirteen or fourteen, was recruited. After all of the original class was gone, the new batch of students became the Second Academy, and so on and so forth. Johanna was the youngest member when the Sixteenth Academy was established, and when she graduated we would become the Seventeenth Academy, and we would receive a new, young member. I secretly dreaded the name change. *Seventeenth* always seemed like much more of a pain to say compared to *sixteenth*.

More than two years after first walking into Weiss's office, I stepped out into the Central Building second-floor hallway. It was the morning after the Beauregard job, and I was still exhausted. A part of me desperately wanted to sleep in, at least for another hour or two, so I could be well rested enough to have made intelligent conversation with the professor. Instead, every other sentence that came out of my mouth was "yes, sir" with the occasional "understood, sir." Down the hall, I could hear the faint sound of clapping. Curious, I walked down only to realize that it was Leon, on the floor, doing clap push-ups. Judging by the sweat dripping off his face, he had been doing them for a while. Once he saw me, he collapsed to the ground, panting heavily.

"You know, you shouldn't be pushing yourself this hard so early in the day," I said, trying to be helpful. Admittedly, the comment sounded a lot more condescending than I would have liked.

"Shut . . . up . . . ," he snarled, in between shallow breaths. Sweat was practically glimmering off of his midnight black skin. He had been at this for a while.

I never liked Leon. I never really disliked him either, though. He was a valued member of the team, and I probably worked with him the most face-to-face out of anyone during missions. However, in the corner of my eye, I could always see him glare at me the same way Weiss did when he was disappointed, except the difference with Leon was that I didn't fear him nearly as much as I did the professor. Leon and I had very different philosophies about training as well. He believed in strength and athleticism above all else. He made sure that he could always lift the most, run the fastest, and strike the hardest compared to the rest of us at the Academy. As the infiltrator for the team, I had a much different approach. I worked on my poker face and tried different exercises to improve my memory. If the information was available, I studied our target and their organizations before missions, helping me get prepared for when my life was on the line. If Eastway were a real school, Leon would easily be the jock and I'd be the theater geek.

"Weiss wants to see you now," I informed him, trying to keep a pleasant air to our conversation.

"Wonderful," Leon groaned, jumping to his feet. "How'd your date with him go?"

"Same as usual," I said. "Killing Beauregard wasn't part of the original plan, so he's going to give Johanna a stern warning not to do it again."

The hulking boy broke into a smile, letting out a small chuckle, "Good, I'm sure a few harsh words will curb her bloodlust. By the way, Chuck's looking for you."

"What does he want me for?"

"How should I know? Just seemed pretty upset this morning. Maybe you should find out for yourself." Leon reared his head up, and his eyes struck me at a threatening angle. I knew he wanted me to go, but I still had questions.

"Is he okay? Where is he?"

Leon glared at me for a few seconds, before shaking his head disapprovingly. My questions were no longer worth answering, apparently, as the muscular student lumbered down the hall toward Weiss.

Giving up on him, I made my way over to the grand staircase, onto the first floor, and out of the Central Building. My conversations with Leon never seemed to end on a cheery note, usually with one of us just walking off awkwardly with a hasty good-bye. Leon may have been about as smart as everyone else on the team, but for some reason he made very poor decisions on missions. Even bringing up said missions would sometimes be enough to set him off, sometimes to the point of physicality. Whether or not he was enraged, in pain, or frustrated, it was a smart idea to get as far away from him as possible.

Walking back to the dorm, I took long, deliberate steps. Mornings in Eastway were silent and lonely. The clap of my footsteps on the pavement was joined by the rustling of ancient gray oaks. These were the only two noises that dared to break the otherwise absolute stillness of the young day. The desolate campus of Eastway, a compound meant to accommodate hundreds of students, was exceptionally eerie when only inhabited by six. Although the sun was out, a brisk breeze from the lake kept the campus cool. In a couple of weeks, it would become unimaginably hot, making anything besides shorts and short-sleeved shirts unbearable to wear outside the shade of the oaks.

Back in the dorm, I found Ozzy sitting on the couch. The first floor was used for recreation and entertainment and had a hodgepodge of furniture and items that didn't really seem to belong, including a treadmill, mini-fridge, and a TV with a cluster of game consoles below, as well as board games scattered around the floor. The latter objects were always out because Charlie wanted us to have a family game night every Saturday. It was partially successful, with him, Mabel, Ozzy, and me regularly participating. The games typically weren't fun if they had anything to do with strategy though, because for some reason Mabel and Charlie would always choose to team up and dominate the board.

I knew that Ozzy spent most of his time on campus here, probably because he still wasn't used to the hard exercise he would have to do otherwise. Just like the previous night, he had his high-powered laptop on him, rhythmically tapping and clicking, eyes transfixed on the screen. He had high-end headphones in his ears, making his head look twice as big. I didn't think he heard me come in, so I silently passed him without giving him a glance and made my way upstairs, to Charlie's room.

I knocked on his door. "Hey, Chuck?" I said. I heard a faint voice, but it was low and seemingly not directed toward me. Another voice, in a higher pitch, spoke up. I realized that two people were having a conversation inside. Confused, I knocked on the door once again, this time much harder. "Chuck? Who's in there?"

When the door opened, Charlie wasn't there. Instead, standing in front of me was a girl a couple inches taller than me. Looking at her face, nothing seemed off until you really started to focus; one side sagged slightly, with strange wrinkles and drooping lips. These were an unfortunate by-product of facial reconstruction, something she underwent years before.

"Morning, Johanna," I said, mustering up a smile.

"Prince," she said, acknowledging my existence. She spoke out of the corner of her mouth, seemingly unable to use the part that had been touched by surgery. Then she walked away, just like Leon, except with less purpose. Instead of having a reason to leave my company, it was clear that Johanna simply didn't want to be around me. I didn't think she wanted to be around human beings in general.

"Davy, that you?" Charlie called from inside his room. I found him lying on his bed, eyes half opened and hair disheveled.

"Yeah, what was that?" I asked, pointing out into the hallway. "Why was she in here?"

"Me and her were having a romantic rendezvous, professing our love to each other while passionately snuggling," Charlie said, rolling his eyes.

I gagged at the thought of someone as unfeeling and robotic as Johanna speaking romantically. "Don't put pictures in my head, man. Seriously, though. Sounded like you two were talking. What's up?"

"None of your business," the boy shrugged, reaching for his glasses. "Just some things on campus that need to be taken care of, nothing for you to worry about. Why are *you* here?"

"Leon said you were upset this morning, and that you wanted to see me."

"Right, right," Charlie nodded and rubbed his forehead. "Yeah, I forgot I saw Leon this morning. Talking to Johanna can really take a lot out of you, y'know? Think I need to go back to bed. What time is it?"

"It's almost eleven," I scoffed. Unlike Weiss, whose inactivity was justified, Charlie was lazy for laziness' sake. It wasn't a habit. It seemed to be encoded in his very DNA, as if his presence radiated the very essence of indolence. "You must have said something to him. What do you want?"

"Right, right," my teammate gave a somnolent nod. "Um, check what's on my desk."

"That?" I walked over to where Charlie was pointing. In the midst of empty soda cans and magazines a white letter lay on his desk, half open. It wasn't the same kind that held our reports. It was smaller, with a stamp and some coarsely typed letters on the front. I reached inside and pulled out a single sheet of paper, which read in loopy cursive writing,

Hello Charles,

Hope you're doing well. Portland has become too breezy for your uncle's taste, so we're taking the yacht down over toward Malta. Professor Weiss says you are excelling in your studies. He seems like a lovely man, but it baffles me that he's always the one to answer my phone calls. I really wish the other faculty was more proactive.

With Much Sincerity,
Auntie Torta

"Cute," I smiled at the letter. Charlie was one of the few among us to have some form of family. They rarely ever saw each other, save for a week in the summer when he'd go and visit them. Leon referred to that time as 'the quietest week of the year.' I didn't know much about Aunt Torta besides her immense wealth, as Weiss discouraged the sharing of personal info, even among friends. I tossed the letter on the bed next to Charlie and asked, "This is what you were so worked up about?"

The bespectacled boy gave an indifferent shrug. "The only thing I did this morning was read that. Maybe Leon saw me upset cuz it was early, I dunno. I went back to sleep after breakfast, so the entire morning's kinda foggy . . . "

"You don't remember what you did this morning?" I said, starting to feel concerned. I watched Charlie very carefully, noting how his eyes were avoiding mine. "Is everything alright man? Is something up with Johanna?"

"No, everything's fine, dude," he whined, sounding more annoyed than anxious. "Nothing you have to worry about, I promise. Help me outta bed, I don't think I have the strength to escape myself."

As I pulled Charlie to his feet and we made our way downstairs, I went through his strange behavior once again in my mind. Leon found him this morning in an apparent panic, he encountered Johanna, then talked to me as if nothing happened.

Once downstairs in the foyer, Charlie announced, "Y'know, I think we need a night to go clear our heads. How about we go in to town?"

"You sure?" I said, tentatively. "I thought you wanted to go back and rest today."

"Yeah, well, I changed my mind."

"Seem to be doing that a lot recently . . ." I muttered, angry at Charlie's lack of transparency. He still wasn't looking at me directly, instead turning his attention to Ozzy.

"Wanna go to town, Oz? I can teach you how to pick up the ladies!" Charlie promised, putting a strange emphasis in his voice that made me wonder whether or not he was being sarcastic.

"Eh, why not?" Ozzy said apathetically, his attention still clearly directed toward his laptop. In the moment, at least, it seemed as though slaying wizards on a screen held his interest more than the promise of meeting town girls with Charlie. Laziness aside, the elder student was probably the most socially active member of the team. If anyone could solve the complex riddle known as the teenage girl, it was him.

Charlie gave a clever smirk, "Sorry, Davy, it appears you're outnumbered. Now, let's get a snack. I'm starving."

The three of us made our way out to the café, a short building with a sloped roof and an abundance of windows. Charlie and I walked in front, making small talk, while Ozzy followed behind, carefully balancing his computer while he walked. Inside, there were tables and chairs, as well as a fully stocked kitchen. Making your own food at the Academy took mild skill and an actually decent attention span, so naturally we opted to either eat out or stick to canned goods. Large chrome machines served a variety of beverages. Ozzy got a hot chocolate, Charlie got his iced coffee, and I got my usual chilled mocha-chocolate frappé with two shots of vanilla. We chose a table near the back, silently sitting as Charlie liberally gave away his tips on how to attract women, even though Ozzy wasn't really listening. "Always brag about what you do at the Academy," he explained. "Like, not what you *actually* do but what they think you do, obviously. To them, you're a wealthy dreamboat with the ability to travel the world, so play the part. Talk about your money and yachts and money and cars and money. Oh, and throw in how your parents don't treat you properly, throwing you in boarding school. You'll get pity-love, which is the best kind."

"Why not just stay on campus?" I asked Ozzy. "Mabel's available, right? She's only a year older than you, so it wouldn't be *that* weird."

Charlie shot me a strange look. The caffeine in his coffee must have perked him up, for his eyes maintained a strong gleam. "Mabel? Don't exactly think she's your type."

"What do you mean?" I asked, speaking for Ozzy, who was still lost in his video game.

"High energy, all over the place. Hard to keep a girl tied down when she's bouncing off the walls," Charlie remarked, lounging back in his chair and taking another sip from his drink. I had to admit that he had a point. Mabel had a lot of good qualities to her, but she was very hyperactive. She never seemed to tire, so hanging around her was an exhausting ordeal. She could find a way to keep any conversation going for hours, and the only way I had managed to get out of it was either running away or politely telling her to shut up. When typing up plans for operations, she would sometimes have it done in a single night. This, naturally, suited the ever-lackadaisical Charlie. However, her plans, like the girl herself, tended to lack focus, leaving her elder student to straighten them out. It wasn't as debilitating as writing the plan up, but it still required a competent, logical mind like Charlie's.

The doors to the café opened. Auric Weiss, accompanied by the sound of his expensive shoes clicking on the tile floor, stepped in, "Excuse me, boys," the professor beamed. "I'd like to have a word with Mr. Parker, if it is convenient."

For a brief moment, the loose, unbothered face of Charlie disappeared. His muscles tensed, and he bit down on his lip and balled his fist. He looked like someone had smashed him in the foot with a hammer.

"Mr. Parker?"

Just as quickly as the apparent frustration appeared, it was gone. "Coming, sir," Charlie called out, giving a loose smile. "Guess I'll have to see you guys later." He stood up and sauntered toward Weiss, like the last soldier in camp to report to roll call. As the two walked out, I thought about Charlie's strange antics. His denial was becoming increasingly relevant the more I was around him. *What was on his mind?* Charlie Parker was a terrible liar, but that didn't mean that he couldn't keep a secret.

CHAPTER THREE

A concrete parking lot by the gate held the Academy's motor vehicles. Thanks to Weiss, all students received their license when they turned sixteen, no questions asked. Despite having mine, I still felt uncomfortable behind the wheel and always preferred to have someone else drive. That night, Charlie drove Ozzy and me into town. "How was your talk with Weiss?" I asked.

Charlie gave a faint shrug, his eyes still glued to the road. "More of the same, I guess. We've got another job."

"Already?" I said, now displeased. "But we just got back. Anything serious?"

I saw Charlie contemplate for a few seconds before answering, "I'm gonna be up all night with Mabel working it out, most likely. I don't think she'll be able to properly account for all the variables by herself."

"So . . . I'm gonna take that as a yes," I sighed. "Is it worse than the one we had in Japan?"

"Which? The one at the Noh performance or the one where that guy shot nails at us?"

Old memories stirred and my stomach instantly grew queasy remembering the "nail gun incident."

"Noh?" Ozzy asked. "What's a Noh performance?"

Charlie smiled a thousand-watt grin, and I knew what would come next. "Well, I don't 'Noh.' What part of 'Noh' don't you understand?" He burst into laughter.

Ozzy and I let out a collective groan. "How long have you been waiting to use those?" I asked.

My older friend didn't answer, far too busy enjoying his own awful joke. "So . . . what are we gonna do once we get in town?" Ozzy squeaked.

"First and foremost, we go to Quickie's. I need to get some things," Charlie announced, trying to restrain his undeserved chuckles. Quickie's was our local convenience store, selling everything from pain medication to slushies. Since junk food was sparse on campus, every member of the team went there frequently. The owners were nice and seemed to like us, although they once threatened to ban Charlie when he tried to buy cigarettes.

The rest of the car ride to town, we remained awkwardly quiet. I had spent the day training and was in no mood for any real conversation outside of Charlie's strange behavior that morning. Ozzy reluctantly flipped on the radio, only to be greeted by a terrible sound of blaring synthesizers and incoherent pangs and beeps. The singer's voice sounded garbled, but due to the music's volume the words were clear: "*Pleased to meet you, can you guess the color of my back? It's all wrong, it's all wrong, let's—*" The alternative music abruptly cut out with Charlie practically slamming on the radio.

"Stupid hipster funk," he said, regaining his grip on the steering wheel. "Jojo must've been the last one to use this car."

I nodded in agreement. Out of all of us, Johanna was the only one who listened to alternative music on a regular basis. I listened to classic pop and rock; Ozzy, surprisingly, favored metal (which I didn't mind, thanks to the magic of headphones.) Charlie liked anything new on the radio, which occasionally dismayed me if there was a new, catchy, annoying song out. I never exactly disliked Johanna's musical choices, but I do have to admit that some of the songs made me feel weird. Johanna seemed to connect to them in a way that I couldn't understand.

It was almost eight by the time we rolled into the parking lot of Quickie's. "You guys wait in here," Charlie ordered. "Play some music or whatnot. I was thinking that after we're done with this, we can go to the park. Lots of cute girls in the park, Ozzy. But it's almost nighttime, and there might be a lot of potheads in the park too, so keep your distance. Last thing you wanna do is get back on campus smelling like weed, believe me . . ."

"Chuck," I called him out, rolling my eyes.

"Right, right, be back in a few." Charlie popped open the car door and stepped out.

I looked back over to Ozzy, "So, uh, how's your video game?"

The boy was absentmindedly looking out his window, almost wistfully. "Fun."

There was a long pause. "Fun?" I said, trying to keep the interaction alive. "Um . . . okay then. Liking Eastway so far? Everything cool?"

"You kidding? This place sucks."

I nodded in understanding, remembering my first months at the Academy, particularly my first mission. "It's a hard transition, I know. One second your life is one way and the other you're here, starting over with no family or friends."

"Yeah, yeah, that's bad," Ozzy shrugged, seemingly glossing over the subject, "but I'm talking about the missions.

You and Johanna get to destroy all the targets while I'm stuck with all the menial stuff."

This response caught me off guard. "Well, Charlie likes how good you seem to be with computers. Maybe in a few years you can be our planner. That's probably the most important job on the team, if you think about it."

"Yeah, screw that," Ozzy retorted, sounding more invested in the conversation. "I want to make a real difference on the team, not just scream orders into a mic. I'm gonna be the sniper."

"The gunman?" I said, increasingly baffled. I wasn't even entirely aware that the boy could shoot a gun, let alone snipe. "You know that requires killing people, right?"

"Why do you think I wanna do it?" the boy said. There was a growing smirk on his face that made me feel uncomfortable. "Most of 'em are criminals. World won't miss them."

"They're still people though," I argued, raising my voice somewhat. *This kid doesn't get it, does he?* "Human life isn't some game. Go behind that scope and it changes you. They're still people you'd be shooting at . . ."

"They're *evil* people," Ozzy growled. I couldn't see much of him in the dark car, but the intensity in his voice told me that I was now talking to someone totally different from the indifferent gamer back on campus. "They'll kill you and everything you care about if they've got the chance. They don't deserve mercy. I know what they can do, Davy. I've *seen* what they can do."

Shocked by this new comment, for a moment I was at a loss for words. I simply stared at him, trying to read his face as it bathed in the shadows. "Is that why . . ."

"I'm here? Of course, man," the boy elaborated. "Karma's fair. I've lost everything to the scum of the earth, but now I'm in a position to exact my vengeance. All I have to do is endure a little more of this awful program and bam! I can be on the front lines of the mission with you, ready to get a heads hot at first sign of danger."

"That's not how we operate," I grumbled, sick of talking to the kid. Ozzy was a strange and dangerous combination of one who had seen too much for his age, and one who had not seen enough of the Academy. The guilt of a possible body count had not set in for him yet, and his idea of justice was skewed and gray. He would, I hope, learn from his mistakes.

"Hey," Ozzy pointed outside his window with a different tone in his voice. He must have been as uncomfortable with the conversation as I was, as it seemed he was changing the subject. "Isn't that the car Leon usually drives?"

"Huh?" I looked outside the window. Sure enough there was a black convertible parked on the other side of the parking lot. The license plate began with the letters 'EAST,' a trait all cars at Eastway shared. *What would Leon be doing in town?* "I'll be right back," I announced. Although slightly relieved that I wouldn't have to deal with a ranting Ozzy, a new, uncomfortable feeling began to grow. I practically jumped out of the car and darted into the convenience store.

The smell of plastic packaging and faulty air conditioning hit me right away, as well as the clean of the squeaky white floors. The sad fact was that Quickie's had better sanitation than the Academy's café. Despite being in a small panic, I tried my best to casually walk up to the man behind the counter. I'd been in there many times and knew his face, but couldn't remember his name. "Hey, have you seen Leon around?"

"Yeah, I think he's around somewhere," the vendor responded. "Came in with some girl a couple minutes ago."

Two people? The uneasiness from within grew. "Was the girl Johanna?"

"Who?"

"That one girl you chased out of the store with a broom after she put a squirrel in your microwave."

"Oh," the vendor looked disgusted as he reminisced about the strange student. "*Her.* Yeah, I'm sure they're around somewhere. Friggin' Academy kids . . ."

As my heart began to quicken from the unknown implications, I sped down row after row of colorful products in the store until I was near the back. From there I could hear voices and stopped dead in my tracks.

"You do realize that this won't end well for any of us here, right?" a male voice said. It was Charlie, sounding very uncertain.

"It's a risk, I know, but you need to have faith," another male voice said. This one was rougher and had less emotion in it, no doubt belonging to Leon. "I'm with her on this one. There might be repercussions, but things will work out."

"I . . . I know, but . . . why do we have to try this? Why can't you just graduate? You're almost out, and then you can put this crap behind you." I had never heard Charlie talk like this before. It wasn't his lazy, laid-back self who had the answer to every question you didn't ask. This was someone deeper, more material than that. It almost sounded like someone desperately pleading for his life.

"Graduating means he's won," a third voice spoke. Female, deeper, and monotone. "Please, Parker. I can't live with myself and what's been done to me. What he's done to *all* of us. If you allow yourself to be his pawn, then you'll die long before your body expires."

"Alright, alright," I could hear Charlie letting out a long, exasperated sigh. "Just tell me Mabel—"

"Hold on," Johanna interjected. "Someone's next to us in the candy aisle."

My heart skipped a beat. I rounded the aisle, entering the back of the store. Sure enough, in their own private circle next to the frozen foods fridge, Charlie, Leon, and Johanna stood. My mind raced; I knew I had to get the first words of the upcoming conversation out. "What is going on here?" I asked, trying to stay calm.

"Davy," Leon said. His voice maintained a higher tone, as if he were in a causal conversation. "How much did you hear?"

"Enough," I snapped back, furious at their deceit. "What's this about not graduating? Can someone just fill me in, please?"

"It's nothing you have to worry about, Prince," Johanna sighed, still keeping a dry, almost quiet, monotone. Everything she said sounded like known facts instead of assurances. "You're not in any trouble. If Charlie wants to explain to you what's up, he's allowed." Then she gave Charlie the most peculiar look, one of her signature intimidating stares. It was piercing, but restrained; less the look of a crazed killer and more the eyes of a calculating mastermind. They were dead eyes, a cold void without any hints of gleam or shine. "Charlie, how about you go tell Davy what he wants to know? I need Leon to stay with me for a few extra seconds, just to make sure we're all filled in."

"But . . ." Charlie began to object, only to let out a deep exhale and shake his head. "Forget it. Davy, let's go. We have to make sure Ozzy isn't too lonely." As the two of us walked out of the convenience store, he added, "Alright, now tell me everything you heard."

"Not much, just something about being a pawn or something," I quickly bluffed. As much as I trusted Charlie and knew he wouldn't purposely try to hurt me, I didn't trust Johanna or Leon. I did have every intention of telling the truth once I believed I had the full story.

"Right, right," Charlie nodded. He looked ill, with his skin turning a shade paler, and his eyes carried dark circles, despite the boy being apparently very well rested. "Johanna wants to get out of the Academy soon. As in escape."

"What?" I said, malice practically dripping from my voice. "Chuck, what's Johanna planning?"

Charlie merely motioned for me to follow him to the car, where he opened the driver's side door and stepped in. I couldn't help but let out a scoff, worthy of a normal girl my age having boy issues. I realized that Charlie had no intention of telling me any further details, at least for that moment. Whatever plan Johanna was cooking, Ozzy clearly wasn't part of it, and even I had trouble believing Charlie would divulge any secrets with our youngest member sitting near him with open ears. Thus, we drove to the park in silence. It wasn't like the gauche quiet we had on the ride out to town, as this one felt justified and necessary for both Charlie and me. I gave him a cold glare any time his eyes drifted onto me, and he would quickly look back onto the road, trying his best to ignore my presence. At one point, Ozzy asked why we were acting the way we were and I explained that Charlie wouldn't let me buy the candy I wanted. It was the second time that night I lied to a fellow student, but it hardly bothered me. To me, lying was a weapon, something I could pull out as quickly as a gun or knife. Like any weapon, it was neither good nor evil. It was what it was: not the truth.

A few minutes later, we arrived in the park. Charlie escorted Ozzy to the grass, pointing out girls and saying hi to people he knew. I knew most of them as well, to different extents. Faces were easy to recognize, and if I looked at them long enough, I could tell whether they were sad or happy, angry or relieved, even if their expressions weren't truly showing it. Names were a different story for me. They seemed to come and go, and those who were not in my day-to-day life disappeared until I saw their face or talked to them again.

I kept a few steps away from Charlie and Ozzy. Without warning, Ozzy seemed to break away from the elder student and disappeared into the crowd of park residents. I instinctively began to chase after him, but Charlie grabbed my arm. "Just let him be," he assured. "You wanna talk? Follow me."

We began to walk away from the crowd, into a quieter part of the park. The streetlamps were sparse and a nearly full moon cast long shadows on the trees, which were just now regrowing their leaves. "You really think it's smart to leave Ozzy on his own?" I asked, concerned. "I don't think he's fully learned protocol with outsiders. What if people start to ask him things?"

"He'll be fine," the boy waved his hand unconcernedly. The unreasonably anxious Charlie I had encountered throughout the day finally seemed to be gone. He walked with a small smile and a contained tone in his voice. His head was crooked ever so slightly upward, observing the evening's stars, which shone brightly due to the sparse light. "You think he'll survive Eastway okay?"

I told him of Ozzy's harangue in the car, and his desire to become sniper.

"Looks like the newbie's got a bloodlust," Charlie cracked a wide grin and chuckled. "Can't believe he's got so much pent-up aggression. Always seems like a real quiet kid . . ."

"I guess we all have our little secrets," I remarked, reminding the elder student that he still wasn't off the hook with me.

We walked away from the path and onto the stiff grass, which crunched under our feet. "Think he's a psycho?" Charlie asked.

"Doubt it," I said. "He's angry, not sick." For an organization that preached justice and decency, Eastway sure had a knack for hiring psychopaths. Along with Johanna, I knew of multiple students of past years who were completely free of any sense of morality. Weiss told me once in passing that he thought they made the best agents, especially when things got messy. They were always willing to pull the trigger. "Speaking of sick, are you sure you're alright? You've got me concerned, Chuck."

Charlie abruptly stopped walking, gesturing for me to do the same. We were on the darkest side of the park, and I could hardly make out my friend's silhouette, let alone see his face. "We'll be safe here, I think. You wanna know the truth?"

"Yes!" I exclaimed. "What's this about Johanna?"

The shadowy boy motioned for me to be quiet. "It's nothing to worry about."

"I'm sick of hearing that. Just saying that isn't helping."

Charlie looked over his shoulders. With a sigh, he explained, "Like I said before, Johanna's escaping. She's enlisted the help of Leon and me to make sure everything runs smoothly. She's going to fly to Europe. The details of the case really aren't important, but what you've gotta know is that it involves an airfield, where I'm planning on making our withdrawal after we take down our mark. You, Leon, Mabel, Ozzy, and I will go on our regular jet. Johanna wants to hijack one of the planes they have there and fly to Europe."

"That's it?"

"See? No harm, no foul," Charlie gave his usual grin. It might have just been the shadows, but something still seemed off. "Now, let's get back to the plaza before I trip on something. This place is freaking spooky!"

Walking side by side, we made our way back to the crowded, lighted square. It was questionable why such a simple explanation needed to be told in a dark, isolated corner of the park, but I figured Charlie's paranoia must have gotten the better of him. Before we fully integrated with the crowd, an arm grabbed my shoulder, stopping me.

Charlie pointed toward the outskirts of the crowd, "Check that out!"

A boy sat close to a girl on a park bench, talking. They were younger than us by a few years. I didn't recognize the girl remotely, but the boy immediately caught my eye. "Ozzy?"

Charlie's arm quickly covered my mouth. "Quiet! Don't wanna embarrass the kid, do you?"

"Right," I said, feeling uncomfortable observing the two from afar, focusing on the younger student. He was laughing with the girl, looking genuinely happy. I couldn't imagine that such a kid could have been proclaiming his desire to kill just an hour before. "Let's leave them alone and get a bite to eat. I'm starved."

• • •

An hour or so later, we were driving back to campus. Charlie had the stupidest grin on his face, glancing over at Ozzy. "So . . ."

"So?" The boy slouched in his seat, looking exhausted.

"Who's the lady friend?"

Ozzy perked up and his eyes went wide. "Ugh, are you kidding me? What did you guys see?"

"Enough," I said, more amused than anything. "C'mon, tell us. What's her name?"

"Ida," the boy mumbled. "We're just friends."

Upon hearing the girl's name, I made a connection in my mind. "Hey, isn't that the name of your character in that game?"

Ozzy's face turned two shades redder.

"That's cute!" I exclaimed, restraining a laugh. "Really weird, but cute!"

"Oz, you sly dog," Charlie continued, "how the heck do you know a town girl? I don't think I knew a town girl here till, like, my second year. Guess I don't have to teach you anything now, do I?"

"Where'd you meet her?"

"Both of you, lay off," Ozzy said. His body was pressed toward the door of the car, as if he was trying to get away from us. "I met her on an old game I used to play. I found out she lived in this town last month and we've been talking since. That's it."

"Gamer girl," Charlie noted. "A rare breed indeed. Nice catch, Ozzy. Now, if you need any tips about making your move . . ."

"She's just a friend," Ozzy desperately reiterated. "Just someone to talk to and hang out with. Maybe give her a tour a campus sometime, y'know?"

"No," I responded flatly. Eastway policy had been ingrained in my memory since my first year. "No outsiders on campus. Ever. Eastway is ten miles away from the town for a reason, man. Lie to her all you want about what's on campus, but bring her on the grounds and she'd have to be, uh, y'know . . ."

I didn't know how to finish my own warning. Something was caught in my throat.

"What?"

"Silenced," I finally blurted out, making an awkward gesture with my neck and throat.

"*Silenced?*" Ozzy said, shocked. "You're kidding, right?"

Neither Charlie nor I replied to his question. Instead, after a few moments, Charlie announced, "Well, leave it to Davy to kill the mood." He then proceeded to switch on the radio and flatly sing along to pop hits all the way back to campus.

• • •

I tried to fit in some exercise after coming back from town. The Academy weight room housed the most expensive and top-of-the-line equipment available. As per usual, I kept to the aerobics machines. The heavy weights were never supposed to be used alone; however, Leon routinely broke this rule. On my first full tour of campus, Weiss happily divulged the story of one of his earlier students who got crushed to death on a particularly ambitious bench press. It was one of the biggest tragedies ever on campus, he explained, because the weight set was stained and ruined. After an hour of aerobic work, anxiety and paranoia soon sank behind a sea of exhaustion. I felt it was finally time to pursue sleep, something that had eluded me for far too long.

Before going to my room, however, I decided to talk to Charlie one last time to make sure everything was clear. Johanna was escaping. The psycho may be a dangerous and unpredictable person, but nothing in her plan seemed to involve me. No matter if things went wrong or right, no one would be in danger except her.

I reached out to open the door, only to be stopped by muffled voices. They were the same I had heard that morning, but this time I didn't call out. Instead, I silently pressed my ear against the wood and listened. Listened to a minor exchange between two voices that would keep me up in my bed for another hour.

"Does he know?"

"No."

"Good."

CHAPTER FOUR

An alarm blared in my room, a sure sign that a new job was beginning. I reluctantly rose from bed, giving a terrible yawn as I got dressed. Four days had passed since I went to town with Charlie and Ozzy, and the previous night Weiss had warned us over the loudspeaker that an operation would begin in the morning. We might have gone out a day or two earlier had Charlie and Mabel finished the plan in a shorter amount of time. They had failed to finish it in one night as Charlie intended, and instead, it took them two whole days, during which I hardly saw either of them, and when I did it was usually in passing.

As the alarm continued to sound off over the loud-speakers across campus, I made the trek over to the Central Building. It was just after four in the morning, and a cool night air drifted across the lake. It was a cloudless night, something that was growing increasingly common as summer approached.

Mission briefings were held in the living area, to the right of the main foyer. I was the fourth to arrive, after Mabel,

Charlie, and Johanna. Leon and Ozzy arrived soon after, and the tedious wait for Professor Weiss began. Everyone seemed to be in a mild mood, excluding Ozzy, who still seemed to be a bit cranky, because he was still not entirely used to waking up at such an early hour. Charlie conversed with Mabel in the corner, most likely discussing what they had written up together. I wasn't surprised by the solemn looks on their faces and the way Mabel furiously tapped on the table in front of her. By now, I had accepted that this job was out of the ordinary.

Much to my dismay, Charlie stood up from beside Mabel and walked over to where Leon and Johanna stood. The three of them together made me nervous, especially right before the mission. I approached Mabel, who looked not only wide awake, but ready to run a marathon. "Is everything alright? Everyone seems to be in a tizzy."

Mabel bit her lip as her eyes frantically searched around the room, avoiding mine. "Tizzy? What are you talking about? Everything's fine! This mission isn't *too* bad!" With every passing word Mabel's voice became higher. With a seemingly petrified face and bulging eyes, she looked like a deer in headlights.

"You don't sound very fine, Mabes," I noted, increasingly concerned. Charlie's deceitful antics alone were exhausting to deal with, and adding the easily flustered Mabel into the mix only made things worse.

"I'm cool, I'm cool, relax . . . relax . . ." Mabel muttered, coaxing herself. "Sorry Davy, I'm just a little off. Every time I try to get some sleep, I just get more awake. Don't think I can think straight . . ."

"When's the last time you had some sleep?"

"Like, three days ago, maybe? Is that healthy?"

"Maybe it'd be for the best if you tried to sleep on the plane," I suggested, worried for the girl's safety. "We're gonna need you at the top of your game, just like any other mission."

"Right, any other mission. This is just like any other job, and we're gonna come up on top!" Mabel gave a small, forced giggle, as if she were trying to convince herself. I partially regretted that she was in control with Charlie, as she would have made an excellent field agent. Whereas my innocence was just a light façade I wore before the moment was right, decency seemed like a natural part of Mabel's personality.

Footsteps could be heard on the staircase, and Professor Weiss gradually descended. He looked especially chipper this morning, with his platinum blond hair combed and his beard finely trimmed. He wore an expensive business suit, complete with a gold chain connected to a watch in his breast pocket. "Morning, children," he chirped.

"Good morning, Professor," we moaned collectively.

"Pryce, Parker," Weiss gave a generous smile, sitting in his favorite armchair in the corner of the room. "You may debrief. Class is now in session."

"Yessir," Charlie said, moving to his laptop in the corner of the room. With a few quick taps, a large glass panel descended from the ceiling in front of the assorted couches we sat on. I heard a machine hum on from some unknown part of the room, and images flickered onto the glass, making a screen. There were two images, both of older men's faces. The one on the right had an olive complexion and looked to be slightly cross-eyed in the picture. The other was bald and had a more serious, threatening look on his face. A white scar on his cheek interrupted his otherwise totally midnight-black skin as dark as Leon's.

"Our target is this guy right here," Mabel pointed toward the man with the scar. "His name is François Demiese. He is the second-in-command of the Liberté Libre Army of San Pablo Island."

"San Pablo?" Leon asked. "In the Caribbean?"

"You bet," Charlie said. "The LLA is a relic of the Cold War. They've been occupying parts of the island for more than forty years. Never had enough manpower to overthrow the president there, but the legitimate government has never really had the funds to finish the LLA off, either. It's basically been a stalemate."

"Who's the man on the right?" I asked, pointing toward the screen.

"That is Julio Santana, the founder and leader of the LLA," Mabel explained, with a certain agitation and excitement in her voice. "He and Demiese are occupying the west side of the island with about fifteen hundred men. Several towns have defected to their side, supplying them with food and clothing." The girl, due to her excitement, began to increase the speed of her speech. "They haven't had new weapons since the eighties, but they could still blow us up if we're spotted too early. They have rocket launchers! Remember the last time we had to deal with rocket launchers? Crazy! We had to—"

"Mabel," Weiss warned. "Take it down a couple notches, please."

"Right, right, relax," the girl nodded, assuring herself. She tapped on Charlie's computer, which brought up a bird's-eye view of an island on the screen. "For some reason, the LLA has gotten much more aggressive with their attacks, taking an old Soviet airbase right here. With the ammunition as well as the abandoned equipment, Santana and Demiese could get the edge they need to push farther inland, and their tactics could lead the island into an all-out civil war."

"So, where do we come in?" I asked. "Army and crazy generals need stopping, what do we do? Incriminating documents, sabotage, what are we talking here?"

The room fell strangely silent. "Well," Weiss began, daring to speak. "We were given very broad terms by our client. They wish to have either the death or submission of both generals."

"Submission?" I pressed. "How are we gonna get the submission of two heavily armed combat generals?"

"Well . . ." the professor gave an innocent shrug. "Perhaps their complete submission isn't necessary. As I told Miss Pryce and Mr. Parker, I believe the quickest way is taking lethal action early."

"So . . . this is an assassination mission? We're just waltzing over there and shooting the guys?"

"It appears to be our only option, Prince," Weiss countered, keeping his cool. "Do you have a problem with that?"

I returned to my seat. It wasn't worth fighting the professor on matters that pertained to the Academy's operation.

"If I may, sir?" A new voice entered the conversation. It was Ozzy, looking cautiously around at his fellow agents. "Everyone seems pretty wound up. I mean, an army's scary, but it's just a straightforward assassination, right? It shouldn't be that difficult . . ."

Weiss nudged his head, signaling Mabel and Charlie to change the slide. The map disappeared, and in its place was a black and white photo. It took me a second to realize what it was.

Bodies.

Five bodies, lined up in a neat row. The image was grainy, but I could spot visible bullet wounds on some of them. On one of the corpses, half of the face was missing, burned black. It was clear no respect had been taken: some eyes and jaws hung wide open. What struck me the most about the grisly scene was how young the victims seemed to be: I could tell they were roughly my age.

"This," Weiss said, standing up, "is the Tenth Academy. They tried to kill the generals a while back, failed spectacularly, and fell victim to the Red Plan. Of course, that was thirty years ago, back when the LLA had up-to-date weaponry and fresh manpower. With your team's luck, there shouldn't be any casualties. Of course," the professor gave a wicked grin, which disgusted me almost as much as the picture on screen did, "I warned Charlie and Mabel to be safe rather than sorry."

"We wrote up a lot of Yellow Plans," Mabel said, looking at the ground. "Professor, may we continue, please? We need to get into our entrance strategy."

"By all means," Weiss beamed, lounging back into his chair.

Charlie hastily switched the slide back to an image of the island. "So, there's an open field over here. With a jet small enough, we could land, but it won't exactly be soft, so . . ." he continued with his presentation. The debriefing was complex but direct and took the better part of an hour. Images came and went onscreen: blueprints for a hanger, diagrams for the LLA's Cold War weaponry, as well as pictures of the jungles and beaches of San Pablo. The only thing I could think of, however, was the Tenth Academy. Their dead, grainy faces and expressionless stares burned into my mind, and I couldn't help but glare at Weiss, hoping he'd notice.

Eventually, Charlie got around to talking about exit strategies and wrapped up, handing each of us our own file of the plan we had discussed, a playbook for the game we were about to partake in. "Your transportation to the airport is waiting outside," Weiss concluded. "This is going to be a tough mission—one of the toughest you've encountered together—but I have every confidence you'll have what it takes to get the job done in the end. You children have the potential to succeed and fail, and in the heat of the moment, it will come down to each and every one of you doing your duty to make sure you all get home safe. Class dismissed."

We stood up and began walking toward the door. Something stopped me from leaving, however. Johanna had approached Weiss, and the two began a conversation. "If it's all the same to you, sir," Johanna said. "I'd like to take one of the school cars to the plane. I'm not in the mood to be driven today."

"You sure?" Weiss asked. "You're going to have to drive it back. You might be pretty tired after the mission."

"That won't be much of a problem. In fact, I'd prefer to come back before the other agents did. There are some things around campus that need attending to," the sniper persisted.

The professor's face brightened into a smile. "Alright, fine. I don't see any problem with it."

"Thank you, sir," Johanna muttered under her breath. She turned away from Weiss and now stood in my direction, passing me as she went out the door. I could see her ambivalent demeanor deteriorate into a face of disgust as she walked farther away from the professor.

Seeing that he was now free, I walked over to Weiss, still angry over the images I had to witness. "Why did you show us that picture of the Tenth?" I asked. "All you did was scare us." Criticizing the professor was always a gamble. You never knew which Weiss you would *really* be talking to—the one who ordered cakes for your birthday and complained about his March Madness bracket getting screwed up or the one that ordered you on missions across the world to collect blackmail on presidents. Occasionally, you could talk to the Weiss that once almost bashed Charlie's head in for failing a field training course twice. At Eastway, I quickly learned that conversing with Weiss was always an option. Speaking out or disappointing him, though, could sometimes be more dangerous than a mission.

"Scare you?" Weiss chuckled to himself. "Oh, my poor little Davy got scared! Maybe after he's done murdering those generals for me, I can get some warm milk and his blankie so he doesn't have nightmares tonight!"

"Your sarcastic tangent is duly noted, but I'm serious, sir."

"So am I," Weiss retorted with a toothy smile. "The Academy does not teach its students how to fear. You feel no fear, Davy; you only heed warnings. This class has had a peculiar strain of good fortune that is bound to run out one day. What better time than going back to San Pablo, the site of the unluckiest mission in Eastway history? The Tenth Academy serves as a . . . caveat for you and the rest of the team in San Pablo. It's just something to keep in mind. Are we clear?"

"Yes, sir," I growled.

"Excellent, happy hunting!" Once he had made his point, the professor proceeded to produce a flask from his coat pocket and took a liberal swig. "What?" he exclaimed, observing the growing look of disgust on my face.

"It's five a.m. Isn't it a little early to be drinking, sir?"

"A.m. or p.m., it's still five o'clock, kid," the professor justified. He then waved his hand as if shooing me away. By then, I was all too eager to take my leave.

As I walked out the door, the unpleasant image of Professor Weiss—overlord of Eastway and master of my future—alone and wasted in the Central Building came into my mind. As terrifying as the thought of an intoxicated professor was, I had never actually seen him drunk. Aside from the occasional expensive wine while listening to our debriefs, Weiss was hardly a drinker at all. Him with a flask in the early morning hours simply added to the uncanniness lurking around campus since this mission had been introduced.

I sat in the limousine with Leon and Mabel. The latter was her typical self, downing three sodas before the sun rose. Because of her caffeine addiction, hard sports drinks were banned from Academy grounds. This hardly curbed her craving, and the resourceful Mabel Pryce worked to find equally caffeinated alternatives. This included sugary sodas, which were arguably even worse. With the toxic cocktail of glucose and caffeine pumping through her veins, Mabel had no chance of sitting still for the car ride.

Leon, on the other hand, did not stir for almost the entirety of the trip. He wasn't sleeping, as his eyes were open, transfixed on the window next to him and the trees zooming past us. With his new, specially fitted Kevlar vest, his bulky frame looked practically enormous. We all sat in one row, and I found it no surprise when Mabel asked, "Uh, Davy? Could you fix your leg? Something's digging into mine."

"Whoops, sorry," I said, reaching in between the two of us. I pulled out my pistol, which was strapped to a holster partially hidden by my coat, creating a bit more space in between us.

"Thanks, that's—" Mabel stopped speaking and gasped, locking eyes with the pistol. "Davy, put that away! You're not supposed to take that out yet."

"What are you two doing over there?" Leon moaned, still staring out his window.

Ignoring the third passenger, I assured Mabel, "Relax. There's no ammo inside. The safety's even on, look."

"If there aren't any bullets, why are you carrying it around with you?" Mabel asked, looking increasingly nervous.

"I dunno, just makes me feel safer, I guess. Kinda forgot I still had this with me, honestly. Should've put it with the other supplies in the trunk."

"Right, right . . ." Mabel agreed, sounding almost lost. Bewildered, she stared at the pistol. "Davy, have you ever killed anyone?"

The question hit me like a brick in the head. "What?" I said, instinctively. I knew what she was saying, but couldn't grasp it immediately.

"Killed someone," Mabel elaborated, picking up my pistol. "You know, *pew pew*." As she spoke, she fired imaginary bullets out of my weapon.

"Oh yeah . . ." I thought hard for a second, looking back on all the lethal jobs I had been a part of. The pain I felt looking back was lessened given the fact that it was almost always criminals in the line of fire. "Almost every time Johanna shoots someone, it's to protect me. So I'd say yeah, a few more people would still be alive if I wasn't around."

"That doesn't count," the girl objected. "I mean . . . like, have you ever actually held the gun and pulled the trigger at another guy?"

"Huh," I kept thinking, trying to recall every mission where I had used a gun. It was mostly to provide cover fire when escaping, and a couple of times during interrogations, but had I ever legitimately shot someone? "I don't know . . ."

"How do you not know?" Leon interjected, placing himself in the conversation.

"Never thought about it too hard," I whined. "Maybe? Probably at one point? I . . . I don't know, Mabes. How 'bout you ask Leon? He's killed."

"Dang straight," the larger boy said definitively. "Shot a guy right in the freaking face. Don't regret it at all. It's a game of survival, and I'm not scared to shoot back."

Mabel seemed more stunned by Leon's definitive attitude than she was by my questionable response. "But don't you ever think about it, though? Decades of human experience gone by the pull of a trigger . . ."

"Not in the mood for philosophy class today, babe," Leon remarked.

"Did he just call me 'babe'?" Mabel scoffed, wagging her finger angrily. "I'm not your babe!"

I reluctantly backed her up, not sure if I wanted to enter the new disagreement, "Yeah, what Mabel said. You shouldn't talk to your teammates like that, man."

Leon finally turned away from his window. His dark brown eyes studied us very intensely before he cracked a smile and said, "You two are pretty freaking cute. Mabel, give Davy his gun back before you find a way to hurt yourself with it."

Mabel politely obeyed and the conversation was dropped as we drove in a welcome silence to the airport, which was nothing more than a small collection of buildings and a runway. The parking lot was not totally empty. Even early in the morning, in a relatively rural part of the state, it was clear that flyers were out and about. Johanna had arrived earlier than the rest of us, standing on the edge of the sidewalk, steel briefcase in hand. It contained her sniper rifle, and she was very fond of walking around campus with it, even if we weren't preparing for a mission.

Together we quietly walked onto the airfield. None of the aircraft were very large, and the only defining feature ours had was a black *E* painted on the door. The inside cabin had a tan rug and six beige leather seats, which were quite easy to fall asleep in. Charlie put on his headset and aviators (sunglasses which he claimed helped him fly better, even at night) and made his way to the cockpit. He typically was the one who flew us to our missions, occasionally assisted by Mabel. I let out a long yawn and approached my usual seat, the one in the front right. "Whoa, whoa, whoa," Charlie raised his palm. "I'm not letting you anywhere near the cockpit."

"Why not? I always sit here," I protested.

"The enemy here has radar," Charlie gave a serious look. "Fly too close to where I shouldn't and kaboom! This mission requires some fancy flying, and you might distract me."

"Distract you? How can I—"

"Just do what he says," Johanna groaned, taking her usual seat in the center right. "I think I'm getting a migraine."

I sighed and complied, sitting on the center seat to the left, across the aisle from Johanna. Ozzy took my typical seat, plugging a ruby jack into his headphones, preparing for a long plane ride. Mabel sat in front of me and Leon sat behind, leaving one spot open in the back to the right. After a brief announcement of the day's trip, Charlie took us to the air. As we sped down the runway, I always questioned what the people in the air traffic control tower must have been thinking, hearing an adolescent boy on the other end. I felt that wonderful sensation of taking to the air, right when the wheels lifted from the pavement underneath. Stretching out, I reached into the seat in front of me to find what magazines were available to read. To my dismay, all that was available was a take-out menu to Beef 'n' Wings. I quietly cursed Weiss and his cruel sense of humor and wished I had brought something along for the ride. My copy of the plan was in the cargo hold, along with the clothes and weapons.

With nothing to do, the plane ride consisted of me drifting through sleep and consciousness, partially aware of my surroundings, Flying above the clouds made it difficult to track how far we had gone. Gradually the skies cleared up, and I realized that we were above the sun-bleached, sandy coasts of Florida, which gradually transformed into the sparkling, blue, midday waters of the Caribbean. I knew that we were approaching our destination, and a mixture of fear and excitement began to build. I started waiting. Looking around at what the rest of the team was doing, I saw that they, too, were all preparing to land, excluding Leon, who seemed to be having a pleasant dream behind me. When the speakers finally crackled on, I felt my anxiety grow.

"*Attention passengers,*" Charlie said in a cheery voice, "*we are making our final descent down to the beautiful island of San Pablo.*"

I peeked outside my window. Sure enough, we were approaching a round, green island surrounded by a ring of white sand. I bit my lip in anticipation.

"*Please keep in mind,*" he continued, "*that we are landing in hostile territory. If we are discovered, you must—*" Suddenly, the speakers cut out.

A second later, I heard them turn back on, giving us a static-like, fuzzy noise. Then, with great clarity, music began to blare: "*Keep on dancing in the shades of your crimson, keep on dancing and dancing and dancing . . .*" A male voice continued to sing as synthesizers played in the background.

Looks of confusion went across everyone's faces. "What's going on?" I asked. "Why is Chuck playing music?"

"I don't mind," Johanna shrugged, maintaining a slight smile. "It's 'Shades of Ruby,' by Electric Sheep in Wonderland. First song on *Stairway to Sirius,* their last great album before they went mainstream."

"Good to hear," Ozzy said, removing his headphones and hanging them on his neck, "but what's going on here? Wasn't Charlie making an announcement?"

"Yeah," Leon agreed. "Someone should go up there and—"

Before his sentence was finished, a powerful, white light erupted in the front of the cabin. There was a horrible screeching noise, and a puff of black smoke and cold air burst into the plane. Ozzy's seat was now charred black, and his part of the cabin wall was gone, revealing the blue sky outside. The entire cabin shook violently, and we began to slope downward, like the final drop in a roller coaster. I heard Mabel let out a small, shrill scream as we continued to plunge, falling downward instead of moving forward.

"We've been hit!" I screamed, clenching my hands around my seatbelt.

"Thank you, Captain Obvious!" Johanna snapped back. "Chuck! If you can hear me, pull up!"

"I'm trying!" I heard Charlie say from behind his curtain. Despite no longer occupying the speakers, his voice was still mighty strong on its own. I felt a small twinge of relief over the fact that he was still active in the cockpit, trying to save us. This assurance, however, was gone once I heard, "Everyone brace for impact, this is gonna be rough!"

The ocean seemed to grow and grow beneath us until I realized that we were on the same level. There was a terrible thud as we splashed down, and what remained of the cabin convulsed violently. I snapped forward, hardly restrained by my seatbelt. Everything grew hazy. I could still feel the plane moving forward, pushing its nose down into the Atlantic Ocean. Along with the tremendous force, torrents of water now gushed into the cabin through the jet's damaged side, over the black, burned heap that used to be Ozzy's seat.

There was one final scream in the cabin before the lights snapped off and everything went black.

CHAPTER FIVE

My first mission happened on a Wednesday in September. It was only fitting, of course, that new students begin their life at Eastway Academy at the same time classes regularly go back in session in normal schools. I had trained every day since arriving at the Academy, but even still I felt terribly unsure of myself. Rex, the senior of the school, had complimented my intuition and guile, the latter of which was apparently a good thing. Johanna scared me for multiple reasons, and when she opted to skip the mission, I was perfectly fine to be down a member if it meant that I didn't have to hear her uncanny voice buzzing in my ear.

The day before the operation, I had practiced saying nothing but lies and seeing how well I could manage. Most were trivial things, like saying I was going to the shooting range when really I was headed for the café. Some, however, were lies that I had been maintaining for some time, for various reasons. The fact I could get away with such deceit probably didn't prove much, but it gave me the confidence

I needed to not have a nervous breakdown the morning of the mission.

I sat alone on a park bench, facing the Third National Bank of Quebec. It was a foreboding building, with thick Corinthian columns that reminded me of the Central Building back on campus. None of the other field operatives were in my field of sight. I silently prayed that they had made it underground okay.

"*Woodstock is ready. The operation is a go,*" Charlie's voice buzzed in the transceiver in my ear.

"*Grateful is ready,*" I heard Rex say. He was the one leading the operation on the roof, guiding a young, brash boy named Leon.

"*Creedence is a-ready,*" Yvette said. She was usually just another field agent, but with Johanna gone she reluctantly became our sniper, scoping out danger. "*I have a clear view of ze stage.*" She was a strange, older, foreign girl whom I had never talked to before. More than a year later, right before she graduated, I would have my first and only real conversation with her.

"*Jefferson is ready to rock,*" Leon announced. Initially, he was pissed that everyone got band code names and he was stuck with a president, but then Charlie explained to him what his name meant. For most of the plane ride over, he had been listening to Jefferson Airplane's greatest hits and had refused to stop talking about them.

I stood up, walking across the street to the steps of the bank. The insanity of what I was doing had not struck me yet. Inside, I was void of emotion, even of the fear that had manifested itself days before. My mind was partially shut down, merely allowing my body to do as it had been told. It might have been because of this that my transceiver buzzed, "*Um, Hendrix? Ready? You there?*"

I snapped out of my hypnotic haze, realizing that I had forgotten to check in. "Right!" I called a little too loudly. Bankers walking around me turned their heads to look, much to my embarrassment. In a smaller voice, I whispered, "Hendrix is ready. I'm moving up the steps." Rex had decided that Woodstock's most popular act had to be my nickname, partially due to the fact that he thought it would be easy for me to remember. I knew that I needed to focus, as many in the team already doubted my skills. It was very strange for a student to start out as an infiltrator, which was arguably the most important and dangerous job in any mission. Objections, specifically by Johanna, were silenced by Weiss, who persisted that I had "something special." Nevertheless, a wave of doubt and uneasiness followed me up to Canada, and I couldn't ignore my comrades' worried glances.

"*Stay on target, Hendrix,*" Charlie responded, his voice sounding stern. "*Remember, if you flunk this mission, I get to choose your code name for the next job.*" I gulped. When I had first arrived, he was more than ecstatic to hear that my last name was 'Prince,' and promptly wanted to pin the code name 'Purple Rain' on me. I was determined to avoid such humiliation at any cost. Clutching my backpack with white knuckles, I entered through the doorway of the bank and plunged into the crowded morning scene.

● ● ●

"*I have a visual on Hendrix,*" Charlie announced. "*Keep your cool. I see someone behind you.*"

I was walking below the bank compound, past large iron doors which I was told were vaults. Even without the heads-up, I knew someone was behind me; the echo of their footsteps gave them away.

"Hey!" a male voice called. It sounded gruff, and when I turned around I found myself facing a tall, gaunt man in a blue uniform.

"Hi!" I said, in a chipper attitude. Charlie had said that since I had a backpack, I might as well play the part of 'innocent schoolboy lost in shady underground of corrupt bank' for as long as I could. "Um, I mean, *bonjour!*"

"Not too good at French, eh?" the security guard smiled, seemingly lowering his guard. His right hand, I noted, remained firmly clutching the holster of what I guessed was a stun gun. "What are you up to down here, little man?"

This mission happened before I hit a big growth spurt, and I was very sensitive about my height. The offhand remark, which I interpreted as an insult, did not go unnoticed. "I got lost from my class . . ." I explained, maintaining my innocuous attitude. "I'm real sorry if I'm somewhere I'm not supposed to be, mister."

"Heh, no kidding," the guard remarked, looking over his shoulder and past me in abrupt movements. He was nervous, I realized. Nervous was a good thing. Nervous meant he could make mistakes. "Now, if you follow me, I'll get you out of here. Field trip, huh? Isn't it kind of early in the school year to have one?"

"Eh, my school's kinda weird," I told him, shrugging. As I moved my shoulders, my backpack made a faint clatter, enough to alert the officer.

"Hey, can I take a look at that?" he asked.

The flutter in my stomach grew. "Sure, no problem." Taking the pack off, I let out a huff as I tried to scoop up the new, immense weight in my hands. "Think you'll need both arms for this, sir, it's pretty heavy."

"Alright," the guard agreed, extending his hands.

With his hand off his weapon, I was free to make my move. With a startling and spontaneous amount of energy,

I swung the heavy pack at his face. Clearly unprepared for such a blow, the officer reeled backward, allowing me to advance and make a move for his stun gun. Before he could get his hands on me to counter, I jabbed the device into his unprotected throat, hoping that I was using it correctly.

A shrill cry of pain was followed by the man losing control of his limbs and flailing for a brief second. Staggering away from me and looking utterly confused about what had just happened to him, the guard collapsed to the floor, making an all-too-loud *thud,* which echoed through the passage. "He's down. We're cool."

"*Nice going, Hendrix,*" Rex noted. "*Search him and get outta sight quickly. Dunno who else could be down there.*"

During a brief pat down, which made me feel highly uncomfortable, my hands found a small, rectangular piece of plastic. "I have a key. I think it could lead to backstage."

"*Great!*" Charlie hollered, ecstatic. "*That just saved us a lot of time. See if it works for backstage.*"

After making sure that the unconscious guard was hidden in the shadows, I picked up my backpack and made my way to the target safe. Like all the other entrances in the passage, the slate door was foreboding, but slipping the key card on a nearby panel made it let out a low, mechanical grown. Very slowly, the slate door disappeared and the safe's inner chamber was revealed. "Hendrix is in. I'm backstage."

"*Roger that,*" Charlie said, still sounding quite elated. "*Give us confirmation and plant the pack.*"

Inside the dusty chamber, under a singly pale light, seven large objects were kept under white sheets. Each was equal in size—each roughly as big as a small car. Walking toward the center of the room made me realize just how expansive the chamber was, reminding me of the gymnasium from my old school. Systematically, I began to tear off the sheets, revealing the true contents of the safe—the true purpose of the mission.

Nine hundred million dollars in high-grade counterfeit bills were densely packed into seven squares. The product of a local mob's new enterprise, our employer needed it destroyed. With each successive pull, some individual bills slipped off with the sheet, spilling onto the concrete floor. *"Any sign of the hostages?"* Rex asked, tentatively.

"Afraid not," I informed. "Just me and the dead presidents. Or dead prime ministers. Or whatever the heck Canada has on its money."

"Roger," Charlie buzzed. *"Now, I believe it's time for Grateful and Jefferson to jam backstage."*

Once again inspecting my surroundings, I carefully positioned my backpack where the plan had mandated it: in the center, up against the back wall. "Detonator's in place on my side."

"Same here," Rex declared. *"Hendrix, it might be smart to get out of that thing's immediate vicinity."*

Diving behind the nearest block of illegal money, my childlike interest in explosions got the better of me and I cautiously peaked my head out. The burst startled me, but it was much more of a hasty *pop* than a grand *bang*. Regardless, the entire wall shook as a blast of equal magnitude erupted on the other side. Once the white smoke cleared above the charred remains of what was once a backpack, a black hole had been created in the wall

With the crunching sound of sneakers on blasted concrete, two crouching figures entered the chamber. Each carried a thin, rifle-like device on their backs. Rex got to his feet first, grinning broadly at me. "See, Jefferson? Kid ain't too bad."

Leon, looking especially severe in the weak light, only gave a passing grunt as he unstrapped the device from his back. Aiming it at the nearest stack, he declared, "Hendrix? I think you oughta step back, unless you want your face melted."

"Hold up," Rex ordered, aggravating Leon. "Shouldn't Hendrix do the honors?"

"Fine," he agreed begrudgingly, practically throwing his weapon onto me.

"It's a lot heavier than I thought it would be," I noted, trying to get a firm grasp on it.

"Just aim it in the general direction of the target, and watch your fingers," Rex advised. He gave me a reassuring smile, but I noticed he was slowly stepping away from me as I leveled the device. Holding my breath, I pulled the trigger.

A light hissing sound escaped the weapon, and for a moment I was afraid something had gone awry. Then a great, hot flame erupted from the nozzle, assaulting the false money. The flames were almost aqueous, seeping onto the stack of cash with yellow, burning whips. The light radiating from the burning notes was almost overpowering, and everything around me became tainted with red.

"Alright!" Rex called, charging forward with his flamethrower like a marine at Normandy, eagerly igniting the next stack of bills. Leon swiftly took back his device from me, to which I had no objections. The burning, however harmless and seemingly justified, scared me. There was a twinge of uncertainty I carried with me when I handled the device, something I was eager to dismiss as jitters.

The two elder students proceeded to burn the remaining stacks, and the chamber continued to illuminate with hues of red, yellow, and auburn. Long and strange shadows were cast on all our faces. Leon's looked especially eerie with a long, toothy smile as he ignited the next heap.

I tried my best to stay away from the burning and smoke, choosing to stand near a corner by the entrance. *"Glad to see everything's going according to plan,"* Charlie spoke simply, presumably trying to find the most appropriate 'burning money' pun for the situation.

"Yep," I agreed, proud of myself. All seven stacks were ignited now, each burning at different stages. "Kind of beautiful, actually."

"Put it on a boat and put a coffin on and you've got a Viking funeral pyre!" the planner said.

Listening to Charlie's words and gazing at the rising inferno, a horrible thought struck me. *"Funeral pyre?* Woodstock, is there any word yet on the hostages?"

"N-no," Charlie said, hearing the intensity in my voice and getting worked up himself. *"Th-they must be in a different location or something."*

"How many are there?"

"We think m-maybe seven; why?"

"Oh crap," I gasped. Without too much thought, I charged at the nearest 'pyre,' pushing it over. Burned currency and flames toppled to the ground, and I began scooping through the remaining pile, trying my best to keep away from notes that the blaze had touched. A few movements later, my fears were confirmed: I found a hand sticking out of the pile. Grasping onto it and pulling with my remaining strength, I dragged a figure out of the scorched mess. "They're under the money! The hostages are under the money!" I shouted desperately, hoping that Leon and Rex could hear me.

Without much of a word between them, I saw them follow my lead and topple another pile—this one with a much larger fire—and begin shuffling through the remainder desperately until Leon exclaimed something and dove further into the pile, pulling out another body. All the while, I checked the status of my own person—an older-looking man—and felt his neck for a pulse. Confirming he was alive,

I dropped him off away from the fire before moving on to the next heap.

"*D-dang it!*" Charlie exclaimed, trying to keep control of his voice. "*They knew we were c-coming to dispose of the bills and set up a deterrent. Save who you can!*"

I felt obligated to say something back to Charlie, but the black smoke swirling around stopped me from opening my mouth. Ignoring the growing pain and redness on my wrists and the dryness in my eyes and face, I pulled out two more hostages from the second and third stacks. The flames had reached the latter and his body was covered in red and black blotches, but he was miraculously alive. Trying to find a new stack in the growing fiery haze, I stumbled into Leon and Rex, both with their sleeves to their mouths. "We need to get them out of here," the eldest agent said. "If not, the smoke's gonna kill all of us!"

"How many did you save?" I said, speaking above the crackling flames, which continued to grow.

"Three. You?"

"Three. We're down one."

I saw Rex's shoulders drop and heard a very audible sigh. He pointed to the burning 'pyre' to the right of us—the one neither of us got to. It was thoroughly engulfed in fire, so much so that I feared the thought of moving too close. It was the first stack we burned—the one I had ignited.

• • •

A glum air lingered over the Academy the evening we returned. As a reward for my first "successful mission," Weiss ordered sweets and a cake and threw a small party in the Central Building. The cake, for some inexplicable reason, was shaped like a bear holding colorful balloons. "You did a *bear-y* good job!" was written on his belly in red frosting.

Before anyone could get a slice, Charlie stabbed the bear with a kitchen knife, an act which made me feel strangely uncomfortable.

The festivities dragged on for half an hour until the professor ran out of candy and everyone departed. Johanna went off to who-knows-where in the woods, and after I was given assurances by both Weiss and Rex that she would be back before the end of the night, I chose not to worry about what she was up to. Charlie, Leon, Rex, and I went down to the shore of Lake Pavus and picked out smooth stones to skip in the water.

Rex had the first throw. He had a conditioned arm and a fluid throw, and his rock flew across the lake in a long series of skips, landing at an impressive distance—halfway across the lake. "Not a bad first mission, Davy," he said. "You kept your cool. Half the newbies have panic attacks halfway through, usually when things get serious. You stayed calm and saved a lot of lives with you observation."

Leon was the next one to throw. His arm jerked violently, clearly releasing a lot of energy. He lacked Rex's refined expertise, however, and after a few short hops his rock sunk only a few feet offshore. "Yeah," Leon said, chuckling. "Six out of seven isn't so bad!"

I balled my fists and approached Leon. Rex's arm stopped me, giving me a stern look. "It's okay, man," he reassured. "You did what you could."

"Is this the freaking Academy?" I asked. All the frustration and black thoughts that had entered my mind on the ride home came to a head. "I nearly suffocated from a fire I started. I burned an innocent person alive. Mission accomplished?"

"Davy, you didn't kill that guy," Charlie chided. Exhausted, he rested by the Lake's rocky shore on his back. Lazily tossing his rock, it landed in the water with no skips, just a single splash. "It's the planner's job to make sure all the variables are accounted for. We should have located the hostages before I allowed you guys to proceed with the burning. If you want to blame anyone, let me have the guilt."

"Heh," Rex let out an inappropriate chuckle, breaking his stoic demeanor. "You wouldn't have even done the first ignition if I hadn't told you to do so. Guess I have a little responsibility too."

"Great," I scoffed, still furious. "So *all of us* killed an innocent person, then. If we weren't there, he'd still be alive!"

"You don't know that," Leon said, losing his patience just as quickly as I lost my temper.

"All the while," I continued, "we're celebrating and eating cake for what? We burned some mob money? Depleted their funds a little bit?"

"It was good cake . . ." Charlie muttered, quietly remaining in the conversation.

"Open your eyes, kid," Rex said, his voice harsher. "We were there to destroy the money, not save hostages. All seven of those guys could've burned up, and we still would have thrown that party. As long as the objective is accomplished, Weiss and the Academy don't give a second thought if a thousand people die. As long as our client pays us, the collateral damage doesn't matter."

I paced back and forth on the shore, my boots stomping furiously into the small rocks. "So what about all that talk about fighting the good fight and protecting the innocent?"

"Freaking newbie . . ." Leon derided.

Rex sighed, doing his best to stay calm. "The Academy is an organization that makes money from clients. We're not superheroes, Davy, but we're also not bad people. We take down the guys we're meant to take down, all the while trying to save who we can. We can't save everyone, though, especially when the bad guys have guns. This stuff happens, and when it does you just have to deal with it."

In my frustration, I tossed my rock across the lake in a wild throw. It miraculously skipped across the water, driving farther than both Rex's and Leon's.

"Not bad," Rex muttered, dropping to the ground, deflated.

"Thanks," I said, surprised by my own strength. The hostile atmosphere began to break away to a quiet evening night. I collapsed to the ground next to him, and we silently observed the crescent moon on the rippling water of the lake. The four of us didn't need to exchange anymore words; the gloomy truth had made itself clear.

CHAPTER SIX

Black water swirled in the cabin, pouring over the first row of seats and lapping on to my dangling feet. The jet was now sinking diagonally into the Caribbean Sea, and taking off my seatbelt would mean a plunge into the rising water below. Regardless, my shaking hands went to work unlatching myself from my seat, and the clicking of metal around me told me that the other students were doing the same.

Freeing myself, I plunged into the seawater below, which was surprisingly tepid. In the dark, dying plane, it was difficult to remember that there was hot tropical water above us. My legs kicked violently, desperately trying to get my footing on the seats below. My arms were spread, feeling the plastic walls of the jet, when one of them felt a strange warmth. I realized that Mabel was next to me, latching on to the one of the windows to keep herself steady. A brief wave of relief passed over me to see that at least someone in the front row had survived.

Another splash rang out from behind, telling me someone else had freed themselves and was now in our position,
trying to stay afloat. I gently passed over my own seat—had
I stayed put the water would have been over my head—and
grabbed onto the chair in the back row, vacant of Leon.
With emergency red lights illuminating the dire atmosphere,
I could tell Mabel was still close. Leon and Johanna were
together on the other side of the cabin; the latter held her
briefcase above her head, protecting it. The gurgling of the
water below us died down, and the creaking, banging noise
became less frequent. It took me a second, but I realized that
the water had stopped rising. An eerie peace settled for a few
brief seconds, where the only sound came from the four of
us, treading water.

A head popped up from the now quiet abyss, lashing out
viciously, taking deep breaths. I quickly recognized the new
survivor by the black aviators over his eyes. "Charlie!" Mabel
cheered, partly startled and partly elated.

"Mabes, is that you?" the pilot said, desperately feeling
around the abyss that surrounded him. "I can't see anything!"

I pushed off from the side of the cabin, meeting my
dismayed friend in the center. With a quick swipe, I tore
the expensive sunglasses off his face. "Oh, oh okay," Charlie
rubbed his eyes, checking his new surroundings. "Thanks
for that, bro. Guys, we've gotta get out of here!"

"The water level's not rising," Johanna noted. "What's
going on here?"

"We've made an air pocket," Charlie explained. By the
distinct splashes he was making, I could tell he was gesticu-
lating as well. "I think there's a big hole down there by the
front row. As water came in, all the air was pushed to the
back of the cabin. Might be keeping us temporarily buoyant."

"What's gonna happen if we breathe in all the oxygen?"
Mabel said, allowing panic to take over her voice. "Alright

everyone! We've gotta make the supply last longer. We can take turns taking deep breaths—"

"Mabel, shut up," Johanna said, snidely. Despite the horrific turn of events, her voice maintained an air of composure that both Charlie and Mabel lacked, to certain degrees. "Chuck, how long do we have?"

"The pressure of this water could make this cabin collapse at any moment," Charlie continued. I noticed trickles of water on the walls, colored crimson by the emergency lights. Our air bubble was bursting. "There's no water pressure in the hole below us. It's the only way out right now."

"I'll go first," Johanna announced. "We need my case, and I don't know how well I can swim with it. Leon, cover my rear. Help me with this if you see I'm struggling."

"Aye, aye," Leon agreed. The two took one last deep breath and disappeared under the water.

"Great," Charlie muttered. "If we're crushed to death in here, at least we have the pleasure of knowing those two survived."

"Who should go next?" I asked.

"Davy," Mabel announced. "You should go. Chuck needs to catch his breath, so I'll stay behind."

Something about the tone of her voice disturbed me. I'd heard it before, like when guards volunteered to sacrifice themselves in an attempt to save their boss. "Mabel, I'm a strong swimmer. If I have to—"

"Just go!" she yelled, giving me a light push. "Now isn't exactly the time to argue."

With one last glance at the two of them huddled close, I reluctantly took a deep breath and allowed myself to drop down into the pool of water. I fought to keep my eyes open. Through the blurs, I could see seatbelts and partially destroyed carpeting floating in the scarlet-tainted pool of the cabin like ruined seaweed. The red emergency lights were consistent along either side—excluding a dark void forward to my right. Assuming that was the way out, I darted toward it, pressing forward. I looked up and saw a very welcome sign: light. I had managed to escape the doomed aircraft, and now it was a matter of swimming up.

Then I heard a terrifying noise behind. The only thing I can recollect comparing it to is the sound of two cars crashing into each other head-on. It was a grinding, screeching sound that traveled throughout my body, stopping me dead in my tracks. At that moment, the plane's cabin collapsed. A powerful force pressed against me, and water now rushed into the breach I had just escaped from, trying to push me along with it. Thrashing with my arms and feet, I was on the verge of panic, with my body sluggishly drifting in the wrong direction. Exhausted by this excess motion, I instinctively opened my mouth to take a quick breath of air—forgetting I was underwater.

When I was about ready to give up and accept the current, the weight pushing me back died. I swam eagerly upward to the shining ocean surface. I took one last glimpse down and saw that our jet had proceeded to sink further, leaving a trail of oil and debris in its wake.

Once above the water, I could feel the mild afternoon air draft into my lungs, revitalizing me. Treading water, I spat out the unwelcome contents I had consumed in my ill-fated gasp the moment before. "Hey!" a voice said. "Who's there?"

"W-what?" I responded. The seawater I had ingested must have traveled to my brain, making it only partially operational. "What? What was all of that?"

"Our jet just got gunned out of the sky, along with almost all our equipment," a wave passed, and I now saw that it was Johanna talking to me. She still held her beloved briefcase above her head, using one arm to tread toward me. "There's the island over there. You can see it if you get on top one of the waves. We should make our way over there before you—" an unexpected ripple splashed Johanna in the face, interrupting her speech. "Before you run out of energy," she finished.

"Th-the others," I inquired. "Oh my gosh, Chuck and Mabel were back there when the cabin collapsed! They could be—"

"'Sup, Dave!" Charlie, practically appearing out of nowhere, swam toward Johanna and me. "That was one heck of a wake-up call, eh?"

"Agh!" I screamed, tempted to hug the man. I found it difficult to put together complete sentences. "How did you . . . ? And Mabel . . . ?"

"Mabel's making her way to the beach with Leon," Charlie did his best to give me a confident smile, while maintaining his balance on the treacherous waves around us. "When the bubble broke, the air pushed upward, practically taking us along with it through a new break. We probably had an easier time getting out than you did, dude. Then again, I had my doubts Mabel could go out the same way you did, with what's down there."

"What do you mean?"

Charlie lost his smile and said, "I mean, Ozzy. Or at least, what was left of Oz . . ."

"You mean I swam past his . . . " I felt a queasy sensation run over me, a discomfort similar to the feeling I get when reading a mission's report. "I had no idea. It was dark, and I couldn't see—"

"Don't feel bad," he said. "It was the only way you saw out. Maybe it was better you didn't see."

I recalled the crash, second by second, remembering how Ozzy's seat seemed to be consumed by fire. "I can't believe it. He didn't even get a chance to react. How'd they shoot us down? I thought—"

"We can talk about it on dry land," Johanna interjected, beginning to swim away from me. "Remember, we're not in the clear yet."

Yearning for answers, I followed Johanna. The island slowly came into view—at first nothing but a green blur to my delirious eyes, although as we drew nearer I could start picking out individual trees and finally a long strip of white sand. The water grew shallow to the point where I could see the bottom, and then my feet brushed against it. I climbed onto the sandy shore and immediately collapsed from exhaustion, feeling the hot sand rub against my cheek. Johanna had apparently done the same exact thing. I could see the soles of her shoeless feet in front of me, along with her ever-present metal briefcase off to her side. Once he reached the beach, Charlie followed suit, collapsing next to me. The two of us stared at each other for a moment, before Charlie cracked a smile and said in a mocking tone, *"What? What? What was all of that?"*

"Oh, shut up," I snapped in between panting breaths. "Don't act like you weren't scared."

"Me? Afraid of death? Ha," Charlie shook his head. "After the crash, I knew things would work out for me. Always aced those stupid maritime classes back at Eastway. Just be glad the ocean gods decided to save your skinny butt."

"Guys, you made it!" the sound of Mabel's voice, along with pattering footsteps, made their way across the beach. Like Johanna, she too was barefoot. A large white cloth was tied around her arm. Despite her apparent injury, she practically pulled Charlie off the ground, giving him a strangely long embrace.

Realizing she didn't intend to give me the same affection, I pushed myself up from the sandy beach. "Mabes," I asked, concerned, "Did you hurt your arm?"

"Yeah," Charlie answered, analyzing how the wound was wrapped. "Before we swam up, the cabin went dark. She didn't know where she was going, and she scratched herself on the wreckage."

"Leon patched me right up," Mabel said, beaming like a teenage girl who had not just gone through a near death experience. I suppose that when one coordinates the demise of others like planners do, nothing can surprise them, even after facing their own death. I realized the cloth around her arm was actually Leon's undershirt, which he regularly wore along with his Kevlar.

"Regardless," Johanna said in a stern voice, clicking open her briefcase. "Let me have a look. It needs to be cleaned. Infection is the last thing I want to worry about with this team."

"How is your sniper gear gonna help clean a cut?" I asked, glancing at her case.

"I keep a first aid kit in here too," she scoffed, as if it were common knowledge. "As well as copy of the plan. Did you honestly think I would keep only a *gun* close to me?"

"Right, right, of course," I sighed, too tired to deal with Johanna.

"Look!" Charlie pointed to the forest behind us. I watched the trees shake as a figure emerged. "Leon! Hey, Leon!"

Leon's face was unreadable. He stomped onto the beach, going straight up to Charlie. Then he balled his fist and punched him across the jaw, sending the hapless planner to his knees. Leon wound up for another haymaker, but I darted between the two and pushed him away. "Dude!" I said. "What are you doing?"

"Chucky here is the one that almost got us killed," Leon shouted, enraged. "He's the one who killed Ozzy! He gave away our coordinates and got us shot down."

"Gave out our coordinates?" Mabel said, in the most calming voice she could muster. "We can't jump to conclusions and say—"

"No, no, he's right," Charlie fought to get back on his feet, rubbing his jaw. "If we were indeed shot down, there's no way that that artillery could have been perfectly pointed like that. Plus we were still over international waters. The Nationalists wouldn't risk shooting down a jet unless they knew exactly who was inside."

"How do you know it was artillery?" I asked, sounding a bit more suspicious than I had intended.

"If we were struck with something and it wasn't an artillery shell, we would have been eviscerated," Charlie explained. "Our jet was built for stealth, not protection. Any larger kind of missile would blow us away like we were nothing."

"You were the one in the cockpit," Leon accused. "You knew our coordinates during every part of the journey. I bet you were also the one who put on that weird song."

Right, the alternative music, I recalled that strange episode.

"Whatever that was, it just popped up on my radio," Charlie insisted, pulling out his real glasses from his soaking wet pocket. "I was just as confused as you guys. And figuring out our coordinates isn't that hard. Any one of us with a GPS could have done it, and all they needed to do was communicate with the enemy. Heck, someone could have ratted us out over Morse code if they had to. Could've been any of us."

"Johanna!" I said, in a rush of emotion. "Was this the plan you were talking about last week? You're angry at Weiss. Maybe . . . you could have tried to get us all killed to get your revenge, and defect to the enemy."

"Don't let your imagination run wild, David," Johanna narrowed her eyes. "You remember that I sat to the right, correct? The aircraft was struck on the right, therefore I had just as big of a chance as Ozzy of getting blown up."

"It was more or less a one-in-three chance," I said. "Not terrible odds, if you wanted to have an alibi."

"I don't take chances," the sniper hissed. "If you ask me, I agree with Leon. Charlie's the guilty party. Remember back when we were boarding? He asked you not to sit on the right side, and Ozzy took your spot. He knew that we would be struck ahead of time."

With the blame shifting back to him, Charlie looked more annoyed than anything else. "So let me get your theory straight. I crash my own plane, sitting in the most dangerous part while it happens, warn everyone ahead of time, and then go out of my way to make sure everyone gets out safely? I must have some truly vile plan I want to execute, if I've been keeping you all alive this long."

"Vile, or desperate," Leon retorted. "Look, it's the only evidence we've got to go on right now."

"What about the music?" I asked. "That was pretty freaking weird. Johanna, you're the only one who likes alternative music. You even recognized the song!"

"Oh, oh, so I *like* the random music that plays before we crash, therefore I'm the mastermind behind this mess? Are you kidding me?" Johanna countered. I had never seen so much emotion in her face. She was glaring at me with unbridled fury, and it was terrifying.

"Well, like Leon said," I remarked, turning away from the girl's unpleasant snarl, "It's the only evidence we've got right now."

"Everyone, quit it!" Mabel shouted. The tension in the air decreased somewhat. "We're grasping at straws here. Charlie's right: anyone could have set us up, and maybe there is some super devious reason behind the music, but we just don't *know* right now."

"I'm with Mabel," Leon growled, still keeping a level of intensity in his voice. "Now we need someone to scout the beach around us."

"*On it!*" Mabel screamed. Without so much as hearing a response, former track star Mabel Pryce burst down the coast away from us, leaving a cloud of sand in her wake.

"Sheesh, that girl can run," I observed. "Guess she wants to help in any way she can."

"That or she wants to get away from us," Johanna suggested, her voice back to a dull monotone. "You three. Scout out the forest. We need to know if there is anything in the immediate vicinity we should be aware of."

"Yes, ma'am," Charlie said, motioning for Leon and me to follow him. I wasn't okay with leaving Johanna alone to her own devices, but the last thing I wanted was a new argument to start in the team. Exiting the beach, I realized that my wet sneakers made an unpleasant sound that could easily be heard. Charlie suggested that I take them off and I complied. The dirt of the forest was tougher than the soft sand. Roots and fallen dead plants littered the path we walked, and even with Leon ahead clearing the underbrush, I still had to be very mindful of where I stepped. Small rays of tropical sunshine broke through the canopy above, and the roaring waves of the ocean could be heard in the background. All in all, it was a very peaceful scene. If we had to crash somewhere, I was glad it was somewhere warm.

"There's a freshwater spring over here." Leon pointed toward a pool of greenish water surrounded by tree roots. "I'd suggest bathing, but given that we're in alien territory, I don't want the enemy to catch us with our pants down."

"Ha, literally," Charlie gave a dry laugh, smiling at the man who had accused him of murdering Ozzy. "So, uh, is the water drinkable?"

"How about you find out yourself?" Leon gave a cold glare on top of the same bitter scowl he had maintained since the argument on shore.

"Eh, I think I'll pass for now," Charlie remarked. "Think I've got enough water in my system already. Ha, get it?"

Leon didn't even roll his eyes at Charlie's awful attempt at humor. He just walked away, back in the same direction we had been walking beforehand. "I'm going to see if Johanna's okay. If you two want to venture further, there's a dirt road further up ahead that you can check out."

As I heard him walk away, Charlie and I sat together in silence. "Y'know," I said, "we should check out that dirt road. Might lead us to some civilization. Dunno whether that's good or bad, though."

We stood up and began making our way forward. My comrade looked behind him. After making sure Leon was out of sight he said, "There's something I need to tell you. Something that's been bothering me."

"What?"

"Remember when I said I heard the music playing too?"

"Yeah, on your radio," I recalled.

"That's the thing," Charlie said, fixing his glasses on his head. "I couldn't use the radio once that music started playing. It was like I was blocked out of the station. Someone could have used that noise to cut me out and send whatever signal they wanted . . ."

"They could've given away our coordinates," I contemplated. "Chuck, if what you're saying is true, then that would have been a solid connection between the music and the artillery strike. Why didn't you mention this back on the beach?"

"They'll just think I'm piling on the lies," Charlie sighed, adjusting his glasses. "I've got nothing to prove it, unless you want to swim out there and get the radio from the wreckage. Plus, it doesn't tell us anything about whoever called the strike. Just says that whoever did also hacked my radio and also played that music."

"Well, it's something," I said. "Don't you think it's kinda weird Johanna was the only one who recognized the song?"

"Exactly. Either Johanna's the smuggest hacker on the face of the earth, or someone's trying to set her up."

"Makes sense," I agreed, astounded by Charlie's quick logic. "So that leaves Mabel—who I guess is an option— and . . ." a new, terrifying thought entered my mind. "Leon. It could've been Leon."

Charlie nodded, looking much more melancholy. "I just dunno, man. We played our cards as best we could, and now it's their turn. There's nothing we can do about it."

We arrived at a small, uneven road. Tire tracks lay fresh on the tan loam surface. I felt no fear at the idea that an army was so close. It was the cold professional in me that casually observed the tire tracks, politely noting the fact that they were from the trained soldiers that just shot us out of the sky. Through years of missions and combat, the idea of my death, and that people wanted to kill me, was something I had long grown used to. Something else, however, was eating away at my mind. "Chuck," I asked, "You didn't tell me everything about Johanna's plan, did you?"

Charlie stood in stoic silence, looking down at the road beside me. "No," he said. "That's cuz . . . I really didn't know what was up. She's kept me out of the loop as best she could, only telling me that she was going to find a way to hurt Weiss."

"Why? What does she have against Weiss? I don't get it."

"She never told you, did she?" Charlie let out a sigh and looked up at the treetops. "Figures, I guess. She never liked you, and you've always kept your distance. Her parents died in a pretty ugly accident. A very *suspicious* accident. She figures, cuz y'know, Eastway can only take orphans . . ."

I realized what he was implicating. "That's crazy," I said, crossing my arms. Johanna was always incredibly bitter toward Weiss, but I assumed that was because she was a naturally awful person. To my understanding, that's how all psychopaths are. "If her parents really did die like that, why would Weiss and whoever he works for go out of their way to get her?"

"Johanna's a lot more talented than she lets on," Charlie maintained, sitting beside the road. "Even by our standards. She's a mentally competent psychopath. One of the highest kill records in school history, y'know. Never missed a shot. Anything she tried to do, she could. Skipped three grade levels. Shook hands with the governor. Qualified for the Junior Olympics at age *eleven*. They probably didn't want her; they *lusted* for her. Her parents' deaths seem pretty convenient in the grand scheme of things. Don't get me wrong: she's a total freak, but hanging around her has benefits."

"What do you mean?"

I saw the muscles in Charlie's throat tense, as if he was forcing words out. "I don't exactly edit Mabel's plans alone. Johanna helps me. I-I didn't ask for it, but they get so complicated sometimes, and she says it makes her feel more engaged with the team, since sniping's a lot of sitting around."

"So you're telling me," I said, feeling a spark of anger ignite within, "that Johanna's been doing your work for you this whole time?"

"No, no it wasn't like that!" Charlie insisted, his voice cracking. "Even back when I started, I worked through most of the plans by myself. A bit like Mabel today, I guess, but without someone there to check for my mistakes. But when it came down to the . . . choices, on the Yellows and Reds, I never really had the stomach for it."

"If the plan went wrong, you couldn't decide which one of us to kill, so you had Johanna choose."

Charlie nodded absentmindedly, clearly ashamed of himself. "All the parts where people could die . . . if people *did* die, she made sure everything made sense. If a plan went wrong or I had to order one of you guys to go . . . I just couldn't handle that! Man, if anything, that proves I didn't kill Ozzy. If I did, I couldn't live with myself. I didn't mean to get . . . " his voice trailed off, whispering words I couldn't make out. I looked at Charlie in a different light. I could no longer see the smiling, carefree almost-college-student who never feared death, but a man who had seen death's steely gaze and had looked away.

"Thanks for telling me that, man," I extended my hand and helped Charlie to his feet. "I think now would be a good time to report to the others. Maybe we can start formulating some plans."

"Right, more plans," Charlie nodded, trying his best to put on a smile. Just as we turned to leave, I heard a faint humming coming from farther up the road.

I grabbed Charlie shoulder, stopping him in his tracks. "There's a vehicle coming. Maybe it's soldiers going to the airbase."

My friend gave a sinister grin and said, "Oh, nice. So, you're thinking what I'm thinking?"

CHAPTER SEVEN

I lay in the center of the road, clutching my knee and feigning agony. Had I determined the situation to be more dangerous, I probably would have cut a small wound to help make my distress seem more real. However, I had faith in my acting skills, and knew that I didn't have to engage in such a façade for very long.

A jeep rolled along the road in front of me. I chose not to directly look at it, and instead winced in pain from my apparent injury. Just as I had predicted, I heard the motor to the vehicle sputter and die, signaling that the jeep had stopped. There was the unmistakable clap of boots hitting the dirt trail, telling me that someone had left the vehicle.

Looking upward with half-shut eyes, the sun-soaked silhouette was hard to make out, but his bulky frame told me that he was definitely a soldier. "Eh!" he said, trying to get my attention. "*Estás bien?*"

Spanish. The man was speaking Spanish. Unlike my French, which had always been poor, I was fluent in the language. *"Please . . . help me, sir . . ."* I moaned, switching to Spanish.

"What's wrong?" he asked. Finally deciding to look up, I was dismayed to see that his rifle was pointed right down to me.

What was *wrong with me, anyway?* I hadn't thought of that yet. Here I was, on the ground and in pain, and I couldn't even think of a good excuse why. *"Urghh . . . help . . . me . . . ugh . . ."*

"What hurts? What's your name?"

Oh crap. Yet another question that I couldn't think of an answer to. I know it doesn't take a ridiculous amount of mental stimulation to think of a name, but keep in mind I was trying my darndest to look weak and injured, which took a lot of commitment. In the midst of thinking of a credible name, I spouted, *"Me llamo . . .* Bob."

"Bob?"

"Si, Bob Mc . . . Somebody."

The soldier's horrendously confused face gave way to a blank one. Before I had a chance to justify my awful name, he fell to the ground face-first. Behind him was Charlie, holding a large rock. He looked just as baffled as the soldier, and even a little angry. "Bob McSomebody? That was the best name you could come up with? What's wrong with you?"

"Sorry man, I'm just not in the right state of mind, I guess," I responded, My face relaxed from wincing, and I began to feel the late afternoon sun sting my skin.

"That man was ready to shoot you, I swear," the older student continued, dropping his rock and reaching down to help me up. "You alright?"

"Thanks, I'm okay. Sorry I couldn't pick a name to your liking."

"Trick is to put a joke in it. How about Seymour Butts?"

"I think he would have been just as suspicious if I said that name instead of Bob McSomebody."

"Yeah, but if you said Seymour Butts he might have had a nice laugh before I knocked him unconscious!"

"Speaking of which," I said, turning my attention back to the soldier at our feet. "Is he alright? That rock looked pretty heavy."

"Eh, as long as his skull didn't fracture, I think he'll be fine," Charlie assured, crouching down and inspecting the body. He then grabbed the soldier by the shoulders and lifted him up with a great heave. "Help me out here, man. We have to get him off the road before anyone else comes."

I lifted the unconscious man by the legs and together we dumped him a few feet off the road. "Do you really think that's going to help?" I asked as we walked back. "I mean, we can't get rid of the abandoned military jeep in the middle of the road."

"Yeah, whatever," Charlie said, shrugging. "So I didn't think this whole plan through, sorry. Why don't we just jack the jeep and crash it somewhere? They'll still find it, but it'd be fun!"

Ignoring the older agent's antics, I approached the soldier's jeep—a muddy mess of a vehicle—and motioned for Charlie to follow my lead. "Looks like it was carrying supplies to the base. Let's see if anything's worth taking. You know, weapons and what not."

Charlie stopped in his tracks. "Crap, I forgot. We should get the gun from our unconscious friend, right?"

"Yeah, you do that," I said, allowing him to leave my side. Too interested in the jeep and its contents to follow him, I cautiously popped open the door using a razor from my sleeve. Inside, there were two tan seats behind a messy dashboard covered in trinkets. Behind the seats, I observed, were large metal canisters, similar to propane tanks, except slightly larger and with smoother tops. I counted seven before my eyes rested on something unusual at the very back of the jeep, near the rear door.

A black, roundish object seemed to bob up and down. It took me a second to realize that I was staring at the back of someone's head. "Hello? Who's there?" I called out, trying to position my small razor to look formidable as the figure turned its head.

"Huh?" it said, with a peculiar high pitch. Now seeing his face, I realized that the figure was nothing more than a young kid, years younger than me. His eyes rested on my small blade, and he turned away frightened. With surprising vigor, he pushed open the back of the jeep and darted outside.

"Hey, get back here!" I vainly ordered, hopping out of the vehicle myself and giving chase. What had just happened had not settled in for me yet, and panic began as I bolted forward. Seeing the back of my target in the light of the forest, I immediately noticed that he was wearing a gray sweatshirt—a peculiar wardrobe choice for the tropics to say the least. His ability to run in such heavy clothes continued to baffle me, and he even managed to keep his distance away from me for at least a hundred meters.

Regardless of his endurance, I managed to catch up to him and tackle him to the forest floor. He let out a startled cry, swinging his limbs furiously. Keeping my grip on him felt like trying to hold down a human-sized, freshly caught salmon. Biting at my hands and kicking with painful accuracy, he eventually overwhelmed me and I was forced to let go. Rejuvenated, but still shrieking, the boy ran further into the forest, while I stood still and recuperated from my pain, giving up the chase.

A minute or so later Charlie appeared, carrying the soldier's rifle. It looked very unnatural for him to be carrying such a weapon, the kind you would see on TV being held by fighters from a different corner of the world. "What's wrong?" he asked, flustered.

"There was a kid in the jeep," I said, huffing. "He got away."

"What?" Charlie said, devastated. "How'd he get away?"

"I had him, it's just . . . " As I spoke with Charlie, I realized that I still had my razor drawn. Discreetly slipping it back under my sleeve, I figured out what I had to say. "What was I supposed to do, kill him? It was just a kid."

"If that kid reports anything to the generals we're all screwed," my friend uttered, now sounding more concerned than angry. "Well . . . between that guy and the jeep on the road, I'm pretty sure they're gonna find out we survived one way or another. We'll just have to act quickly to get off this island before they hunt us down."

"Sounds like a plan," I agreed, finally catching my breath. Regardless, a certain pain below the skin lingered, and the boy's frightened look facing my dagger was stained in my mind.

CHAPTER EIGHT

We're baaaack!" Charlie announced, trudging onto the shore, rifle bouncing on his back. A dying sun in an orange sky nearly touched the ocean ahead, which caused shining ripples on the water. I followed closely behind Charlie, carrying two canisters of oil in each of my hands. Despite taking breaks, the thick liquid had taken a toll on my arms, and my muscles had become unbelievably sore.

"Where'd you get that stuff?" Leon asked. He sat by a tree, looking quite docile.

"We ambushed a jeep full of it back on that road you told us about," Charlie explained. "They were carrying high-grade motor fuel, the stuff used in aircraft, typically. My guess is it was going to the airbase."

Johanna walked over to the two of us, arms crossed. She easily looked the most put together compared to the lot of us. Her hair appeared to be neatly combed and her clothes were perfectly dry, with hardly any wrinkles. "Why did you bring it back?"

"Stuff's highly flammable," I responded. "Charlie thought we could use it for something, maybe rig it to a timer and set it to blow."

Mabel studied me with excited, almost bulging eyes. "How many soldiers were there?"

"Just one," Charlie said, practically beaming. "Don't worry about him; we knocked him out cold and dumped him on the side of the road. When he wakes up, maybe he'll wander back home or something. He didn't know who we were, so it's nothing to worry about."

"Smooth," Leon scoffed.

Johanna turned back to me and continued to press for answers. "You ambushed the army on the road, yes? Is their jeep still there?"

"Yeah," I said, "if it's discovered—or more likely, *when* it's discovered, the LLA will know that we survived the plane crash. Hopefully, by then it'll be too late for them though. Charlie thinks it'd be smart if we made our move tonight."

"Interesting," Mabel said, snapping out of her uncomfortable daze. "Sounds pretty bold."

"Totally!" Charlie chimed in, "I say we make a dash for the airfield under the cover of night."

"You intend to escape? What about our mark?" It occurred to me that Johanna had no concern in her voice. She sounded painfully disinterested.

"Well, I wouldn't call it an escape, more of a strategic retreat. We get out of here, get our weapons back, formulate a new strategy, and come back swinging."

Johanna looked down at her nails, saying in a monotone voice, "Cool. The two of you can scope out the airbase and formulate a more specific plan. Leon, go with them for protection."

Leon began to object, "But—"

"*Leon*," Johanna coldly glared. In silent submission, Leon walked next to Charlie, and they set out into the jungle. "Prince," Johanna continued, "go scope out the beach in that direction."

"I was over there already, so I don't think that's necessary," Mabel objected. She soon joined Leon as another victim to Johanna's stare and added, "But it never hurts to double check!"

"That's right," the sniper gestured for those around her to move out. Leon, Charlie, and Mabel disappeared into the thick forest, and I departed our makeshift base for the coast without any objections. Still highly suspicious of Johanna being alone, once I believed I was out of sight I hid behind a dune and observed her.

The girl got up from where she was sitting and began pacing. In the rare moments where I could see her face, I saw her lips moving, as if she was talking to herself. Her movements were quick and abrupt, seemingly deciding to go in one direction before suddenly changing her mind. Every so often her head would shake, and she'd reach out her pointer finger, accusing the air.

Minutes passed before she finally stopped, crouched down and picked something up. When some time passed and there was no more movement, I thought it would be a good time to return back. Arriving, I found Johanna crouched over, prodding the sand with a stick. "You're back early," she noted without looking up

"What are you doing?"

"Alleviating boredom," she informed me. As I continued to approach her, I saw that she was prodding a small crab with her stick. Every time it tried to distance itself from the girl or bury itself, it received a quick prod. It wasn't enough to kill it, only to break or disfigure a part of its body. As Johanna tore off limb after limb, the crustacean became more and more cracked and immobile. When she finally landed the killing blow to its midsection, the crab had one claw and one leg left and was still furiously squirming about. When she noticed I was still observing her, she added, "What are you doing back so soon?"

"Just like before, there was nothing on that side of the beach," I said, eyes still transfixed on the remnants of the mutilated crab. "Of course, I also didn't want you to be lonely, especially when it's getting dark out."

"You don't trust me alone, do you?" Johanna asked. She didn't wait for my answer. "That's fine. If I were you, I wouldn't trust me either. I don't even trust *myself* right now, and I *am* me."

I tried to make sense of the sniper's sentence. "What?"

"Never mind," Johanna said, keeping the same icy tone in her voice. "It's stupid trying to explain myself to you. After all, I'm the big, bad psycho. You're the good guy, the reluctant enforcer of the Academy's will, right? So are you here to ask questions? Pick my diseased brain for info, hm?"

Even without investing any emotion into her voice, it still seemed to bleed with disdain. "I just want us all to be on the same page here. Ozzy deserves that, you know." It had been hours since I had last thought of the kid, something that made me immediately guilty. It was strange to think of him as dead. He was someone with so much aspiration, so much anger that needed to be dealt with. For it all to go away in a burst of fire seemed unnatural, with all his unfinished business disappearing with his body.

"Hm," Johanna pondered, still poking at the sand with her stick, as if fighting another crab. "I can show you the truth, if you want. You're gonna hate it, but I won't lie."

"You still think it's Charlie, don't you?"

The psychopath finally looked up from the ground with her cold eyes displaying an opulent gleam. "Two hundred percent."

"What makes you so sure?" I said, trying my best not to inject any more hostility into the tense conversation.

"Because he was lying to you on the beach. His arms and eyes were dead giveaways. You would have seen it too, if you were looking for it. You're usually pretty good at catching liars."

The words 'Charlie' and 'liar' triggered something in my head, and a dormant thought came back to life. "I know Charlie's lying about something," I said. "But I think it has something to do with you and your supposed 'plan' after this mission."

Half of Johanna's lips curled into a smile. The other half, on the damaged side of her face, remained still. "Oh, *that*. I was wondering if you were still curious. How much do you know?"

"Not enough," I remarked. "But frankly, right now I don't care about what it is or what it's going to do. All I want to know is who's going to get hurt. Charlie wouldn't be a nervous wreck if there was no risk."

Johanna once again looked as though she was pondering, even taking a solid minute to stare out at the ocean before looking back at me. "I've got plans, Prince. They were shot out of the sky along with the plane. My plans, if you really must know, have been put on hold and will probably die with me on this stupid rock in the ocean."

"Charlie and Mabel are gonna think of a way out," I stated. It would be a while before I realized she had changed the topic away from her plan. "We're getting out of here as a team."

"*Team?*" the sniper asked, raising her voice. "What team? This little group of ours is eating itself alive. You saw what happened here on the beach. How do you expect us to break into a military base and live?" In a rare moment of anger, Johanna snapped her stick and threw it to the ground. "Do me a favor and get me another branch. This one's too flimsy."

I remained standing over her. The newly risen moon cast a light down on me, covering the girl in front of me in a black shadow.

"And yet," the sniper sighed, "the mighty David Prince still graces me with his saintly presence."

"I want answers, Johanna."

"I gave you answers," she insisted, moaning. "Charlie's lying. My plans have been put on hold. What more do you want?"

"You're not gonna tell me what you're scheming, I know that," I said. "But I can make a few guesses. If you're conspiring off campus in Quickie's, my guess is you're planning something that will harm the Academy as a whole."

"A fair observation," Johanna admitted, sounding mildly interested. "I'm not the traitor though, if that's what you're trying to conclude."

"What I want to know is why. Why are you trying to hurt the Academy?"

The sniper looked up blankly. She ran her finger along the disfigured part of her face, the part that never looked quite right. "Surgeries can't fix all wounds, Prince. What Eastway did to me . . . I want to make them suffer. Even if it's a fraction of what I've endured, it'd be worth it."

"They gave you that?" I asked, pointing to the artificial skin on her face.

"The Academy wanted me as an agent," Johanna elaborated. "Unfortunately, I had a happy family, and they couldn't have that. So they made an *accident* happen."

"So now you're out for their blood?" I pressed. I knew I was prodding an open sore, but I needed some kind of peace of mind knowing that with all the new questions being presented, I had at least gotten some explanations. "That isn't the way you should face your problems. Even if they did what you're saying they did, revenge will only put you and the ones around you in dire danger."

"Thus, Saint David Prince begins his next gospel reading," Johanna proclaimed sarcastically.

"It's pretty easy to look like a saint next to someone like you," I countered viciously, frustrated. "Have you ever cared about anyone besides yourself and your little vengeance scheme?"

Johanna gave another half smile. "So high and morally righteous, aren't we? Deep down, we aren't that different from each other, you know. Ever wonder why it's so easy to lie through your teeth? To watch men die at your feet, and step over their corpse and try your best not to get blood on your shoes? Deep down, you wouldn't care if one hundred people died, as long as you didn't have to be the one to pull the trigger. I shoot our enemies down so you can keep your clean conscious and do your job. So no matter how high the body count is, you can be here, lecturing me about what's right and wrong because you're the good guy."

"Shut up," I yelled, beginning to feel fury build up in the back of my throat. "This isn't about being good or bad. I just want to get the facts down. It's the right thing to do, and you know that."

"What a load of crock," Johanna hissed. Regardless of her severe tone, her smirk was growing. "You're surviving for Ozzy's sake? Wanting to know everything is just the right solution? No, you want to know every minute detail because you're scared of what you don't know. Inside you, Davy, you're just a confused, scared kid who couldn't face the *real truth* even if it was to save your life."

"*Real truth?*" I asked. "Now what are you talking about? I think I've hung around the Academy long enough to be able to handle all the bad things."

"No, you can't," Johanna responded flatly. "You can't handle the *worst* things. Never could."

I stared her down, egging her on to continue.

"Fine. Tell me what happened two years ago, July 23."

"Huh?" I immediately knew what day she was talking about. My heart sank.

"That's right," Johanna said, half-smirking. "The day you lost them. The day you lost *everything*. Do you remember what you did that day?"

I wanted to speak but knew I couldn't. Instead, I walked away, too sick of Johanna to continue the vile argument. I didn't look back at the sniper, but I knew she was triumphantly grinning.

CHAPTER NINE

Charlie wanted a multipronged assault. He explained it over our only map of the airport compound, which came courtesy of Johanna's briefcase, an item which I had a begrudging respect for. We were to meet at a specific plane south of the landing strip. Charlie and Leon both thought it looked to be in pristine condition, and the soldiers milling around it seemed to confirm their suspicions. Leon, arguably the most skilled fighter of the group, was to escort Mabel and Charlie to the aircraft, coming in from the eastern side, which was protected by a high chain fence. The fence would set off an alarm when crossed, so a bomb would be planted outside of the base to alert the soldiers prematurely, and hopefully draw them away from the airfield. "Even with the distraction we have planned, we three might run into a couple of patrols," Charlie explained. "That's where Leon comes in. You . . . do what you gotta do."

Next came my role. I was to take the more dangerous route, coming in from the western side of the compound, around the main terminal. I was more or less the insurance of the group. If the other three got captured, I still could manage to escape with Johanna. "If you come across a patrol, promise me you'll hide," the sniper said. "If you get spotted I'd prefer not to clean up for you.

I nodded in agreement, recalling how a soldier had held me at gunpoint that afternoon. In close range combat, I could handle myself if I maintained the element of surprise. However, even with my training and weapon proficiency, I could still easily be overwhelmed if I was by myself, just like anyone else in the Academy.

"Jojo, you're gonna plant our little surprise. After that's taken care of and the timer's set up, take a position on this knoll, here," Charlie pointed toward the map. "If things go awry, especially for Leon, Mabel, and me, I don't want you to hesitate in taking down the enemy. Once we meet up with Davy at the aircraft, you can give up your position and meet us down there. I trust you can make the trip on your own." Johanna agreed with our plan, but I was uncertain that her being the one to handle the explosive was a good idea. "Alright, guys, given the way the stars are out I'd say it's a little past ten. That gives us an hour or two to get into position and strike at midnight!" Charlie said, practically cheering, pumping his fist into the air. "We can do it! Let's go shoot some suckers and get outta here! Whoo!" My friend's energy astounded and befuddled me. I had never seen his eyes so wide, so full of life. His words came out in rapid-fire precision, with the same intensity Johanna's had when she was in an argument. This came from the lax, sleepy boy on campus that practically needed to be ripped away from his bed in the morning.

"Keep it down, Parker," Johanna ordered. "With your mouth you'll probably alert the army before we even get close to the air base." She turned her attention to the lot of us, stating in a monotone voice, "Everyone be on your guard tonight. Remember your training if you want to get out alive."

"There we go!" the bespectacled boy cheered. "These guys may have guns, they may have explosives, and they may have two hundred times the manpower, but we have something better than that. We're fighting for our lives, and if we work together and watch each other's backs, there's nothing we can't do!"

"Whoopee," Leon sarcastically grumbled, "let's go destroy an army using the power of teamwork."

The Academy dispersed into the woods, excluding Johanna, who opted to stay behind and put the finishing touches on our bomb-distraction. Stepping into the forest, I looked one last time at the psychopath hunched over her bomb. I think she knew I was looking, as I saw a spontaneous, sinister smirk sprout on her lips, reminding me of the one that grew during our conversation earlier that evening. As I walked through the darkened jungle, my mock shoes—strips of leather tied to the soles of my feet—made an unpleasant squishing sound, which bothered me, considering our mission centered on stealth. Leon was directly in front of me, and I walked carefully behind him, trusting him to get me to the main road, which led to the air base. I was curious to see if the jeep and body I had dispatched remained on the road. Lo and behold, once we arrived on the dirt path, there was neither car nor corpse in sight. My body shivered at the emptiness, as I realized that the LLA must know by now we were on the island. Perhaps they had even dispatched troops to search for us, and there were soldiers wandering through the black forest, just like we were.

We continued walking down the path until Leon signaled to halt and then pointed in front of him. About a hundred yards forward the jungle stopped, and there was an open clearing and a long chain fence, just close enough that I could see it clearly. The entire compound was dark. No spotlights beaming from towers or illumination from the buildings. It was an encouraging sign, as darkness naturally made stealth much easier. *I guess General Santana can't pay his electric bills,* I thought. I heard footsteps approaching from behind me. It was Charlie, accompanied by Mabel. Back in the forest, they must have followed behind me in the same fashion as I did with Leon. I noticed Charlie was holding something in his hand. "Everyone take one of these," he whispered. Although quiet, I could tell that his voice was still brimming with energy. "They're transceivers from Johanna. Just like any other mission, right? We need to stay in touch."

I took one of the convenient devices and stuck it in my ear. The oh-so familiar static crackle of the machine adjusting its transmission was a welcome sound, making me think of missions past. They always seemed to work out in the end, and I had growing confidence that this one would too. I parted from the group, moving back into the jungle to my left. The map of the compound materialized in my mind, and I tried my best to picture where I was and where it was I had to go to enter the air base. Banter soon arose over my transceiver, which didn't help my state of mind. *"Guys,"* Mabel asked, *"did we forget to give ourselves code names? What if we're hacked?"*

"No worries," Charlie responded. *"I think I've got code names covered. You hear that, Purple Rain?"*

"Charlie," I said, trying hardest to keep my voice down as a new impulse of rage flowed through me, "that is not my code name, especially on a mission like this."

Mabel gasped at the mention of Charlie's name. *"Dude! You just compromised the whole mission! Do you want Charlie to be discovered and hunted down?"*

"Keep it down, Mabel, please," I remarked. The more I spoke, the more nervous glances I gave to the metal fence

beside me. "Code names are just a formality. These soldiers have decades-old equipment with them, so I doubt
they'll be able to hack our conversation. Besides, how many
people in the world have the name 'Charlie?' It's not exactly
uncommon."

"*I've gotta side with the lady on this one,*" Charlie chimed
in. "*There may be a lot of guys with a name like 'Charlie,' but
only one has as sexy of a voice as mine.*"

Mabel girlishly giggled at the previous comment, further infuriating my inner professional and increasing the
temptation to switch off my transceiver. As I made my way
to my entry point, I couldn't help but become unnerved by
the stillness of the air base. Even with the lights out, I had
expected to see at least some soldiers in the moonlight, on
patrol or resting. *Where were they? On patrol? Were they all
around me?* I thought. It wasn't encouraging when the only
thing you knew about an enemy is that they managed to
shoot down your top secret stealth plane. Taking every caution possible, I finally arrived at my destination: the western
side of the chain-link fence. The main terminal now stood
directly in front of me, and I'm ashamed to say that my
fear of the unknown then truly culminated within. Staring
down a seemingly empty military base, with one of my
teammates dead and the rest of us in seemingly permanent
mortal danger, I couldn't help but take a step back and hear
my heart call out to not press forward. *Am I walking into a
trap?* My voice didn't listen to my instincts, and it whispered
into my transceiver, "I'm . . . I'm in position. I'm ready when
you guys are."

"*Roger that,*" Charlie said. "*Um, is the bomb in position?*"

"*Yes, and so am I,*" Johanna announced. "*Flip the switch
whenever you're ready.*"

"*Alright, Davy, Find a place to hide,*" Charlie ordered.
"*They're gonna go right past your gate, down the western road.*"

"Alright," I said. Instinctively, I leapt up onto the nearest tree I could find and climbed, balancing myself at the base of one of the higher branches. I may not have aced the maritime program at Eastway, but when it came to our course on forestry, I was at the top of the class. The army complex was much larger than I thought it would look. Even from high up, I couldn't see the other side of the forest. "I'm ready . . . I think."

"*You think?*" Leon scoffed. "*Prince, are you okay?*"

"*You just gave out Davy's last name!*"

"*Mabel, shut up,*" Johanna hissed, her poisonous words dripping from a toxic tongue.

"Guys, I'm fine," I assured. Gazing at the structure, I remember the impact of the plane as we went down and the aura of despair that hung over our team. This wasn't like any other mission. My pulse was racing too fast, and a hard worry burned in the pit of my stomach. Ozzy was dead. We all almost joined him. We could still join him. There was an army before me waiting to see it happen. "Maybe . . . just a little too anxious."

"*You can have your freaking anxiety attack when we're done with the mission,*" Johanna scolded, her voice reeking with authority and entitlement. "*I'm sick of the tropics. Charlie, blow the bomb, now.*"

"*Yessir,*" Charlie responded, dutifully. "*Alright guys, let's see if we can make General Julio go down by the schoolyard.*"

"How long have you been waiting to use that?" I said, groaning.

"*All night,*" Charlie chuckled.

"*Was that a joke? I don't get it,*" Mabel chimed in.

"*It's alright, Mabes,*" Charlie assured. "*Y'know, I'm in a kinda Paul Simon mood. When we get back, remind me to make a playlist with—*"

"*Blow the bomb!*" Johanna barked.

"*Sheesh,*" Charlie said, grumbling a couple words I couldn't pick up on. Then a loud noise erupted behind me, similar to the crack of a gunshot. The explosion was a brief flash of light followed by black smoke rising up through the jungle, visible in the bright moonlight. Then a small orange light began to glow in the area. It was small at first, but it grew rapidly, and soon orange flames were licking the treetops. An alarm blared from somewhere inside the air base, and voices could be heard. I couldn't help but breathe a sigh of relief as I saw soldiers mill out of the terminal and surrounding buildings. Some were only partially dressed, no doubt awoken from a lazy and unjustified slumber.

As the large crowd—I counted at least two hundred—talked in cautious voices amongst themselves, I heard one lone voice scream out, and I saw a man pointing in my direction. Briefly panicking, I realized that he was pointing to the fire brewing *behind* me. The voices of soldiers soon became frenzied and they rushed out of the compound passing the tree I clung to. The men were a variety of ages, some slightly older than I was, but most seemed middle-aged. My guess was that the last time this army got a steady recruitment of soldiers was at least twenty years ago when these men were young. Most didn't look to be anywhere near top form, and some could even be called plump. Seeing their faces cautiously stepping into the dark forest to confront a simple fire made me relapse back into a degree of confidence. I kept my cool as the soldiers passed, trying my best to count them.

Then I heard the buzz of a motor starting up, and I saw a jeep zoom past down the road, with soldiers in all the seats as well as hanging off the doors. In the driver's seat, I spotted a man I instantly recognized as the general himself, Julio Santana. He was better dressed than the other soldiers—his jacket even had black shoulder pads—but nevertheless he looked as disheveled as the soldiers under him. I couldn't help but disrespect a general that seemed to drive his own soldiers around, like a soccer mom taking her kids to practice. With the general driving and the amount of people in the jeep reaching clown-car proportions, I couldn't help but find my previous fear of the LLA to be downright silly.

Just as Santana's jeep passed, another vehicle zoomed down the road. This one moved much faster, with only a single man behind the wheel. The driver zoomed past his fellow soldiers, and I saw a couple nearly get hit, but the car wouldn't slow down until it was bumper to bumper with the general's. I realized that the man alone in the jeep was Demiese. I kept quiet and coolly watched him pass.

As he did, the most peculiar thing occurred. For a brief second, at the last possible moment he could do so, Demiese turned his head. I gazed down and saw the general's serious brown eyes look up and *seemingly meet mine*. It was just a simple glance, but it was unmistakably centered on the treetops, where I sat. His eyes narrowed into what I interpreted as a wince, then went straight back to the road, dutifully following behind Santana's automobile. I watched the party disappear into the forest. I knew this was the time to press forward with the mission, but I couldn't resist watching the back of Demiese's head as he drove off, trying to look for it turning back to have a double take at a white teenage boy crouching on a jungle branch. Of course, he didn't look back, and I quickly assumed that he had not seen me. Shaken by his passing glance, I immediately tried to reassure myself. *He couldn't see me. With the way the moon's coming down in front of my tree, I'm in the shadows.*

"*Prince!*" Leon's voice beckoned. "*Status report?*"

I jumped down from my tree, landing on the soft dirt road in a tan cloud of dust. "Y'know," I whispered, "the soldiers were marching under me a couple seconds ago. They probably could have heard you scream like that."

"*Please just give me your status, man,*" Leon pressed, clearly not in the mood.

"It looks like Julio went down by the schoolyard," I informed. "He, Demiese, and some soldiers went out to see your little blast. Turning into quite a pretty fire." As I spoke, I briskly walked into the open gates of the air base, trying to look as natural as possible. I saw some armed soldiers in the corner of my eye, climbing up into one of the terminal towers. Spotlights were going to be lit. I needed to find some cover.

"*Yeah, we can see the smoke from here. How many soldiers?*" Mabel inquired, trying to sound as official as Johanna.

Checking through my count one last time, I said, "Two hundred and thirty-three. Thirty-one if you don't count the generals."

"*So we've still got thirteen hundred soldiers in here?*" Johanna said, sounding more depressed than bothered.

"*At the most,*" Charlie assured. "*Our statistics for the plan were kinda spotty. Maybe the forces aren't as consolidated, or they've had some desertions. Um, by the way, Leon, Mabel, and I are in. The alarm's been activated, and it's only a matter of time before they realize it wasn't triggered by that explosion. Johanna, get ready.*"

"*I see you three,*" the sniper responded. The spotlight switched on. Two shining beams danced across the concrete landing strip, over the decaying planes. "*Prince, why are you just standing there?*"

"Right, right, sorry," I muttered. I dashed toward the central terminal. Making my way around such a large building was long and arduous, but it was painfully necessary for the sake of the mission. As I ran around, I passed old garages and a couple hangars. The doors to some of them were only half-shut, revealing a black, empty void beyond. More soldiers must have dwelled beyond that void, soldiers that could, perhaps, see me. I tried not to think about such exposure too hard.

As I rounded the corner, I found myself confronted with a black silhouette. At first, I wanted to believe he was just going back to his quarters and sleeping for the night. His eyes were bloodshot, but the way he clutched his gun told me that he was a man on current duty. *"Hey, you!"* he said, in a foreign language I couldn't immediately identify.

My body worked faster than my mind deciphering the language, and I spouted out, "Who, me?" in plain English. I regretted those words immediately. *What's wrong with me today?*

"Eh, you American?" he asked in a thick accent that sounded vaguely Creole. "Why you here?"

Since I couldn't speak such a language for the life of me, I quickly responded, "Yeah . . . I'm with my family at a resort on the other side of the island." Speaking slowly, I tried to distract him from the fact that I was reaching for the gun on my back, an item which I believed he hadn't noticed yet.

"You . . . you no good," the soldier said, shaking his head. "You—" His voice seemed to cut out strangely. He just stood there with a blank expression on his face.

"I . . . ?"

The soldier fell to the ground. I now saw that he had a wound in his neck: a gunshot by a skilled sniper. "Thanks," I said, sighing. A wave of displeasure passed through me upon the realization that Johanna had saved me yet again. However guilty, another human life had been taken for the sake of my own.

Johanna didn't respond to me immediately. Instead, she announced, *"I'm going down the hill to meet with the lot of you by the plane. Unless you want to stay in this tropical paradise, I advise everyone to get over. Stay clear of the towers, if you can."*

I sprinted the remainder of the terminal, now with much less regard for how much noise I made. I could now see figures standing around one certain aircraft. It was smaller and certainly cleaner than the rusty, disjointed planes parked around it, and it seemed eerily similar to our old plane. Charlie was the first to see me approach and waved me over. "It's called the *MacVeagh*. I think it must've been used for tourism before it was captured."

Behind Charlie, Johanna stood with her briefcase held protectively in her arms. "Where's Mabel and Leon?"

"Inside the cabin," Charlie tapped on one of the *MacVeagh*'s glass windows. Leon's face became visible. He looked down at me and gave a quick nod. "If you guys are ready, I believe it's time to test my skills once more."

Johanna nodded and opened the door, stepping on to the plane. I briskly followed suit, but turned back around to ask, "What do you mean by 'skills?'"

Charlie grinned heartily. "My flight skills. Getting shot out of the sky can damage a guy's ego, y'know."

I couldn't help but smile at the comment. It may have been in poor taste after what happened to Ozzy, but hearing Charlie's wisecrack felt like a return to normal, a sign that this mission was almost over.

The interior of the plane was much less posh than that of our former plane, but given Eastway's saturated taste for luxury, the *MacVeagh* could certainly be seen as quite comfortable on its own. Besides black mold on the ceiling and the corners of the cabin, the white carpet and walls looked brand-new, and the seats were plush, first-class airline quality. There were only four, as if some god of fate knew that that would be just enough for our diminished party. I cautiously sat adjacent to Johanna on the left, keeping as close an eye as I could on her. Charlie stepped into the cockpit—not shutting the metal door behind him. This may have been out of pure laziness or out of fear that he might have to quickly escape from the cockpit once more, but I liked to interpret it as a gesture of transparency, as in proof that he wouldn't do anything his team behind him wouldn't approve of. "Alright passengers," Charlie said, strapping on headphones, "Our super-secret operation thing was a success. Get ready for takeoff ladies and gents, for I believe we've got smooth sailing ahead."

Like a systematic machine, Charlie flipped switches all around him. Outside, I saw the wings of the plane adjust, making a squeaking sound that was loud enough for me to worry that it might have been heard. Then, just as what I believed to be an engine hummed on, a piercing voice exploded through the cabin.

"Keep on dancing in the shades of your crimson, keep on dancing and dancing and dancing . . ."

It was the same music as before, the one that played when we were originally struck. This time, however, it was blasting at a ridiculously high volume, making the cabin walls shake. "Agh! Alternative music! Make it stop! Make it stop!" Mabel screamed, cupping her ears. I couldn't tell whether she was disapproving of the music's volume or the genre choice.

"Ugh, it's not that bad!" Johanna called back. Although her voice was calm and assertive, I could by the look on her face that she was just as distraught and confused as the rest of us. "Chuck, what the hell?"

"I don't know!" Charlie screeched, his voice in full-blown panic, slamming his arm on the dashboard. "It's on the radio! I can't turn it off!"

I peeked outside my window. I saw soldiers—at least twenty, maybe more—were running toward us, and even more silhouettes could be spotted approaching the entrance gate. The men sent to put out the fire, including the two generals, must have returned. Before I could see anymore, white light consumed my window, briefly blinding me. A spotlight was now pointed down at our plane. "I think they can hear the song out there too," I announced. "They're coming toward us."

"Start flying!" Johanna shrieked.

Charlie fluidly moved his hands around the cockpit. With every pushed lever and turn of the wheel, it seemed just as stressful and exhaustive as if he were outside pushing the jet with his bare hands. The aircraft rocked forward, pushing us out of the spotlight. I could now see a mob assembling. The army had guns pointed at us. *They were shooting at us.* With a vicious turn of the wheel, Charlie positioned the *MacVeagh* as best he could on the runway. All the while, the ghastly, explosive music continued to blare in our cabin.

"Dance away and maybe I'll walk with you, walk with you, walk with you . . ."

The engines made their own sound, firing up. The plane once again lurched forward, this time with a quickening pace. Just as I was ready to lean back in my seat, a bright flash of light passed my window. Then, another sped past on the right side. "They're firing rockets at us!" Mabel shrieked, furiously clutching on to her seatbelt. *"See!* I told you they had rocket launchers! They've got—"

Another shining ball whizzed past my window, this time erupting into a bright light. The plane's wing had been struck. The entirety of the *MacVeagh* jerked to the right, violently shaking. Inside the cabin, the lights flickered. My body flew forward, only to be painfully restrained by my seatbelt. Despite the damage, the engines must have still been intact, as the plane pushed forward, smashing violently into the ground nose first. The entire cockpit, along with Charlie, seemed to break away from the plane and disappear, as concrete took its place. As we pressed forward, I realized that it was the second time in a single day that I was in a plane crash. Instead of ocean water, we had the cold runway to greet us.

The *MacVeagh* continued to jerk and falter, but it no longer moved much distance. The cabin had almost been flipped on its side, but it thankfully managed to right itself. It was then, as the engines died and the lights flickered to black, that the music finally stopped. *"You can't dance with me, dance with me, dance with me—"*

"Wha-what?" Mabel said. Her voice sounded as though she were choking. Through the blackness of the darkened cabin, I could make out a small trickle of blood coming from her mouth.

"We've been compromised," Johanna muttered, sounding way too calm to be coming from someone who had survived two plane crashes in a row. I could see her clutching her shoulder as well as undoing her safety belt. "That music . . . it made them discover us. We must retreat back into the forest and recollect ourselves."

Following her example, I tried my best to get my shaking hands to undo my safety belt. However, I objected, "What about Charlie? We have to find him." The space where the cockpit had been was now a gaping hole in front of us, letting in the night air and revealing the remainder of the runway we had yet to cross.

"If he's alive, he knows what to do," Johanna insisted, eerily decisive. "Now we must cut our losses and regroup."

If he's alive? Cut our losses? My mind couldn't process Johanna's words. I angrily tore open my safety belt and stepped onto the jet's ruined floor, wary of my mock shoes. "I'm going to find him. If you guys want to run away, that's fine. He can't be that far away, and I'm not leaving a man behind."

"I'll come too!" Mabel cried, with a surprising amount of strength in her voice.

"No," Leon uttered, in a deep monotone. "You stay with me. Davy knows what he's doing, but you could get hurt."

Mabel's jaw tensed, and I saw that frustration clearly burned within her. She didn't say anything, though, and with a calming, but still very much shell-shocked aura hanging over the remainder of the group, I set out to find Charlie.

CHAPTER TEN

The cockpit was no more than ten yards away from the rest of the wreckage. It was tattered and black, with streaks of long white scratches from where it pressed against the runway. I hurriedly made my way to the other side. Pieces of debris were scattered around, ranging from large half-broken panels to small plastic triggers I had seen Charlie flick no more than a couple minutes before. I found Charlie still strapped into his seat. Red gashes decorated his face and his own seat belt dug into his skin, which I realized was due to his body leaning forward. One of the lenses of his glasses was gone and the other was shattered. The spectacles' frame was certainly also broken, almost hanging off his face. "Chuck! Charlie!" I called out, grabbing his shoulder. *This isn't possible*, I thought.

Charlie's chest heaved and he breathed in a great gasp of air. "Davy . . . is that . . . ?" he said. Before he could continue, he got into a coughing fit. Crimson blood ran down his chin.

"Charlie!" I said, practically squealing. I felt a faint rush of hope enter my heart. "We've gotta get you outta here. There's a freaking army after us." I nervously looked over my shoulder, down the runway. I saw no figures yet, but I heard small, distinctive sounds that might have been voices.

"Heh, we've faced worse, right?" Charlie strained to smile. Some of his teeth were missing, and the rest were stained blood red. I moved my hands to undo his seat belt but he swatted my hands away. "No, no, just listen to me." His voice sounded coherent, but I could tell he was struggling. His eyes hung open lazily, the same way they did before he was about to go to sleep.

"I'm getting you out of here," I insisted. "You can make it—"

"Look," Charlie said, almost aggravated. He gestured toward his lower body. Both limbs seemed unnaturally twisted under the dashboard, bent in different directions. From his torn pants I could see a drops of blood falling down into a larger pool growing under his seat.

It was then I knew. The same feeling of terror conceived in the afternoon's plane crash, the one that had haunted me the entire evening, had returned and struck me down. I could no longer feel. I couldn't speak. I could only observe my friend's distraught, fearful face as he continued talking to me.

"The plane, earlier today," Charlie said, now practically choking on his own words. His glasses slipped further down the bridge of his nose, and I could clearly see his bloodshot eyes. "I gave away the coordinates. I had to . . . it was part of the plan. It was always part of the real plan. I'm sorry. I almost killed all of us and now I did it again . . ."

"You killed Ozzy," I said, mustering the courage—or, perhaps, the rage—to speak. "He was only a kid and you killed him!"

"No," Charlie shook his head. With the gesture, his shattered glasses fell to the cockpit floor. "No . . . when I gave away the coordinates, I knew the plane would be shot down . . . but it didn't happen. The more I think about it . . . it didn't."

"What are you talking about?"

With every word he spoke, Charlie's voice grew softer. He sounded exhausted and raspy. "There was no artillery. Nothing showed up on my radar. At first I doubted it but . . ." Charlie took a second to swallow something, perhaps blood. "But there was nothing. No one was shooting at us. It's all clear now. Something must have detonated under Ozzy's seat."

"A bomb?" I gasped. I clutched onto Charlie shoulder, feeling as weak as he probably did. "Who would put a bomb there?"

"I . . . dunno," Charlie looked away from me. His eyes lazily stared at the cockpit window. "I was told to follow a plan, but that plan didn't work out the way I thought it would. This . . . this is all a setup. The music, the planes, the targets . . ."

"Why did you send the coordinates?"

Charlie's eyes flickered back to me, but only for a brief second. "I had to . . ." he muttered. "It was the only way to . . . stop . . ." My dying friend's breathing increased rapidly.

"What? What?" I asked, panicking. I could feel my eyes begin to cloud with tears. I felt like crying, not just for Ozzy, but for what had happened to us. *This is so wrong . . .*

"Listen!" Charlie jammed his teeth together, hissing out the word. "Johanna . . . watch . . ." The boy's jaw loosened and his head hung forward. There was no more labored breathing, no more garbled words. Silence reigned once more inside the broken cockpit.

Charlie was dead.

It was impossible, something that seemed like nothing more than a terrible idea that you hazardously thought about in the middle of the night, something that you tried with all of your might to dispel as quickly as it had arrived in your subconscious. On missions, Charlie was just a voice. Someone who always seemed far away from the action, safe in a locked room with Mabel. He was the one that helped me get confident during missions. The one who always had a plan, no matter what occurred.

That day, Charlie had a plan, and it had failed, and it had cost him his life. Charlie, the one who actually liked smiling on campus. The one person in the Academy I always felt comfortable around, the one person always free to talk. The one of us who had friends in town. I didn't know how long I held onto his limp shoulder. At one point, I didn't care if they found me by his corpse, crouching in a pool of his blood, and shot me on the spot. I almost wanted to die. I didn't know what was left for me to do.

"Prince," a voice called out. I turned around and saw that Johanna stood before me, her arms crossed. "You found the cockpit. How's Charlie?"

"He's gone," I choked out. "Why are you here? Weren't you running into the forest?"

"I will, but developments have been made, and I thought it would only be fair if you were filled in," the sniper spoke, observing that blood now surrounded her shoes. "Judging by the red, he bled out. Did you manage to catch him alive?"

Charlie's dying words echoed in my head: *Johanna. Watch. Watch Johanna?* I couldn't figure out what it meant, but it certainly made me feel a lot less comfortable standing by the older student. "Yeah, he said he was the one who gave away our coordinates," I told her. I withheld the information about the bomb under Ozzy's seat. I figured such a revelation could somehow be used to my advantage later. "It didn't sound like he was responsible for that loud music, though. Didn't know who did it. Told me in his dying breath."

"Did he have any clue who did?" Johanna cocked her head, seemingly curious. It was then that it occurred to me that she had her sniper rifle in her hands.

"No, he couldn't get too many words out in time," I said. Although it was partially true, I couldn't help but feel I was outright lying to her, and I prayed that my face wouldn't give off such a vibe.

"Pity. Well, it looks like this mission officially has a body count," the girl sighed, giving the boy she had worked four years with a simple, unsympathetic gaze. Then she looked behind over her shoulder and said, "The LLA is coming down the runway. It looks like they're not bringing any vehicles down, so we have a minute or two before they can clearly see us. I need to shoot you in the foot."

"What!" I exclaimed, much too loudly for my own good.

"Shhh!" Johanna brought a finger to her lips. "This is Mabel's idea, not mine. We need to have someone captured, someone who can keep up an act and stay on the inside until the moment's right. Say we took you hostage. They won't believe you unless you have a wound."

"So you want to shoot me in my foot?" I said, enraged at the idea of further pain. "From your sniper rifle? Seriously?"

"Come on, it's just a lousy bullet," Johanna coaxed, now partially mocking me. She swiped the transceiver from my ear, crushing it in her deceptively petite hands. "You've taken worse."

"Why not get Leon to do it? Or better yet, Mabel? It's her freaking plan, apparently!"

"Shhh! Neither of them can withstand the physical and mental abuse you will no doubt face once in captivity," Johanna explained. "This isn't up for discussion. Stick out your foot out and raise it off the ground. I promise the bullet will go cleanly through."

At this point, after two plane crashes, my best friend's death, and now probably the most suspicious person I know promising me that I'll be captured, my mind couldn't handle the idea of getting shot, anywhere. Now only partially thinking, I stuck out my foot, tearing the strip of leather off of my sole. I then said, "Is there any other—"

Johanna pulled the trigger on her rifle, and a small flash of white came out of the muzzle. My foot jerked backward, and physical agony was added to the list of ingredients in my emotional cocktail, along with terror, fear, angst, and distrust. I gasped in pain, but didn't scream. Biting down on my lip, I collapsed to the ground, clutching my wounded foot. "Well, that settles that," Johanna said, sighing.

In as hushed a voice as I could muster, I exclaimed every swear I knew. Some were directed at Johanna and some were addressed to the concrete below as I cringed in pain. Despite my insults, Johanna seemed unfazed, keeping the typical steely look in her eye. "It was Mabel's plan," she repeated, calmly stepping away from me. "You can yell at her after this mess is over with. Put on a good act for the Nationalists. Remember, all of our lives are at stake. Have fun!"

Through winced eyes, I watched her step off the runway and disappear into the jungle forest. The idea of turning myself in and confessing everything seemed strangely plausible, if only to mean that Johanna would die. I never believed that a teammate should be left alone with the enemy, bleeding. Even if it was part of Mabel's new stupid plan, Johanna should have known better than to follow through with it, especially when it was so quickly conceived.

Voices grew louder in the distance. The army approached and surrounded me, keeping an arm's distance away from me, looking at me with bulging, terrified eyes. Some made their way in the direction of the plane, others walked over to the cockpit. I hoped that they would drag me away before they had to take Charlie's body out. While the soldiers watched me, I did my best to seem as innocent as possible. I still held my wounded foot in my hands, but now instead of curses I sobbed quietly. Some of the men threw questions at me, like who I was or what I was doing here. None of them pressed me too hard, and it was clear that they were waiting for someone.

Eventually, General Demiese broke through the ranks and approached me. His green military uniform was tainted gray from soot, no doubt a product of fighting a fire. Once his feet nearly touched where I sat, he stopped. I held my breath, waiting for him to speak. I looked up and saw him staring down at me, his eyes piercing like the bullets from Johanna's rifle. I knew I had to get the first word out, then. "*Monsieur*," I gasped, choosing French as my false language. '*Demiese' sounded French, right?* "Monsieur, s'il vous plaît—"

Before I could say anything else in my wonderful foreign accent, Demise kicked me in the head. The horrible, colorful emotions that had been coursing so passionately through my veins died away and were replaced by the blank slate of an unconscious black.

CHAPTER ELEVEN

I woke up in a gray, airless cell that had walls that gave off the impression that they were closing in on me. There was a bucket in one corner and an old mattress in the other. The mattress had sharp springs poking out of it, leading to an unpleasant surprise if one chose to lie down. With that in mind, I chose to stay on the tile floor, resting my back and sore head against the wall. Outside of my bars, I saw a soldier I did not recognize lounging in a chair, no doubt the one who was assigned to watch over me. Closer to my bars, I found a small figure sitting cross-legged, watching me. Carefully studying him and his clothes, I realized he was the same kid who managed to escape my jeep ambush. He even wore the same sweater, with a logo for an old sports team I didn't recognize. The presence of such an individual set me off enough to yell, "Hey, you!" Regrettably, I spoke in English.

The kid, realizing that I was awake, perked his head up, terrified. "I didn't tell nobody!" he exclaimed, leaping to his feet and darting away from my cell. The soldier must have heard our words, and he began to stir from his slumber, groggily waking up. He looked down at me in my cell like I was some sort of fascinating zoo animal. I raised my eyebrows and gave a small wave—a gesture that wouldn't support the young, scared boy persona I was trying to adopt, but at that point I really couldn't find the strength or energy to care. The soldier gave a surprised look and ran away, just like the boy.

Now alone, I was beginning to feel insulted. It's one thing to shoot down my plane, assault me, and imprison me, but when you ignore me afterward, that's a whole different ballpark. In the moment of solitude, I inspected what damage had been done to me the previous night. My back felt incredibly sore and burned, making me suspect that I had been dragged at some point that night. I felt my forehead, making sure my skull hadn't cracked under the weight of Demiese's boot. The intense physical pain that had manifested in the area began to subside, but my headache continued to rage. Besides my heels, which were bleeding from possible dragging, my feet were surprisingly well cared for, with new white gauze wrapped around my gunshot wound. The fact that it didn't hurt made me think that I was under some sort of drug, which I didn't mind. I ran my fingers through my hair, trying to pull out any dried blood. Once satisfied, I combed it over to the side, making myself that much more presentable. Mabel had suggested before that I borrow one of her hairpins in case a lock needed to be picked, and in that moment I seriously regretted not taking her up on her offer. I then thought, however, that even if I managed to open my cell door, I was still in very unfamiliar territory, with strangers with guns around every corner. Plus that would go directly against Mabel's supposed plan, which had cost me one of my good feet.

The soldier returned sometime later, now accompanied by two other men. By a light outside my cell, I recognized one as General Santana. Seeing him up close, he looked much older than his picture, with thin white hair and unfortunate crevices in his face. He had large brown eyes that reminded me of a certain nice elderly person I would occasionally see back home in Twin Lakes. Like the lone soldier and the boy before, they seemed to just stare at me, transfixed. I decided to break the ice by smiling and waving my hand. It may not be the most appropriate thing to do when one was in a prison cell, but I had to think like a scared little child, looking up at a figure of authority who wasn't the guy who kicked me in the head.

One of the men whispered in Santana's ear. The general nodded slowly, with an indifferent look on his face. This interaction bothered me, if only for the sole reason that I couldn't hear what they were saying. Such ambiguity was not welcome, especially from the people I was trying to take advantage of. The general motioned his hand upwards, which I interpreted as an order to stand up. Gripping the wall behind me, I climbed to my feet. With pressure on my wounded foot, I let out a startled cry in genuine pain. If they had given me medicine to numb the gunshot, it might have been wearing off. Santana's two subordinates opened my cell and helped me out. Leaning on their shoulders, I hopped on my good leg over to the general, who proceeded to yet again gesture, this time to follow him.

The prison was small, which I didn't find surprising considering that this was only an airbase. The three prison cells lined against the wall were most likely only intended to be used as holding. The fact that there was such a small area designated for prisoners, as well as the fact that two of the cells were currently vacant, made me wonder what exactly the LLA did with the prisoners of war. We walked out of the designated prison room and into a dilapidated hallway. High-placed windows filtered light through broken panes— a sign of daytime. I pictured the warm, tropical sun and an open blue sky and focused on the raw, pleasant feelings they gave off. This wishful bliss helped me tolerate my physical agony and aided in helping me block out the painful memories of the previous night. General Santana, who had been stoically quiet, finally broke his silence as we walked. "You . . . you American?"

My mind panicked at the sound of English directed toward me. I quickly countered with, *"Non, je ne suis pas américain, monsieur."* The general didn't respond immediately, which made me fear that I had overdone the accent, or that it sounded different from whatever type of French they spoke here. I had always dreaded the language and for some reason had a much more difficult time becoming fluent in it, compared to Spanish and Italian. Leon—whose last name was Andre, and who had family in eastern Canada—had it as his second language and made it his goal my first year to teach me.

One of the soldiers pushed me off his shoulder and went to open one of the doors to the hallway. To my satisfaction, it contained a plastic table with two chairs on either side. *I'm going to get interrogated,* I realized, relief washing over me. At that time, interrogations were basically my forte. It was one thing to keep up an act while you walked, talked, and occasionally ate. It was a whole different ballpark when I was strapped down to a single chair around suspicious men who may or may not be trying to kill me. There, all I needed to focus on was the words that came out of my mouth, and I always knew the perfect way to divert hostility, or in some cases even manipulate my interrogator. Due to the questionable amount of missions we went on that required me to get detained in one form or another, I had mastered my craft. In

war of words with a known enemy, I took comfort in knowing that I reigned supreme.

I sat at one side of the table, flanked by a single man to
my right, and Santana sat on the other side, with his own soldier. *"Please tell me your name, son,"* he said, in a kind voice.
His French didn't sound as natural as I was used to hearing,
and I could easily tell that it was not his first language.

In a timid voice, I gradually articulated, "David . . . Parker,
señor." Using Charlie's name felt borderline sacrosanct, but it
was at least better than "Bob McSomebody" and "Seymour
Butts."

"How old are you, David?" the general said, proceeding
to the next question.

"Fifteen, sir," I said, before adding sweetly, *"My birthday
was last week."* I lied about my age because I always had the
impression that sixteen-year-olds were more dubious than
fifteen-year-olds. Maybe it was because we had a lot more
legal freedom in most countries. Plus, I figured the younger
the captive, the less likely they were to be considered for
execution. Depending on my tone of voice, I could probably pass as a straight-up fourteen-year-old if I was really
trying, but with the pain in my foot and the repression
of Charlie's death clouding my mind, I doubted I had the
mental strength to convincingly act any younger.

"Oh! Well, happy birthday," the old man said, surprised
by my comment. Catching your interrogator off guard was
one of the best things you could do in a situation like mine.
"Where are you from?"

"Canada," I responded, trying my best to remember
what a French-Canadian accent sounded like.

The general studied my face intently. The more I looked
at him, the more he reminded me of an eccentric uncle, the
kind that would magically pull a coin out of your ear. *"That's*

mighty far away," Santana noted, talking to me as though I was years younger. "*Were you on vacation with your family?*"

I smiled. A subtle degree of acceptance was enough.

"*What were you doing last night on our runway?*"

Taking a deep breath, I chose an answer: "*They took me captive. I didn't know what language they were speaking. They hardly talked. They wanted to take me to their country; it was horrible. When the plane crashed, I was in the cockpit. I was this close to dying! It was horrible!*" As I spoke, I scrunched up the muscles in my face, making it look like I was on the verge of tears. On the inside, I was smiling. It was probably the best lie I'd managed to tell since I convinced a Mexican kingpin I was at his hideout to deliver pizza.

Santana gave me a sympathetic nod and pressed, "*How did you get that wound on your foot?*"

"*The plane crash—oh, it was so awful!*" I pouted. "*I ran away as fast as I could from the wreckage and one of them—the kidnappers, I mean, was shooting at me!*"

"*You should be thankful we were there to rescue you,*" Santana added. "*Now, we'd love to send you back to your family, but we have to make sure that there's some . . . compensation for our heroic efforts.*"

At this comment, I subconsciously rubbed my head. If getting kicked in the head was their idea of a rescue, I did not want to be around to see their hostage negotiation. "*I understand, sir,*" I whimpered. "*It was so kind of you. Those kidnappers were so awful.*"

The general broke into a smile, revealing to me that he had quite a number of missing teeth. "*Glad you see it our way. Now, how about you get some rest?*"

I rubbed my nose pathetically and quietly agreed, "*Oui, merci. Gracias, señor.*"

Santana seemed to appreciate my bilingual speech and motioned for me to leave. A soldier helped me out of my seat and we made our way to the outside hallway. Just as I reached for the knob, however, it began to turn. The door swung open and General Demiese stepped into the room. He had a limp in his step and carried a cane, two features I didn't notice the previous night, making me playfully consider the idea that he broke his foot on my skull. No words were exchanged, and we silently passed each other, just like we did the previous night when I was in the trees. I forget which one of us was the first to look away, but someone did, and we continued to go our separate ways. I asked the soldier who was handling me, *"Who is that?"* as it seemed appropriate.

"General Demiese," the soldier responded, his French strangely accented, just like Santana's. *"A very angry man who lost his family a few years ago and doesn't have very much to live for outside his work."*

Sounds vaguely familiar. Trying to relate my own losses to the man seemed almost possible, if I didn't have so much hate to block out the sympathy. All I could feel in my heart for him was disdain.

Back in my cell, I thanked the soldier and slumped against my wall, not sure what to do with myself. Contemplating for a few moments, I decided that it was time I accepted Charlie's death and reviewed what had happened that night. First, of course, there was the music that played, which gave away our position. Then there was my final conversation with him, recalling the mysterious reference to Johanna, his final words.

"Pssst, hey," a small voice whispered. For a moment I thought it was Mabel or Johanna, only to realize that it was a male. It was the same boy who was by my cell when I woke up, the one with the sweater. "Didn't I tell ya?"

"Tell me what?" I said, groaning. We might have been speaking English; I don't quite remember. With the growing laundry list of languages on this strange island, I wouldn't have been surprised.

"I didn't rat you out!" the kid said proudly. "So, we're like, bros, right?"

I flashed him a confused look. "You *are* the same kid I tackled in the forest yesterday? You do realize I might have been trying to kill you?"

"Meh, forgive and forget," the boy innocently shrugged. Something about his demeanor was certainly off, but nothing about him struck me as suspicious. "Besides, you're locked up now, so you can't kill me even if you wanted to. You don't scare me!"

I recalled the way he had run in terror when I had originally awoken. "Just get to the point," I said. "What do you want?"

"A deal," the kid replied, smirking. "A little exchange of information. You obviously don't know what's going on around here and I'm kinda curious about you. Let's trade off stories."

Feeling compelled to roll my eyes, I looked away from the child. "I'm sorry," I said, "I'm not exactly the type to liberally give out info. Besides, you might be in cahoots with the generals." I heard the boy begin to giggle. "What's so funny?"

"You said 'cahoots.' That's a funny word," the boy bit his lip, trying to stop laughing. "Look, if you won't tell me who you are, I just might report to the soldiers. By the way, nice French, Mr. Napoleon."

Great, now he's threatening me. "Okay. My name's David, but people call me Davy. What do you want to know?"

"What the heck are you doing on this island?" the boy asked, happy that I was paying attention to him. "I mean, I don't think tourists wander off into the jungle and steal war supplies."

"My life's a little complicated," I said, uncertain about how I should explain. "I do certain tasks for people that don't exactly always agree with the law."

"Like what? How bad are you? You a hitman? Drug pusher?"

"No, I'm against those people . . . in a way," I continued, stumbling over my words. "Sometimes I steal evidence to indict them, or if they have a company, I can find a way to ruin them. I have to do it stealthily, and sometimes they don't even know I'm operating against them."

"So you're a secret agent!" the boy said, hardly containing his excitement. "That's awesome!"

I was a secret agent. For some inexplicable reason, the notion surprised me when I thought about it. I could not fully make a connection because—unlike the dashing gadget-wielders in movies who worked for a prestigious organization to protect people, I worked for an organization which was always looking for a profit in contracts. "Yep, just like James Bond," I half-heartedly confirmed, "except there's fewer sexy women and more moral turmoil."

"That's alright!" the kid chirped, hardly dazed by my nonexistent enthusiasm. "Y'know, for an international man of mystery, you're doing a pretty bang-up job."

"As long as they don't know my intentions, I might be safe," I stated, defending my skill. If the boy said anything to the generals I was screwed. He didn't report on me earlier, though, so I figured it unlikely he'd report on me now. It was poor logic that I would've rolled my eyes at had I not been rotting away in a cell with burning injuries. Telling him about myself was strangely a relief, as though I was breaking away from the secrets and the isolation that came from working at Eastway.

Satisfied with my reply, the boy eagerly continued with his questions. "So who was that they found on the runway last night? He didn't look any older than you."

"Charlie," I said, trying my best not to focus on the words I was saying. "His name was Charlie. Our plane was sabotaged and we were shot down before we could get off the ground."

"Were you and Charlie friends?"

My chest heaved. My heart quickened. I lowered my shoulders, realizing how tense I was. "Yeah, we were close."

The boy ran his hand through his hair. I recognized the gesture, as it was something I would do frequently when I didn't know what to say. I realized that I had put him in a very awkward situation. "I'm sorry for your loss," he finally articulated, no doubt trying his best to sound sincere. "Did he do any secret agent stuff?"

"Nah, he was . . . he was behind the scenes. He . . . he shouldn't have been one of us to die."

"*Us?* How many of you guys are there?" he asked. I glared at him, signaling that the question was off-limits. Even if he could be trusted, it would still put my free teammates in danger to some degree, something I would avoid at all costs. "Sorry," he said, getting the message. "Um, anything you wanna know about me?"

"Right," I said, realizing I still knew absolutely nothing about the kid I was having a heart-to-heart with. "What's your name?"

"Nope," the boy shook his head, getting back part of the obnoxious grin he had lost when the conversation turned serious. "Ain't gonna tell you."

"Fine, what can you tell me?"

The boy looked to his left, and then his right. "Things are getting dicey here. People are saying there might be a coup against General Santana."

This news surprised me, mainly because it wasn't in Charlie and Mabel's initial report about the mission. "A coup? Why? Who's leading it?"

"Demiese," the boy said, now whispering. Clearly, he was nervous about divulging such information. "Lots of people are angry about how long it's taking to overthrow the government. It's been what, like thirty years? Some guys have even started deserting. They're saying Demiese is gonna take power and march us toward the other coast, destroying everything in our path and end the war."

"Sounds bold," I remarked. *Bold, but stupid.* With only fifteen hundred poorly equipped men (or less, if the stories of desertions are true), any assault on one of San Pablo's modern cities would end in disaster. Even if the LLA made headway, stronger powers in the north would perceive the nearby threat and annihilate them without a second thought.

"That's not all," the boy continued, "there's—"

The iron door to the prison block swung open, and three soldiers stepped inside. The boy I had been speaking to was struck with terror and fled to a dark corner of the room. "*You!*" one of the soldiers said to me, "*General Demiese would like to have a word with you.*"

"*I just spoke with Santana!*" I pleaded. The men didn't seem to listen and pulled me out of my cell, dragging me back into the same interrogation room I was in minutes earlier. The elder general was nowhere in sight, and Demiese sat alone on the other side of the table. "*I was already with your partner,*" I repeated to the general. For dramatic effect, I rubbed my forehead, making sure he knew that the events of the previous night had not been forgotten. Demiese said nothing. This silence seemed to allow his malevolent presence to surround me. He flashed me something of a quick smile—nothing more than a quick twitch of the lips—and rose from his seat. Although the usual chemical rush of fear had not registered in my brain yet, I could feel my heart quicken as Demiese made his way toward me, hobbling on his cane. His right leg seemed to remain perfectly straight as he sauntered around the table that divided us.

Soon, the general towered over my seat, glowering down at me. "David Parker?"

"*Oui?*"

"*Tu t'appelle David Parker?*" Demiese asked, "Or do you go by Davy?"

Before his comment could register, a blunt pain erupted on my side and I toppled out of my seat. The general had struck me with his cane. Momentarily panicked, I couldn't think of what to say.

"Your French is awful," the general continued. His English was flawless, with no hint of an accent. "Only good enough to fool senile old men. No wonder Santana took a shine to you, eh?"

Regaining some grasp on my current situation on the cold concrete floor, my interrogator looked like an ever-growing giant. Willingly staying silent, I looked up at Demiese cautiously, anticipating another blow.

"What's the matter? Cat got your tongue?" he taunted. He wound up his right leg and delivered a hard kick. His leg felt metallic, and the force of the impact was enough to send me rolling toward the wall. "I know a lot about you, Monsieur Prince. I know you still have some friends on the outside, yes?"

Either from fear or pain, my hands began to shake uncontrollably, and my chest and stomach heaved. A vicious hand pulled at my hair, making my head jerk upwards, face-to-face with the general, now crouching down at my side.

"Look at me when I speak to you," he hissed. "You really are just like they were. The Academy kids, I mean. So much bravado, so professional. Then, when the wrong person finds out too much, you break. All the training and drilling doesn't prepare you for when reality hits. When the big, scary men with guns catch up to you, and the only thing you can do is turn around and face the bullets. Of course, before *you* do, I want to make sure you watch your fellow 'students' die first. I'm a firm believer that one needs to see the fruits of their efforts."

Staring down my interrogator and with the distinct taste of blood flooding through my mouth, I decided to take a small chance. I spat at him, and red specks landed on his face, causing him to flinch.

The general retaliated with another heavy kick and laugh. "That's the spirit! And here I was thinking you were going to make this boring." Although unfazed by my brief defiance, Demiese stood up and stepped out of my line of sight. "I'd really like to continue with the fun, but I must prepare for this evening. *Take him away.*"

Seemingly from nowhere, two hands picked me up from the floor and began to drag me across the room.

"Au revoir, Davy Prince!" Demiese chirped, still chuckling. "Don't worry, I'm sure we'll meet again *very* soon!"

CHAPTER TWELVE

Despite my wounded foot—which, compared to my new injuries, seemed like an inconvenience more than anything else—I found a way to pace nervously around my small cell. I held a small cup of porridge in my hand, a relic of my previous meal (the soldier had called it 'dinner' when he gave it to me). I didn't know how to act properly. Through my years of experience at Eastway, I had never had my cover blown. If I could recollect correctly, I didn't think it had *ever* happened before, save for the Tenth Academy. *Another failed mission in which Demiese was the target.* The more I thought about the desperation of my situation, the more flustered I became. "What's wrong with you?" a voice said. I turned to see that the boy with the sweatshirt was once again sitting diligently by the bars of my cell. "They gonna kill ya?"

"I don't know," I responded. As I spoke, I realized how tense my jaw was.

There was a brief silence. The boy ran his fingers through his hair, trying to think of what to say next. "So I take it your talk with the general didn't go very well?"

"No, he knew about me," I said. "He knows. I don't know how, but he knows Eastway's secret. Who could've tipped him off . . . ?" My voice trailed off as I came to a realization. I darted toward the bars, grabbing the boy and pulling him toward me. "You! You little—"

"Nononono!" the boy cried, struggling against my grip. "You went with him while we were still talking! I wouldn't have had time to tell him anything."

"Right," I muttered, loosening my grip. The boy pushed himself away from me and the iron bars. "Sorry, I guess I'm just getting paranoid," I continued, my voice calming down. Demiese had known information I had not told the boy, so him being an informant seemed unlikely. "That was some quick logic. You're pretty smart."

"Back when I went to school, I was at the top of my class," the boy said, with a small smirk. "'Cept for Algebra, but screw that class. Teacher's a witch."

"Ha, true that." I smiled, reminiscing about my own troubles with that math course. I gave the boy a pat on the shoulders feeling that he must have been wearing multiple layers. "Y'know, I don't exactly think that sweatshirt's appropriate for the weather down here."

"Yeah, well," the boy said, shrugging, "it's pretty cold for July."

"July?" I said, cocking my head. "Dude, it's still spring."

"How do you pick a lock?" the boy said, totally ignoring my statement. I decided to follow suit, and considered the strange remark harmless.

"I was thinking the same thing, actually," I admitted, testing my cell door by shaking it. "It's harder than it looks in the movies. If I were on a mission, another member of the group—his name was Ozzy—would go about unlocking things and mess with a building's infrastructure. Had a big tool kit he would carry for stuff like this, with lots of different rods." I knew I had let it slip that there was yet another person in the Academy, but his death as well as my tentatively growing faith in sweatshirt-boy made me not think much of it.

"So you don't know how to pick a lock?" the boy said, unimpressed.

"Well, I can do it on common doors . . . sometimes, with the right tools, but," I crossed my arms and shook my head, "I honestly have no clue."

"Huh," the boy scoffed indifferently. "Some international superspy you turned out to be."

"Hey, shut up. I'm good at my job!" In frustration, I rattled my door once again. The hinges were so brown and rusted, they seemed ready to snap off. In that position, a strange light caught my eye. I realized the light came from the boy's pocket. "What do you got there?" I asked.

"Oh, this?" Much to my horror, he pulled out a large, clean kitchen knife. "Everyone on base seems to have a weapon, so I've got mine."

I gazed at my own distorted reflection in the knife's gleam. I looked like a mess: my face was dirty, my shirt was unrecognizable, and one of my eyes opened much larger than the other. "You should be careful with that thing," I remarked, slowly stepping away from the bars. "Get some leather and make a sheath, or something. You could cut yourself."

"It's alright," the boy said, glancing down at his shiny knife, perhaps looking at his own reflection. "I've already had to use it, y'know. Killed people."

For the second time that day, I felt an impulse of both shock and terror run through me, "What? What did you just say?"

"It was just like you said," the boy said, his voice now void of emotion. Like my first conversation with him, the room's aura shifted dramatically. The air now felt dry. The voices outside the cell block seemed to quiet. "I killed. Not really sure who they were or how many of them were my fault, but I know I did something. I dunno how to live with that."

"K-kid," I said, realizing that my voice was uncontrollably shaky. "You didn't kill anyone. Th-that's ridiculous. How old are you, twelve?"

"Thirteen," he said, under his breath. "Sorry, I gotta go now." He turned and began walking toward the door, placing his weapon back in his pocket.

"Hold up!" I called, reaching my hand through the bars. "Come back here! Tell me what happened!"

The boy was gone, and I was once again alone. I slumped against the iron bars of my cell, unsure of what to do with myself. Not knowing whether to be frustrated or worried, I began to feel increasingly sleepy.

• • •

A terrible crashing sound woke me up. Several cracks erupted through the air. *Gunshots. That can't be good.* I hobbled my way toward my cell door, now shaking it furiously. The cracks continued to erupt outside as the rusted hinges screeched and squealed. I didn't care how much noise I made, but if guns were firing and I was locked in, it wouldn't end well for me. As I pushed my weight on the weakened bars, I heard the door to the prison block open. Briefly panicking, I realized it was my new best friend, sweatshirt-boy. As he ran toward me, I could tell he looked every bit as terrified as I felt. "We can't talk now," he explained. "A patrol's coming down this hallway and if I'm seen with you I'm a goner."

"What's going on?" I said, trying to maintain a hushed voice, for the boy's sake.

"Demiese just announced that he's executed Santana," he answered, panting heavily. "Then someone shot at Demiese and now . . . now everyone's crazy!"

"Are they fighting out there?" Just as I spoke, another volley of sharp noises erupted.

"No, they're shooting off fireworks," the boy scoffed, rolling his eyes. "What do you think? The base is in chaos. Some guys shooting other guys for running away, some guys shooting the guys who are staying, and some guys who probably don't even know what they're shooting at."

The realization came over me that the LLA was falling apart and we had hardly fired a single shot. It shouldn't have been that surprising, given that the base seemed to be quite disorganized, with terrible morale, but I expected Demiese to have some form of a plan to deal with the aftermath of his coup. "Is General Demise still alive?"

The door began to rattle behind my visitor. "There's no time!" he exclaimed, once again unnerved. He dashed away to a dark corner of the room, out of my line of sight. The door opened and two men stepped inside, both brandishing rifles. I slumped against the wall and pretended to be asleep. This act wasn't very hard to pull off, given that I had just been awoken minutes before. I heard the sound of one set of footsteps cease while another proceeded. Briefly opening my right eye, I saw that a figure was indeed approaching, his gun now raised. I heard a heavy mechanical click: the sound of a gun ready to fire. *He's gonna shoot me in here? This is how I'm going to die? Getting gunned down while pretending to be asleep in my prison cell?*

Thankfully not. The other shouted and I heard a scuffle between the two. I decided to "wake up" at this time, fluttering open my eyes and sitting up straight. The soldier furthest away from me was clutching his comrade's arm and said in

French, "*No, the general wouldn't want him shot in there. Take him out and put him against the wall. It'll be cleaner.*"

My fears were once again confirmed: they were there to execute me. Fully understanding the severity of the situation, I tried my best to keep a blank face and feign stupidity. "*What's cleaner? What's going on, guys?*" The soldier in back covered his mouth and made a strange exhaling sound, like he was trying to repress a laugh or a sneeze. As the soldier in front unlocked my door, I stood up and meandered toward the opening to meet him. I didn't know how I would get out of that predicament, but I knew I still had some element of surprise. The soldier took me by my arm and pushed me against a wall, placing my hands on my head. I formulated a loose plan in my head: at the last second, before he pulled the trigger, I would spin around and knock the gun away from me, knock him out, then jump on his partner—who would hopefully be paralyzed by shock in the sudden turn of events—and take him out too. In my defense, I was half asleep, and as good as I was at reacting to events and following orders, I was never one to think too far ahead. On missions, I had planners do that for me.

Standing up against the wall, I imagined the soldier getting in position. I could practically hear him raise his gun and then . . .

I heard a short, dry snapping sound. Turning around, I saw that my shooter was now collapsed on the floor, slouched over at a very strange angle. The other soldier stood on top of him, gun still firmly in his hands. Confused, I opened my mouth to speak, but I couldn't think of what to say. I had no idea what had just happened.

The living soldier's next comment—in perfect English—cleared things up for me, "That was by far the worst French I had ever heard spoken in my life. You still slur your *r*'s and emphasize your vowels too little. If Santana believed a word of that garbage, he deserved to die."

"Leon!" I exclaimed, gasping in relief. "I've never been so happy to see you in my life. How did you get in here? Where are the others?"

"Up on the roof," Leon said, pointing upward. "We need to hurry. The situation's deteriorating outside."

Acknowledging there was a serious chance I could still die horribly, I allowed myself to produce a smile that would put the Cheshire Cat to shame and diligently followed Leon out of the prison room. "How did you know I'd be in here? Did Demiese send you personally to do me in?"

As we entered the narrow hallways of the base, the sound of gunshots and the occasional scream could still be heard coming from different directions. There was a loud crash and the entire building seemed to shake, and it didn't help that the buzzing lights above flickered ominously. "No, but I think the other guy was. Demiese isn't very active around here, I think. Only saw the man when we were drilling yesterday. Couldn't have shot him then, of course, with all the guys around. Tried to get near his quarters earlier today, but then the coup started and now everything has been thrown out of whack."

"What do you mean Demiese's quarters? He could be there right now?"

"Creep likes to hang out in the radio tower, for whatever reason. It's on the other side of the airfield, where most of the shooting's going on right now. Johanna said we can go around and check it out after things quiet down."

The thought came across my mind that Demiese could escape. I pictured watching him disappear into the thick jungle around us, a place where it was easy to get lost and never be found. Another explosion rocked the building, causing the lights to once again flash. I had to hang on to the wall to support myself as the tremors passed. "Whole army's killing each other. Kind of crazy things have come to this."

Leon looked back at me and gave a quick smirk, "Not really."

"What do you mean?"

"I'll explain later," Leon said, waving his hand at me. "But now, you need some good shoes." He darted into one of the rooms, signaling for me to stay put. When he came out, he held a pair of dirty brown boots in one hand and a pistol in the other, handing them both to me. "Thought you'd be more comfortable with that," Leon said, meaning the gun. "It's still an old firearm, though, so I wouldn't shove it in your pants if you want to conceal it. Trigger's a little sticky, and the last thing we need right now is an unfortunate misfire."

After taking a moment to put on the old boots—they were horrendously uncomfortable on my bare, bleeding feet, but it was still better than walking barefoot—I clutched the pistol in my hand and continued to follow Leon through the deserted terminal. The gun felt heavy and awkward in my sore hands, and it repeatedly hit my side as I walked. I paid very little attention to it, and didn't bother to cock it or prepare it. Johanna was going to be the one to kill Demiese, I was sure.

Following Leon through the twisting office hallways, we eventually came across a dead end with a metal ladder propped up against the wall. It led to a hole in the ceiling and the starry sky above. "It's built for emergencies," Leon explained. "Became a godsend to us when we arrived on the scene. They're right up there. Before you see them, there's one more thing I have to tell you."

"What?"

"Don't bring up Charlie in front of Mabel. She's emotionally unhinged enough as it is."

This comment struck me as very odd. Mabel did have spastic tendencies but she was still a member of the Academy, and I'd never seen her lose her cool during a mission. The idea of anything being off-limits during such a crisis seemed peculiar.

After climbing the ladder (which was a surprisingly difficult process considering my wounded foot) I arrived through a metal hatch onto a slightly sloped platform. This was, based on the height relative to other buildings on the compound, the roof of the main terminal. I mentally retraced our path through the building, only to come to the conclusion that I must have been kept somewhere near the outside of the main terminal itself. Below me, I could finally see where all the terrible noise was coming from. Hundreds of soldiers were running frantically around on the runway, shooting at those around them seemingly at random. Some were hidden by concrete blocks or by one of the ruined planes, shooting at each other and those lucky enough to make it to the chain-link fence. Directly before us, Johanna was down with her rifle and seemed to be in intense focus. Mabel was crouched next to her with binoculars. Both wore the same clothes I saw them in yesterday, and the only real difference was that Mabel had bandages wrapped around her head.

"Sorry to intrude, ladies," Leon said from behind me. "I'm back."

"Oh, hey," Johanna said, not bothering to turn around. "You're back. Is Prince dead?"

"Oh, you wish," I scoffed, insulted by the casual tone of her comment. At the sound of my voice, Mabel dropped her binoculars and looked over at me in awe.

"Davy!" Mabel chimed, clearly overjoyed. "You're alive! My plan worked! We've managed to get everyone on the inside! We can move forward now, and—"

"Mabes! Calm down, please," I stated, trying to process the girl's words. Mabel's electric joy was contagious, and staring at her wide-eyed, excited face, I couldn't help but allow myself to smile a little bit. She ran to embrace me, but I grabbed her shoulder before she could get her arms around me. I partially regretted rejecting her; a hug probably could have done me some good. "Whoa, whoa, whoa," I raised my finger, taking an authoritative tone. "Your little plan got me shot in the foot."

"You needed to be wounded to be taken prisoner," Mabel explained, panting as she tried her best to articulate. "If you were just lying there, they would have assumed you were one of us and shot you on the spot. That was my train of thought, at least. I told Johanna that you had to look hurt, I didn't say anything about you getting shot."

I angrily gazed down at Johanna, who was still in her sniping position, looking down her scope. "Sorry," she muttered. "I guess when situations get so dire, I think with my rifle. Would you have preferred me to smash a few of your bones with my briefcase? The injury would have been a little less . . . clean."

"Couldn't I have just had Leon's job?" I asked. "I mean, I *am* the infiltrator of this team, right? I could've snuck in just as easily."

"No, you couldn't," Johanna responded flatly. "Looking beyond the fact that you're whiter than Wonder Bread and your French is awful, I have my doubts you could take such a serious role."

"Serious role?" I asked. "What is this, a play?"

"I think she means," Mabel softly interjected, "that you could pull off the 'affluent, innocent hostage in distress' image much more than 'hardened rebel guerrilla.' Davy, I'm really, *really* sorry my plan was so hard on you. If you need someone to blame, it's me."

I bit my lip, swallowing my rage. It was very hard to stay angry at Mabel for very long.

"Everybody drop!" Johanna called out abruptly. Quickly we fell to the floor and watched a shining ball of light pass over us, leaving a trail of smoke. It was an RPG, similar to the one that had struck the *MacVeagh*. It sailed above us, exploding in a great flash of light. As we pulled ourselves off the roof, Johanna fired five shots in rapid succession into different parts of the field below. "More people are catching on down there," she announced. "We're gonna have to change our position again."

I took another good look at the carnage below. "I still can't believe things are turning our way. This is incredible!"

"You can thank Mabel for that," Leon said.

"What do you mean?"

The younger girl blushed, brushing hair off her face. She looked like a nervous elementary school girl who had just won the science fair. "Well, the infiltration plan with Leon had a couple . . . layers," she explained. "After he got in, I ordered him to say certain things to some of the soldiers. Spread a couple conspiracies and whatnot, y'know? Knowing the coup d'état was going to happen gave us a big edge, as did the LLA's disorganization. One thing led to another and then . . ." the girl pointed down to the soldiers shouting and shooting at each other. "That happened."

"Making our enemies kill each other. Huh. Mabes," I said, smirking, "that plan was pretty devious of you. Didn't know you had a diabolical bone in your body. I'm impressed."

"Yeah, I guess," Mabel said, now beet red. The fresh-faced girl probably had never been called "devious" or "diabolical" in her life, and certainly not affectionately.

"If we're done here," Johanna interjected, "we've still got a mission to do."

"What should we do? There's no way we can go down *there*," I said, pointing to the war zone below.

"We need you two for reconnaissance," the planner instructed. Although she spoke confidently, I noted that her leg shook and she kept running her fingers through her hair—a sure sign of restrained anxiety. "We can observe what's going on outside, but we're in the dark when it comes to indoors. There might be a patrol or two still active within the compound that hasn't broken yet."

"Account for all the variables," I remarked. "I like it. And what about Demiese?"

Johanna scoffed, "Too dangerous. The purpose of this mission was to *degrade* the army, remember? We wanted to do that through killing the generals, but that's no longer necessary. Our main focus now is to hold out, and when the coast is clear, we find a working vehicle or plane and escape."

A part of me was frustrated that I wouldn't see Demiese get what he deserved, but I knew that escaping alive was our first priority. "Sounds good to me," I agreed. "Leon, ready to roll out?"

"Hold up!" Mabel said. Her calm, placid voice gave way to a familiar, excited squeal. She was so loud that I briefly worried that the soldiers below could hear her over the gunshots. "There's something I need to tell you guys!"

"Yeah?"

Johanna, Leon, and I stared at the younger agent and waited. Mabel stared back. Her eyes grew to be as big as saucers and she took a big swallow. I couldn't tell whether the information she wished to share was that nerve-rackingly awful or if she was just pitifully anxious. "N-never mind," she muttered, looking away from us. "It can wait. It's . . . it's not important now."

Leon rolled his eyes and walked away, back toward where we entered. Not wishing to press the seemingly emotionally confused girl, I followed suit. Gunshots and explosive fire continued to erupt, making the metal ladder shake in my hands as I gripped it. Before I descended back down into the compound, I gave one last glance at the air traffic tower beyond.

CHAPTER THIRTEEN

Leaving Johanna and Mabel to their own devices on the roof, Leon and I were back on our own. The general anarchy outside made it easy to deduce that Leon in his soldier outfit would get shot just as quickly as I would. Given that I could react to danger faster than him, I took the lead. Taking calculated, methodical steps, we traversed the same hallways we had walked through minutes before, going in the opposite direction. The second time through, I noticed bullet holes lining portions of the wall and the disrepair of the collapsing ceiling.

The garages were similar to the hallways, as in they were bleak and abandoned. The lights seemed to have permanently decided to stay off, something that might work to my advantage if we encountered soldiers. The noises of battle still raged outside, although there seemed to be less shooting and more shouting. Occasionally the sound would die altogether, in which case Leon and I would have to stop moving in fear that our footsteps echoed outside. Broken wood, tools, and other objects lay haphazardly across the floor. I silently thanked Leon for getting me shoes. "Think we can use one of these?" he said, pointing to the vehicles next to us. There were two of them in the garage. One was very similar to the jeep Charlie and I had ambushed, with high wheels and a large frame. The other was small and had only two seats, reminding me of a dune buggy.

I dismissed Leon's suggestion with a hand gesture, pointing to the car's wheels, or where they should have been. Both vehicles were on cinder blocks.

"Oh, I see," my teammate muttered, disappointed. Leon was never the one on the team to give good suggestions on a mission. To be fair, I never offered anything, but that was because I trusted control's judgment above my own. Leon would occasionally point things out and would always get shot down by Johanna or Charlie.

We made our way through a second garage, which was a similar scene: three cars, all on cinder blocks, no doubt broken down. The interesting thing about this room was that the last car we passed was not a jeep or a buggy, rather it was an old, expensive, high-end car with a big grill and a distinctive hood ornament. The doors and hood were rusted to the point where I could not tell what the original color of the car was. Its apparent age and elegance made me wonder if it belonged to the air base's old owners, who worked there before the Nationalists took it over.

"So," I whispered over my shoulder, "what's up with Mabel and Charlie? Why did I have to be so cautious?"

Leon stopped dead in his tracks and let out an exaggerated sigh. "You're really something else, Dave," he began, now speaking normally. "You and Charlie were close, but him and Mabel were something else."

"Something else?" I said, pondering. Then it struck me: a bolt of surprise, realization, and confusion. "Wait, they were a thing? They were a thing! Are you serious?"

Leon nodded his head, partially amused by my reaction, although still quite serious. "Mabel's athletic, pretty, and smart and Charlie was outgoing, funny, and decently attractive. I mean, when you lock two people like that in a dark room together during missions, things happen."

"They were . . . what even!" I exclaimed, trying to wrap my head around such a ridiculous notion. The idea had never even come across my mind. I quickly ran over every time I saw them together alone on campus. Charlie would drive Mabel into town usually, but that never struck me as odd given as he did the same thing for Ozzy and me. Then I remembered the tenseness in Charlie's face every time Mabel was brought up in a romantic light, or the way Mabel had clung close to Charlie after our jet crashed into the ocean. The open campus was wide enough to hide any kind of romantic affair, especially if I wasn't looking out for it. But the biggest question I couldn't wrap my mind around was, *Why keep it a secret from me?* "How long were they . . . together?"

"Dunno, few months?" Leon shrugged. "Saw them by the lake together in January. Chuck asked Weiss if they could go ice skating while most of us were out in town, I believe."

"Wait, so *Weiss* knew they were together and I didn't?"

"Yep," the large boy confided, flashing a sucks-to-be-you smirk and patting me on the shoulder. "We can play high school gossip after this is all said and done, bro. Just be happy that Mabel took his death as well as she did."

"Yeah . . ." I contemplated, "Do you think it's sunken in yet?"

"Huh?"

"Chuck dying. Do you think it's sunken in for her yet?" I clarified. "When you lose someone close, it sometimes takes a while for you to feel it. You're in shock, you know?"

"Sure, whatever," Leon responded flatly, shrugging. It was the kind of shrug you'd see from a classroom delinquent who didn't understand what the teacher was talking about.

Before I could find out more about the relationship, a clanking sound erupted from the other side of the garage. The loud tapping of military boots was followed by multiple voices shouting unrecognizable words. Leon leapt behind the fancy car, quietly releasing a string of frustrated profanity as he did so. Standing feet away from the car, I did not have the luxury of a hiding spot.

The soldiers' shouting seemed to intensify once they sighted me. As they approached, a clearer picture broke out of the darkness. Seven human-shaped silhouettes pointing seven rifle-shaped silhouettes surrounded me. In the midst of the shouting, I picked up individual words in French, Spanish, and Creole. Knowing that men pointing guns at me was a bad sign, I decided that my only course of action was to take advantage of the confusion by adding some confusion of my own.

"All of you, shut up!" I bellowed.

The garage fell dead silent. One soldier even staggered backward, seemingly astonished.

A gruff voice spoke against me. *"Quien es usted?"*

"Who am I?" I countered, insulted. "Who am I? How dare you! Get out!" I dramatically pointed out, away from the garage.

Either out of bravery or bewilderment, a lone soldier, different from the first speaker, stepped forward. *"Qui?"*

"You heard me!" I spouted, stamping my foot down. "Scram! You guys have no business here. What? *No hablas inglés?* Get out!"

At this point, all the men had lowered their weapons. They began distancing themselves from me. With no visible weapons, I knew that I wasn't the least bit intimidating, but

I didn't let desperation seep into my voice. Instead I was angry and demanding, hoping that something would somehow trigger with them to make them go away.

Much to my amazement, a few at a time, they began to walk away. The last one looked at me closely before shaking his head and joining his comrades, rifle still strapped to his waist. When the coast was clear, Leon poked out, looking just as stunned as some of the assaulting soldiers. "What was that?"

"I didn't think they'd fall for 'innocent French boy,'" I explained, very proud of my work. "So I decided to go for 'angry American.' I'm not too surprised that these men blindly follow orders. I'm sure they do it all the time with Demiese."

Leon opened his mouth to speak, but apparently couldn't immediately decide what to say. He only shook his head and motioned for me to follow him, briefly reminding me to stay quiet in the future.

The next hallway we entered was somehow even darker than the garages. My eyes adjusted gradually, but I still needed to focus hard to see anything clearly. The floors were decorated with gashes of broken and rotted wood, and I was reluctant to put much pressure on any step. Treading lightly, however, proved similarly painful on my aching feet, and I had to be mindful not to step directly on my wound.

Although the walls were of similar quality to the main terminal, the wooden floor and lack of doors to the surrounding rooms made me determine that that building must have been abandoned. Peeking into one of the rooms, my suspicions were confirmed. Moonlight from a small window revealed the metal skeleton of what was once, I realized, a bunk bed.

"C'mon," Leon softly urged. He was already on the other side of the hall, by the door. "I think this is the way outside."

Using the wall for support, I hobbled down the remainder of the hallway, motioning for Leon to open the door. A blue beam of pale light struck me and illuminated the area around me. It was nothing but some weak moonbeams, but in the dark void I was in it was almost blinding. When the light settled and my vision cleared, nothing prepared me for what I saw on the other side.

CHAPTER FOURTEEN

I saw Charlie's legs first. His feet floated above the ground, toes pointed downward. His head was crooked downward, with his face shielded by a mess of dirty, uneven hair. A long, thick rope connected his neck to a flagpole above.

I forget what my initial reaction was. I remember seconds later, though, when I was on the floor and my throat hurt from screaming. Leon had to cover my mouth in case any nearby soldiers heard. "Take a deep breath," he instructed. Removing his hand, he helped me to my feet. "It's okay to look away."

I bit my lip and stared at the ground. I was shaking. My vision was hazy. My stomach hurt. Once I collected myself to talk, my voice came out like a strangled cough. "They . . . that . . ."

"He was already dead when they hanged him," Leon said, still trying to keep me calm. "You saw him when he went. He didn't suffer. We need to keep moving, man. We've got a job to do."

My thoughts turned away from Charlie and the flagpole and back to Demiese. Only now, thinking of his face and the wounds he'd given me, I wasn't scared anymore. I didn't bother to think about the traitor, or the team, or even much about Charlie. It was just Demiese and his horrible, piercing eyes. I felt a cold anger ignite. It wasn't the kind that boiled over, where you screamed and cried and couldn't think clearly. It was a whole different beast, giving me a clear, but narrow mind. I wanted to find the general and nothing else.

The courtyard with the flagpole was surrounded by the terminal on three sides, and opened to the runway on the fourth. The compound had fallen eerily quiet, with only the rattling of the flagpole in the evening breeze resisting the total quiet. Without talking to Leon, I made my way out to the runway. He yelled something at me before reluctantly following suit. "Are you crazy?" he asked, struggling to keep his voice hushed. "We can't be out here exposed!"

"Things have quieted down," I assured. My voice sounded perfectly normal, a far cry from my hysteria moments before. I sounded void of emotion, like Johanna. "Can we be covered?"

Leon whispered something in his transceiver, before relating to me, "Johanna's got us in her sights. She doesn't know how much longer we can go before we're out of range, though."

I drew my pistol and motioned toward Leon. "Stay close. We're moving out."

Fifty yards down, the traffic tower stood, casting ghostly spotlights on the cracked concrete. A wall of concrete blocks, about waist-high, surrounded the base. A perimeter, I speculated, keeping Demiese away from his unruly subjects. Cautiously approaching, we could see very little of the massacre that had taken place. The dark night probably covered many of the bodies, and the ones I saw were partially covered by shelter or shadows. Occasionally we'd hear the rattling of the fence—possibly another soldier escaping.

Just when we reached the block perimeter, Leon winced and clutched his ear. "What?" he called in his transceiver. "I can't hear you when you're screaming like that, Pryce." There was a pause as the planner spoke and his face turned serious. He turned to me. "Get down."

"What?" was the only word that managed to come out of my mouth before Leon tackled me to the ground, over the wall. A round of high pitched cracks erupted, and dust from the cinder block in front of us was kicked into the air from the incoming bullets. Just when I thought it was safe to poke my head up, another round of bullets erupted. "Thanks for the heads up, Mabel," I whispered.

"Hey," Leon now crouched next to me and growled, "where's my thank-you?"

"How many guys are firing at us?" I said into the transceiver, ignoring Leon.

Leon relayed the question back to the planner. "Thirteen," he said. "Everybody who's left in the area." I didn't know whether to be happy so few men remained or sad that so many were trying to kill me. "Johanna's out of range too. Gonna take her a few minutes to reposition."

Another round of bullets crashed into our protective cinderblock. Just as the round finished, Leon peeked his head up and fired shots with his rifle, just for a split second. "They're approaching," he announced. He then plucked his transceiver from his ear and handed it to me. "Talk to the girl. I need to put some pressure on these guys."

"Mabes, we need a distraction," I ordered desperately, watching Leon sit up to fire another round.

"*I got it! Check this out,*" the youthful girl chirped. Instinctively, I looked up above my cover. It was true that a mob of men were now dangerously close to us—so close, in fact, I could see holes in their bullet-proof vests—but they also all had their heads looking away from us. I saw that they were looking on the roof of the main terminal further down the runway. I saw a figure jumping up and down, waving their hands and making whooping noises. "Hey, all y'all! Look over here!" Mabel screamed.

The surviving soldiers, perhaps confused, perhaps agitated, began shooting toward Mabel. I saw the girl's silhouette disappear and heard panting over the transceiver. "*That was fun!*" she exclaimed.

"'Look over here'? That was your idea of a distraction?" I said, stunned.

"*It worked, didn't it?*" Mabel countered. Looking at the soldiers, I realized she was right. They had their backs facing us, and were still shooting up at the roof, where they saw Mabel. The soldier's brief shock turned into a lingering confusion, and a couple looked back our way. They would be back in just a few moments.

"Go up and kill that man," Leon said, pointing to the tower's entrance. It was painted blue. Another big iron door.

I realized that Leon was calling the shots, something that hadn't worked well in the past. "You can't take all those guys."

"I can hold them off and wait for Johanna," Leon insisted. He pushed me away from our hiding spot, leaving me no choice but to make a break for the door. I pressed myself against it until it broke, presenting me with a winding stairwell to climb. *I'm almost there. I almost have you, General . . .*

Leon's shouts and the hostile gunfire became more distant with every flight I ascended, until I couldn't hear it at all. Instead, there were my pattering feet echoing with each step. I kept climbing until I reached a single red door, which had *Communications* written in English and Russian. By now my feet and legs were once more sore, but the pain was bluntly ignored. I pulled myself inside and got to my feet before looking around. Large paneled windows lined the walls, which was something expected in a tower meant to observe. Tables, chairs, and ancient radios stood around the walls, eerily vacant. *Where is everybody?*

My eyes finally rested on a single man sitting in the corner. He was hunched over, fiddling with one of the radios. He turned around and our eyes met. Everything became a blur. He picked up his cane and hobbled toward me, scowling. "You see what you've done? Isn't it enough? Come to put me out of my misery?"

The gun in my hands was shaking violently. My finger froze, unable to give that little bit of strength needed to pull the trigger. Demiese took my hesitation as a sign of fear and gave a big smile. "A scared little boy in a grown-up's world." He reached out past my gun and swatted me with his cane, causing me to stagger back and lose my weapon. He followed up with another quick blow to my legs, leaving me to fall to my knees. He turned away from me and moved for my gun. I instinctually leapt after him, catching the general on his bad leg.

Finally detecting resistance, Demiese pushed back. When he saw that I wouldn't budge, he threw down his cane and picked up a nearby chair and swung at me hard, making contact with my chest. I heard a sharp snapping noise come from my ribs and I instantly tasted blood in my mouth. "There's room on that pole for a couple more" Demiese hissed. He wound up to kick me again, but this time I grabbed his steel-toed boot and pushed it in an awkward direction, knocking him off balance. I launched myself to my feet as Demiese toppled over, darting to find something to fight him with. I had lost sight of my gun, so I settled for Demiese's dropped cane. As my enemy tried to rise to his feet, I gave him a wild blow. The cane connected and he fell back down with a hard thud.

Without detecting any movement, I hit him again. And then again. I was no longer in control of myself, now just a spectator to a movie I didn't want to watch. At one point, the general tried to resist, but I coldly beat him back the same way he had struck me, and followed up with a strike to his head. This blow broke the cane, but I didn't notice. I just kept hitting, now all over. I kept hitting until his face was unrecognizable, just a darker blur mixing in with the crimson that already obstructed my vision. My hands were wet with blood. Pools of red gathered at my feet. Demiese tried to say something to me at one point, but I couldn't hear because my hearing was blurred too.

I wish that I felt something inside when I was doing this. It could have been my conscience crying out or a hot anger taking hold of my muscles. I didn't feel anything like that. Just the feeling of resistance in the cane with every hit I gave as it met with my victim's body.

I stopped when I got tired. By then my hands and some parts of my arms were maroon and sticky. Demiese was gone, and I struggled to look at him for more than a few moments. He was still. I was still.

Silence regained control of the tower.

Reviewing the room once again, one object caught my eye. The radio Demiese was sitting at was a newer model and, upon further inspection, was American made. The device looked very out of place next to the other, more antiquated technology, and I made a mental note of it.

I heard a light thud behind me and spun around. There was a dark figure partially concealed by the shadows approaching me. I held Demiese's walking stick—covered with his blood as well as my own—outstretched. A broken Cain stared down a new enemy.

"H-hey, Davy?" the figure spoke. He stepped out into the weak light. It was the boy who wore the sweatshirt. I lowered my weapon, relieved he somehow had made it out alive. Then I saw where his eyes were looking: down at the ground, at the bloody wreck that use to be Demiese. He then looked at me with eyes as big as dinner plates. He was scared of me, I realized. "D-did you . . . ?"

"Run," I ordered. I wanted him to escape the base, but I also wanted him to look away from me. Me, the bloody, tired killer who rightfully deserved his fearful gaze. "Get out of here!"

The kid disappeared out of my sight. Maybe he went down the stairs or through another door I didn't see, but he was no longer near me and therefore off my mind. I finished catching my breath and collected my gun, remembering that there were still things left to do. "Is Leon okay?"

"*No,*" Johanna said, her voice more threatening than concerned. "*You have to get out of there, now.*"

Something inside me switched back on, and I bolted down the stairs to help Leon. I found him slouched over a wall, bleeding profusely. A lone soldier, just as beaten up, stood above him, weapon pointed down. "Hey!" I shouted, pointing my pistol menacingly. "You better run."

The soldier only grinned and leveled his rifle.

"Fine," I muttered, "have it your way." Before he could get his shot off, I fired. His foot blew out from under him and he collapsed to the ground. As I advanced toward him, the already bloodied fighter staggered to his feet and bolted without his weapon.

I turned my attention back to Leon. "Are you okay?" He shook his head "no" and began squirming. He was in a lot of pain, but he was still alive. His arms were trying to cover the right side of his neck, where small streams of blood were flowing out. "Johanna, you need to get down here now."

"We're coming!" Mabel yelped. *"Keep him alive!"*

"I'm working on it!" I tried to help cover the wound on his neck. But Leon twisted at my grip, shaking his head downward. I then saw the three dark holes over his military jacket. Practically ripping it off, I tore off bits of it to apply pressure to the holes. Just as the dark spots grew wider, a familiar voice rang out.

"Get back," Johanna ordered, crouching next to me. Relieved, I dutifully obeyed as she went to work, taking out bandages and instruments from her briefcase.

I scanned the desolate runway around us. "Hey, where's Mabes?"

Johanna shrugged absentmindedly, absorbed with her work. "She freaked out in the courtyard. Might still be there. I'm sure she's fine; no one else seems to be left in the terminal . . ."

"And you just left her there?" I said, my relief quickly turning to disgust.

"I was in a hurry, and Leon needed help," Johanna remarked, half-heartedly defending herself. "As long as she can do her job, it doesn't matter if she's mentally scarred. It's just a corpse. There are plenty of those floating around. Wanna go get her? Fine."

Enraged, I left Johanna to her own devices and bolted toward the main building, praying that the sniper's words were lies.

CHAPTER FIFTEEN

I found Mabel standing in the courtyard, her back turned. I couldn't see her face, and I genuinely had no idea what she might be feeling. *Fear? Rage? Confusion?* Reluctantly, I called out to her. "Hey, Mabel."

Mabel didn't answer, staying still. *This isn't going to end well*, I thought, quietly approaching her. "Hey, Mabel," I repeated, this time with a bit more emphasis in my voice.

To my surprise, the girl spun around and embraced me, burying her face in my chest. Her jaw was tight and she was shaking, but she wasn't crying, weeping, or hysterical in any sense. I could just hear her breath, my own, and the hard tropical breeze blowing around us. Eventually, I felt compelled to speak up. "It's okay," I cooed. "We can go home now. We're done here."

She looked up at me. Finally staring at her eye to eye, I was surprised to see that she looked to be in relatively stable shape. Her eyes were bloodshot from tears and her lip trembled, but her face as a whole was stiff and strong. "No," she stated quietly. "We're not going home. We have no home. We're going back to school."

I didn't know how to respond to her. For more than two years of my life, Eastway was the place I knew. I lived there, slept in its beds, and ate its food. It was always the place I thought about returning to when I was away, but maybe it was because I had no home in my life to think about instead. Eastway may very well be a prison—one with very nice food, very nice people, very nice toys, and a very nice promise of the future once you were free. It was a prison most of the time I really didn't mind living in. After all, it was my free choice to be sentenced there; my free choice to give up my freedom in exchange for a shining future. A part of me still wanted that, but another part of me was looking down at a broken Mabel, who had just laid eyes on Charlie hanging on a flag pole. "I'm going to take him down, now," I said softly. "Go back to the hangar. I won't be too long."

"I'm not going to see him for a while," Mabel objected, clearly trying to look away from the flagpole. "I-I don't want my last image of him to be this."

I silently agreed, but as I did, I fell into a coughing fit, crouching over. On the last hack, blood flew out of my mouth and onto the wild grass.

"You okay?" she asked, her voice still quiet and reserved.

"Yeah, yeah, just got a few broken ribs," I said, still crouched over.

"That makes sense," Mabel said, rubbing her face. "I think one of them poked me in the eye." Her light comment almost made me smile and gave me hope that things might return to normal for her.

"I'm fine," I declared, walking over to the pole and grabbing on to the rope. "How do you cut this thing?" Just as I uttered those words, a sharp pain struck me deep in the chest. I heard Mabel shout, but it sounded oddly distorted.

The sky above me warped and soon faded to black, and all that was left was the stinging I felt inside.

• • •

I didn't know where I was. Someone could have walked up to me and told me I had died and gone to hell and I probably would have believed them. Then again, given the light atmosphere and the generally peaceful feeling I felt, they might have even been able to convince me I had gone to heaven. I was in my old room, the one I slept in before I lived at Eastway. I was in my old home. The walls were painted a navy blue, and rock 'n' roll posters surrounded my bed. I had just started getting into classic rock, and posters of Freddie Mercury and Sting hung next to artwork I had drawn in school. I wasn't a bad artist, by any means, although I never seemed to be able to draw people correctly. People and horses. My horses really sucked.

It was an unusually cool day for July. The sun was gone, the skies were dark and overcast, and a bitter wind cut through the trees outside my window. It was unfortunately cold inside the house as well, and as I sat in bed, waiting to fall asleep, I couldn't help but clutch my blanket and shiver. Downstairs, I heard people yelling. I guessed that it was Mom and Dad. It really didn't bother me until Mom started to raise her voice and then started screaming, yelling something unintelligible.

Concerned, I rolled out of bed and put on a sweatshirt. It was gift from my father, back when he was trying to get me into sports. I opened the door to my room and yelled downstairs, "Mom? You okay?"

No answer. I still heard a male voice speak. *Dad?* As I descended the stairs, I realized that there wasn't just one male voice, but two. Coming to this realization, the walls beside my stair melted away into black, and the stairs under me disappeared. I looked up to see a giant, bright light above my head.

"Someone hand me the scalpel." I turned to my right to see several figures in hospital attire standing sideways, studying me intently. Another one, right next to me, seemed to be doing something to the side of my chest. I realized I was on a hospital table. Out of all the people standing around me, I thought one seemed out of place. She had no equipment in her hands. The masks everyone wore around their mouths were a pale blue, except for hers. Hers was a clean white, and even though I couldn't see it, I could tell she was smiling. She had these brilliant eyes, a bright, otherworldly violet. I knew this woman could not be a doctor; no part of her belonged in the dark environment of an operating room.

"He's awake," she said. Her voice somehow managed to be sweet and melodic, yet also deep and regal. "Would someone kindly put him back down?"

"Of course, Ms. Scott," one of the doctors said. I felt a plastic mask be placed over my mouth and nose. The operating room disappeared, and I laid alone in a black void with the violet-eyed woman. She stood above me, looking down and beaming. *Ms. Scott . . . I've heard that name before . . .*

"Don't worry," I heard her say, her voice now faint and distant. Her body began to disappear, and all that was left were her brilliant, hypnotic eyes. "You're safe now. Rest easy."

• • •

The next time I woke up, I was very much grounded in reality. My mind processed my surroundings quickly, no longer encumbered by strange feelings or hallucinations. I was once again lying down, but I was on a bed, not an operating table. After spending a day stuck in a concrete cell, it felt like heaven. Everything around me was white: the blankets, the curtains, the walls, and the floors. Even the TV was perfectly white, making its black screen seem terribly out of place. To my right, there was a wide window. Lying down, all I could see was the black night sky, void of stars.

"Welcome back to the world of the living."

I sat up in my bed, startled by the voice. A short, blond-haired man stepped toward my bed, seemingly out of nowhere. "Professor!" I exclaimed. "Where—"

Weiss silently put his fingers to his lips and pointed to my left. I realized that there was another occupied hospital bed in the room, although I could not see who inhabited it. The professor pressed against my shoulder and pushed me back onto my pillow. "I've been waiting for you to regain consciousness," he said softly, in his usual laid-back voice. "The doctors heard you stirring earlier in the night and they called me down. Leon's still in intensive care, but he'll pull through. The team survived, Davy. You made it."

"Where am I?" I said. As I spoke, I realized I still had a focused pain in my chest. The left side of my torso was artfully wrapped in white bandages, which made me worried.

"The Empire State, naturally," Weiss said, giving me a fatherly smile. "Thirty miles drive away from Eastway. I'll be back in the morning, and I'll explain to you what's been going on. Get some sleep tonight, Davy. You've earned it. You're almost home." With those parting words, the professor stepped away from my bed and walked out of my room. Now alone in the darkness, I closed my eyes to sleep, only to feel disturbed. I recalled the violet-eyed woman and her stare, and the mysterious yet unsettling impression it gave me. I felt the same sensation right then and there, as if somehow she was still watching me.

CHAPTER SIXTEEN

As it turned out, Mabel was my roommate in the hospital. I had no idea how Weiss managed to get us co-ed rooms, but I was thankful. The only other male on the team was hooked up to a bunch of machines that were—according to Mabel—very noisy. When I first woke up in the morning, around seven, I found her in bed, quietly solving Sudoku and crossword puzzles in the newspaper. She looked almost as bad as I felt, with black circles under her eyes and a single Band-Aid on her chin. She had cut her hair. It was now a short bob, hardly longer than Johanna's. The change was surprising because I knew Mabel couldn't stand the mandatory Academy haircuts, not bearing to have it cut any more than necessary.

Her pencil strokes became less and less frequent and her erasing became more common. As I watched, I saw her face grow into a frustrated grimace, eventually crumpling up her newspaper and throwing it to the ground. "Can I have yours?" she asked, in our first interaction of the morning.

Her voice sounded like someone had shoved a grenade down her throat. "I need to restart."

"I'm not giving you my newspaper," I said, frowning. "I gotta get caught up on what's been going on."

"All the catching up you need," Mabel said, "is on page three."

I flipped to the third page of the bulky paper. Line by line was covered in black ink, making it illegible. The only readable articles were colorful ads on the side promoting used cars and women's lingerie.

"I think that's an article about San Pablo," Mabel explained. "Weiss just said that 'clean up' got a little bit messy, or something. I found a news website saying that there was a big fire on some island in the Caribbean, but the article was taken down real quick."

"Huh," I pondered, "so there really are people out there besides us, cleaning up our tracks."

Mabel went on to explain how, after I fell unconscious and was treated by Johanna, the two girls successfully flew a functioning plane they found in the hangar to Florida. Weiss bought us tickets for the Atlantic Bullet Train and we were all checked into the hospital. Although the girls were in much better shape than Leon and me, the professor had said that he would only check us out as a group, citing that having some students in the hospital and some students thirty miles away on campus would be troublesome, since there was only one of him. Mabel seemed ready to fall asleep throughout most of the conversation. I had never seen the girl be anything close to tired before, and with her new haircut she even looked like a completely different person. Charlie, or what became of him, was never brought up in the conversation. After wrapping up her adventures while I was unconscious, she began to complain about the hospital. "I've been stuck here for three days now," she whined. "I don't know what else to do. Weiss brings me books to read but he always gets the wrong ones. I swear he can't tell the difference between the *Code of Nesilim* and *The Great Hymn of Aten*!"

"Yeah, what a dope," I commented, unaware if Mabel caught my sarcasm. She seemed pretty out of it, even when talking directly to me. After a moment of silence, I heard scribbling and found that the girl was writing once more, this time on a napkin.

"What are you writing now?"

"Trying to see if I can write down the *Gettysburg Address* from memory."

"Why?"

"Cuz I already wrote down Cicero's *Philippicae* and I want to take a little break from ancient antiquity."

"Why are you writing down historical transcripts?"

"Passes the time, I guess," Mabel said innocently, as if what she was doing was a common hobby. "Three days rooming with an unconscious guy really isn't that fun. Writing's kinda a force of habit. I used to have to write down all this different stuff back in real school."

"You had to memorize crap like this back at your old school?" I asked, baffled. "That sounds pretty harsh."

"No, no," Mabel objected, taking a second to yawn. "No teacher *forced* me to do it, I just got good at memorizing the stuff I read. Half the kids depended on me to write their essays for them, among other things. I ran a really big cheating operation at my school."

This new revelation hit me like a truck. "You," I pressed, "Mabel Pryce, who though that 'Uzi' was a Japanese rapper, ran a cheating operation."

"You bet," she said nonchalantly. "One of the biggest operations in Connecticut, I think. Got six or seven grand a month doing other kids' homework."

My jaw dropped. "*Seven grand*?"

"I was a fast worker," Mabel said, sounding happier, but still not smiling.

"So, did they find out? Is that why you were sent to Eastway?"

Mabel frowned, "I got sent . . . no, I got to come here for the same reasons as everyone else. Everything I had in my life was gone. It's still gone." She girl paused, gazing at the empty space across from her. "I remember being in a hospital like this, right after it happened. I had never felt alone before in my entire life. It felt horrible . . . everyone had these really fake smiles and when they talked to you, and they didn't sound like they meant what they were saying. Maybe they didn't know what to say. They just felt bad for me and wanted to be polite. Then Weiss came in and told me about Eastway. He told me all the things I had to do here, and I still went." The girl let out a wistful, exhausted sigh. "I . . . I was weak. I was scared of Weiss and the Academy, but I was even more afraid of being on my own. I needed something to stand behind . . . I wasn't strong enough to stand on my own."

"I know what you mean," I softly agreed with her, lounging back in my bed, trying to process Mabel's woeful words as they slid out of her mouth. There was a twinge in my gut as I remembered sitting in the police station alone, thinking the same way. The only difference was that she was scared of the ambiguity of her fate, and I was scared of the certainty of mine.

"Hey, hey, hey!" an enthusiastic voice rang in the hall. Professor Weiss stumbled in, haphazardly carrying two trays of breakfast food. "Good morning, children!" he chirped, delicately placing a tray on Mabel's bed. On the rim of the dish I saw two brownish-orange pills, which the girl looked at with disgust. "I'm sorry, Mabel," the professor added, noting her distress. "They didn't have any Adderall, so we're gonna settle for Dexedrine, okay?"

Mabel reluctantly took the pill.

"Good morning, Professor," I said, watching him place my breakfast on my bed. To my hungry eyes, it looked delicious: fresh scrambled eggs with steamed sausages on the side. "You seem in a chipper mood today."

"You did it!" Weiss beamed. "François Demiese is dead! You beat his freaking face in! I love you. I could just kiss you right now."

"Please don't," I muttered fearfully.

"I don't think I've ever seen you this happy after a mission, sir," Mabel noted, chewing on her breakfast.

"I knew this one was gonna be hard," Weiss elaborated. "After I lost contact with Charlie on the radio, I thought you guys were already done. When Johanna contacted me and told me that Demiese was dead and the base was abandoned . . . sheesh, I almost lost it right there. But as dramatic as this ordeal was for all of us, we must have a formal report," the professor snapped his fingers at Mabel. "Miss Pryce, now that we have a witness awake and present, I believe now would be a good time for you to stand up and recount the mission."

"Yes, sir," the girl moaned, rolling out of her bed and standing up. "Um, status of the mission is complete."

"Status of the target?"

"Deceased. Cause of death: blunt wounds sustained in an engagement against David Prince. Three hundred and twenty-one non-target hostiles were neutralized. Most of those casualties were inflicted by other soldiers." Sometimes I wondered how planners got that kind of information, but I was too afraid to ask.

"Mr. Prince, can you attest to this claim?" Weiss inquired.

"Yep, they're all super dead," I stated, more interested in my scrambled eggs than the report.

"We followed a variation of Yellow Plan AV-37 with some elements of Green Plan AA-01," Mabel continued.

"Status of the team?" the professor asked, maintaining his tone of voice.

"Leon Andre sustained multiple gunshot wounds and is in serious condition. Osmond Lee was struck with what is believed to be a land-based artillery strike and is deceased," the girl began, keeping an even tone.

"Wait, Ozzy's real name was Osmond?" I interrupted. Weiss immediately shot me a look, effectively shutting me up.

"Charles Parker is," Mabel hesitated for a second, "deceased. David Prince—"

"Hold on a second," Weiss raised his palm. "Please elaborate on Mr. Parker's death and postmortem treatment of the body."

"Sir . . ." Mabel seemed to begin to object to him, but she swallowed the lump in her throat and said, "Mr. Parker's death is attributed to a combination of blunt force trauma and blood loss. Postmortem, his body was moved on to the compound and hung on a flagpole for intimidation purposes. David Prince received complications with his broken ribs and was in serious condition, now recovering. Mabel Pryce is active, as is Johanna Wills."

"Very nice," the professor signaled for Mabel to go back into her bed.

"Sir, how was I in serious condition?" I asked. "I mean, Demiese just gave me broken ribs."

"Yes, but they happened to be the worst set of broken ribs ever," Weiss elucidated. "The broken bone penetrated your pulmonary artery, 'bout a centimeter away from your heart. Some of the doctors were afraid you might not survive the surgery."

"The surgery, right," I said, recalling my lucid experience in the surgery room, as well as the woman who was looking down at me. "Professor, do you know a woman named Ms. Scott?"

An unmistakable spark ignited in Weiss's eyes. The muscles on his face shifted, but not in an immediate look of disapproval or acceptance. It was as if he was unsure of how to react to the question. "Right, right . . . she said you woke up at one point, and you looked up at her. I guess it makes sense if you remember her . . ."

"Who is she?"

"She's uh . . ." Weiss stopped for the briefest second and looked to Mabel, perhaps fearful of who heard what he was about to say. "She's my boss. The headmaster of the Academy, if you want to put it that way. You see she's um, she's taken a certain interest in you. Quite concerned about your condition."

The idea of Weiss having a boss shocked me, and I wasn't entirely sure why. I knew that the organization we worked for must have had more people than Weiss, and there was a good chance Weiss had to answer to a chain of command, but I couldn't picture someone ordering the professor around. He seemed to be in total control of himself and those around him at all times. "There's one more thing I need to talk to you about concerning my report, Professor," Mabel added.

"Of course; what is it?" Weiss said, his face returning to its usual casual smirk. I wondered if he was relieved that the conversation pertaining to Ms. Scott had been dropped.

"There is evidence that the mission had been sabotaged," the planner explained. "Well, our coordinates were given away, resulting in the artillery strike that killed Ozzy. Then, once we tried to make our escape following Yellow Plan AA-51, bizarre music began to play which compromised our position, and we were shot down on the runway."

"Are you suggesting that *someone on the team* purposely sabotaged the mission?" the professor said, turning his head to the side in interest. "To what end?"

"To kill the rest of us, possibly," Mabel said. "Sir, you do have to realize that it's totally within the realm of feasibility that a student feels a strong animosity toward Eastway and you."

"Duly noted," Weiss said, unalarmed and amused by Mabel's sarcasm. "Johanna told me something very similar about these . . . complications. Perhaps we should talk," the professor glanced back toward me, "in private."

Is he suspicious of me? I was frightened of what Johanna might have told Weiss. "Sir, when can we get back to campus?" I asked, eager to get back in the conversation.

"Sooner rather than later," the professor informed. "Leon's making a remarkable recovery, as I knew he would. Takes a lot to take down a strong boy like that, and even more when he's got a future to aspire toward. After he starts walking, I'd say a day or two, tops."

"Professor," Mabel asked, "hate to be a bother, but did you get that book I asked for yesterday from my room?"

"Right!" Weiss darted into the hallway then ran back, now carrying an incredibly thick hardcover book, reminding me of one of those expensive family bibles. "*Plutarch's Lives*. Had to read this back in college. Ah, the good ol' days . . ."

"Some more light reading?" I asked, cocking my eyebrow.

"Uh-huh." Mabel smiled and nodded enthusiastically. Once again my sarcasm seemed to have gone undetected. "Maybe it'll be a critique of Plutarch's comparison between Cimon and Lucullus."

"I don't really know what you said, but okay," I said before turning back to Weiss. "Anything else I need to know about, sir?""

Weiss moved toward the door, but paused for a second, snapping his fingers. "Oh yeah! There's one small matter I want to take up with you about your assassination of the target."

"What about it?" I reflected back on the unpleasant memory of me in that tower.

"Well, I want you to listen to something," he said, producing some small, triangular device from his sleeve. "Your transceiver picked up some very interesting things concerning your altercation with the general." He glanced over at Mabel, "Miss Pryce, feel free to cover your ears."

Mabel ignored the command, instead lounging back in her bed. Seeing that the girl wouldn't obey, Weiss reluctantly switched on the device's playback feature, and an unmistakable audio crackling radiated throughout the otherwise dead-quiet room. The crackles began to range in frequency, at some points becoming hardly noticeable and at others deafening and unpleasant. "*No!*" a voice cried out in the midst of the noise. "*Stop! I surrender! Please—*" Before any more could be made out, the transmission went silent, switched off by Weiss.

"It sounds like Demiese was ready to submit," he elaborated. "That *was* our objective, if you can remember."

"Death or submission," I recalled. My gut felt tight.

"Killing a target after they capitulated is against Eastway policy," the professor explained with an authoritarian kind of ambivalence. "What do you have to say for yourself?"

Feeling threatened, I thought on my feet, smiling at Weiss. It was the sweet, insincere smile I would give to targets during jobs. "Naturally, the general couldn't be trusted, sir. After his murder of Santana, it's clear that he would use underhanded tactics to take me out, like pretending to surrender. I believe I played it safe."

"Are you sure you didn't keep hitting him because you were blinded by rage?" Weiss pressed.

"Yes," I lied through my pearly white teeth. "Also, to be fair, sir, Demiese spoke French. I'm pretty sure 'I surrender' is a pretty common part of their vocabulary."

The severity in the professor's face dissipated and he returned to a lazy grin. "Glad to see that injury can't stop your wit, kid. I guess your logic about Demiese's treachery makes sense. If you did keep a cool head there, that's commendable. Only the strong can do their duty without investing emotion," Weiss took a deep breath, observing the two exhausted agents in front of him. "I believe that's all I have to say for now. I'll be around, if anyone needs anything. You kids have fun, but not *too* much fun!"

Once he was gone, Mabel shot me a look. "Was that true? You really figured Demiese was gonna deceive you?"

I shrugged at first, but was quickly overwhelmed by guilt. I couldn't lie to Mabel. If anyone deserved the truth now, it was her. "I was angry," I confessed. "That's the reason why I kept hitting. It didn't feel like anger, though. My head felt clear, and it felt so easy to do it's just . . ." my voice trailed off.

"What?"

"I don't know how to describe how I felt," I said. It was the truth. "I only know that I never want to feel like that again."

"Wow," Mabel said feebly. An awkward pause followed, with the girl seemingly unsure about what to follow up with. "I have a confession to make," she blurted out. "It's what I wanted to tell you and Leon before you went out."

"Yeah?" I distantly recalled Mabel having a secret she wanted to spill during bloody action at San Pablo.

"You know how I told you guys I was track team captain at my old school?" she said. "The thing is, I lied. I was co-captain. I told you guys that so maybe you would like me more."

"What?" I said, shocked. "*That's* your big secret? Why did you feel the need to tell us that?"

Mabel clutched her sheets hard. She seemed to shrink in her own bed. "S-sorry . . . I just wanted to be straight with you guys. I don't usually lie about things . . . sorry, it was inappropriate to bring up."

Realizing that I had frightened the girl, I did my best to calm myself down. I was now concerned, though, about Mabel's new behavior. "What happened, Mabes? You're not usually this timid."

Mabel didn't answer, instead returning to her book.

After a difficult silence, I added, "Well, maybe I've gotta couple secrets too. There's something I need to tell you about what happened when I talked to Charlie for the last time." The false detail of the artillery strike in Ozzy's death bothered me too much to keep to myself, especially after Mabel mentioned it in her report to Weiss.

"Don't," Mabel said, not looking up from her book. She held the object with one hand and wrote on the pages, scribbling notes she would occasionally transfer to a loose leaf sheet of paper.

"Mabel, it's important," I insisted.

Mabel sighed, scribbled something quickly down in her book, and—to my astonishment—handed me her heavy, ancient book. "Look at the passage at the top right about the Battle of Eurymedon," Mabel said. "I need you to review my notes."

I stared at her, perplexed. "I don't see how—"

"Just do it," the girl stated, lowering her voice to a menacing level.

"Alright, alright," I relented, glancing down at the part of the page she had pointed out. It read:

The room is bugged. What do you have to say to me?

I nervously looked up at Mabel, instantly uneasy. "Seriously?"

"I know, right?" the girl said in a highly exaggerated voice. "Two hundred Persian ships were compromised. Pretty exciting battle, huh? Now, if you have anything to add, please write!" Reaching between our beds, she handed me her pencil. Carefully, I scribbled down,

Ozzy wasn't killed in an artillery strike. There was a bomb planted under his seat. Charlie told me he saw no coastal action that would indicate a strike. He also said he sent out our coordinates to the enemy, but I couldn't find out why.

By the time I had finished writing, my revelation took up the remainder of the column on the page. Carefully, I handed the hefty tome back to its owner. I watched Mabel's eyes dart over my words, her face gradually getting more and more disconcerted. She forcefully flipped to the next page and wrote down a new message, practically throwing the book back at me. Her new comment, written in less tidier cursive, read:

Charlie was the traitor?

I looked up at Mabel and shook my head. I could see the relief in her face. In the book, I calmly wrote,

The traitor is still at large. They were the one who put a bomb under Ozzy's seat and made our escape plane play music. I think they might be going after Weiss and the Academy.

Handing it back to Mabel, she took a second to read it. Then, giving me a quick nod, she flipped to the back of the book and jotted down a message with just as much urgency as she had with her previous one. Instead of handing the book back over, she merely displayed the last page for me to see. In big capital letters, it read:

WE CAN TALK ABOUT IT LATER. THIS CONVO NEVER HAPPENED.

"Thanks for the help, Davy," she added. The room got quiet again. Nurses came to take our dishes away, and I noticed that Mabel—typically a big eater—had hardly touched her meal. When a nurse asked about this, she replied that she wasn't in the mood.

Once they had left, I felt increasingly obligated to say something. "You and Charlie really were close, weren't you?"

At first, Mabel looked shocked at the audacity of the question. She took a long time to answer. "He was the only person on campus I could talk to, but in the end he probably made me feel the worst."

"What do you mean?"

"After Johanna told me he had died," Mabel continued, her voice on the verge of cracking. "It felt surreal. I didn't cry or scream, obviously, but I also really didn't feel that sad. I focused on the mission and prayed that you were alive. I had to keep planning—stick to my work so the rest of us could escape. I didn't even remember he was gone until I saw him in the courtyard."

"That's very strong of you," I said, remembering how down on herself she got earlier. "You're a part of the Academy, Mabel. That alone makes you incredible."

"'Only the strong can do their duty without investing emotion,'" Mabel muttered, her voice increasingly strained and empty. "I think that's what Weiss said. If that's what strong is, I want to be weak. I want to cry when someone I love is killed, and I want the grief to be terrible."

"Grief like that can be unbearable," I reminded her.

"No, *this* is unbearable!" For the first time in the conversation, Mabel raised her voice. She was now almost shouting. "It's unbearable to let him die and then move on like he never existed. Human life means more than that. If I can't feel anything for him anymore, what does that make me? What do I become?"

"The perfect student," I said, sighing, understanding what the girl was implying. "Exactly what Weiss wants you to be."

"I'm scared, Davy," Mabel said, her voice retracting back to nearly a whisper. Her eyes were turning bright red, just like they were in the courtyard. "I'm scared that I'm gonna become what Leon and Johanna are. Even if I leave Eastway, and even if I get whatever they promised me, I'm scared I'll never get back what they took. In a way, we're stuck at the Academy forever. We're all just prisoners here of our own device."

I couldn't help but now smile at Mabel's words. "*You can check out any time you like, but you can never leave.*"

"Did you just . . . sing?"

"'Hotel California,'" I told her, giving a light smile. "It's an old song I like . . . just seemed kinda appropriate. Listen," I remarked, "I know what you feel, Mabes. I feel it too. You don't have to be scared, cuz you won't become like that."

"How are you so certain?"

A bizarre burst of strength erupted through my body, between my broken bones and sore muscles. I sat up from my bed and stared at the girl directly in the face, demanding her full attention. Once our eyes locked, I began, "Because you're Mabel freaking Pryce. You decide who you are and what you care about, not Weiss. They can try to change you, sure. They can make you see things you wish you could unsee. They can threaten you and hurt you, but in the end, who you are is something you own." In retrospect, I only partially knew what words I was saying as they came out of my mouth. I knew it *felt* right, though, which must have counted for something.

A moment passed, and the oddest event of the morning occurred. Mabel Pryce smiled. It was a terrible smile compared to her usual standards, a far cry from the gleaming, toothy grins I was used to seeing from her. It was something, though. Some color seemed to return to her cheeks, and her exhausted eyes became just a little bit wider.

"Thanks, Davy," she said. "I needed that." Just as she finished, I heard a strange growling sound come from her bed. The girl placed a hand on her stomach and said, "Maybe . . . I should've eaten a little more when I had the chance."

Then the two of us laughed. In the mix of the continual anxiety and fear of the past week, laughing was probably the most unnatural sensation I could have felt, but at the same time it felt undeniably amazing. Just for a brief, passing moment, Mabel's face lit up, and everything felt like it was going to be alright.

"I think I'm gonna go downstairs for seconds," she stated, sitting up in her bed. "Wanna come?"

"Nah, too much of a hassle," I remarked, still chuckling. I sat back in my bed, watching Mabel disappear into the hallway. Now alone, I contemplated my conversations with Weiss and Mabel, quietly singing to myself, *"And in the master's chambers, they gathered for the feast. They stab it with their steely knives, but they just can't kill the beast . . ."*

CHAPTER SEVENTEEN

My room with Mabel was on the second floor of the hospital. On the first, along with a food court and a visitor center, there was an impressively sized workout room. Bikes, treadmills, and other equipment lined the outside of the gym, with yoga mats and much smaller machines. Judging by the shiny wooden floor and paneled ceiling, the area had been built or renovated recently. The medical staff provided me a free change of clothes and shoes as well as a card detailing protein shake recipes I could try later at the juice bar. As tempting as a chocolate-banana smoothie sounded, I desperately needed to teach my body what the whole moving-like-a-regular-human thing was like again. Out of all my injuries, the bullet wound on my foot was the most persistent. The pain had steadily dulled, but the only way I could walk was with a hard limp.

Entering after breakfast the day after my talk with Mabel, I chose a treadmill and began a steady walk. Not many people were there when I arrived, but they gradually sauntered in. Most were old people, who occupied the yoga mats, sometimes assisted by a personal trainer.

I tried my best to not walk like Igor with scoliosis, but it nevertheless proved to be a surprising struggle. I didn't know how much weight I could put on my injured foot or how far I could push myself. Lost in thought and more focused on walking than I had ever been, I didn't notice a familiar figure approach.

"Good morning," he said sweetly.

"Gah!" Surprised by the voice in my ear, I tripped over myself. The treadmill, set to walking speed, gently pushed my aching body to the floor.

"Whoops! Sorry 'bout that," Weiss exclaimed, coming to my aid. He wore the same suit as yesterday, sticking out next to those in exercise attire. Half the gym was looking at the two of us as I lay next to the treadmill. "He's alright, folks," Weiss assured, beaming. His smile faded and he crouched over me, concerned. "What hurts?" the professor asked, quietly.

"Ugh . . . everything," I answered, letting out a quiet moan of pain.

"Eh, you can walk it off, champ!" Weiss's smile returned and he extended his hand to pick me up. Once I was off the floor, he remarked, "You shouldn't go moving like that after your foot's been screwed up, y'know."

"Just wanted to see how far I could go," I said confidently. I wasn't a track star like Mabel, but I took great pride in my speed, as it was one of the few athletic things I could outclass Leon in. My body ached from the fall, but painkillers numbed any serious hurt.

"That's the spirit," the professor said, glancing over at one of the machines. "I haven't tried one of these things since college. I considered the exercise I got at Eastway was enough to last me a lifetime." The man patted his stomach, remarking, "Guess I'm paying for it now."

"Um, why are you here, sir?" I said, my voice keeping a slight edge due to the pain I had sustained.

"Oh yeah! Leon's condition has greatly improved over-night. He's been able to stand, and he's been eager to take a walk with you outside."

Why me? "I'll head right over," I promised. "So, when are we getting out of here?"

"As soon as the limousines arrive. I scheduled them to come at noon, but you know how late they can sometimes be."

"Do we really need limos?" I asked. "I mean, don't we have cars on campus?"

"Oh please. None of the cars can carry all of us, and like I'd trust recently hospitalized children behind the wheel," Weiss said, waving his hand dismissively. "Now, you go to Leon. I'm going to check on Miss Pryce."

We went our separate ways. I learned that Leon had been moved overnight from Critical Care to a regular room, down the hall from mine. I found him with Johanna by the door to the courtyard. Judging by the agitation on their faces, they were arguing about something. Before I could get within earshot, Johanna turned away and stormed off, seem-ingly talking to herself as she went past me. "What was that all about?" I asked.

"Girl's gone crazy. Don't worry about it," Leon said. His voice was gruff and weary, and it was clear by his distant gaze that he was under the influence of stronger medication than I was. Aside from bandages on his neck and chest, he looked to be in decent condition.

We stepped out into a spacious courtyard, with fresh green grass and flowers planted in the soil around us. Along the walkway thin trees stood with new, bright green leaves.

They were young saplings, needing wooden poles to stand up properly.

Leon produced a pack of cigarettes from his pocket. "Want a light?"

Wishing to be on good terms with the guy and under the influence of strong medication, I agreed, taking one and positioning it in my mouth. Leon then pulled out his lighter and ignited the tip. I inhaled, only to break into a coughing fit. The cigarette slipped out of my mouth and fell onto the walkway.

Leon laughed hard. So hard, in fact, that he needed a minute to catch his breath. He then crushed the smoldering cigarette and motioned for me to walk with him. "You're a funny kid, Dave," he said, proceeding to go to work with his own smoke. "One of these days, we should trade places. You can handle the soldiers, and I'll handle the old guy with the chair. A freaking piece of furniture, man!"

This time the laughing was mutual. "Thirteen soldiers though, man," I added. "It's pretty impressive that you got through that. You kill the lot of them?"

"Nah, I just did cover fire," Leon groggily reminisced. "Johanna sniped a few. The rest panicked and ran. I'm sure no one wanted to be left in that compound by that point. The guy who you scared off jumped me. Got a few lucky shots in, that's all . . ." Leon's voice drifted off, and he let out a quiet moan and clutched his chest.

"You okay?"

"Fine, fine," Leon said, waving his hand dismissively. We walked for a bit more until we were in the center of the courtyard, with no visible doors in sight. The spring sky was crisp and the morning rays felt very serene. "I want you to know I'm thankful," the large boy said, leaning by a tree and taking another puff. "You saved my life back there. We don't see eye to eye on too much, but I respect that you did what had to be done."

"Thanks," I said, trying to sound sincere, realizing what he was talking about.

"Wish I could've seen it," Leon said, grinning wistfully. "What did his face look like?"

"He looked the way you'd think he'd look," I said, trying to get away from the topic. "Why'd you bring me out here?"

Leon inhaled from his cigarette and then puffed out a fresh wisp of smoke. "For the fresh air. Maybe it'll give us clear heads."

"Something on your mind?"

"I know they're still out there," Leon proclaimed, his dazed eyes gazing up at the flawless blue sky. "The traitor, I mean. I know they're still alive, and they want to take us down."

"Is that what you were talking about with Johanna?" I asked. "You both seemed pretty on edge."

"We're all on edge. Don't kid yourself, Davy." Leon still wasn't looking at me; instead he was now crouched over, fixing one of his bandages. "Your room bugged too? Guys in suits standing by your door?"

"Yeah," I said, "maybe we work for the men in black."

"Probably just hired muscle," Leon said, not paying attention to my humor. "Weiss wants to make sure that everything ran smoothly while we're off campus. He's scared."

The professor is scared? The notion seemed almost laughable. "I've never seen him scared before in my entire life. You really think he's afraid of anything?"

"I know if I were in his shoes and two agents got murdered during a mission, and no one knows who really did it, I'd be terrified," Leon said, explaining his reasoning. "We don't know who started that music or who gave away our coordinates. Ambiguity's the scary thing, Davy."

"You've got any suspicion on who it is?"

"Eh," Leon shrugged, "I'm half sure it's you."

I laughed. I laughed hard. The only problem was that when I was done and I looked back at Leon, he was staring down at me with bleak eyes, with his weak smile all but gone. "Oh crap, you're serious."

"I'm looking at the possibilities, man," Leon said, absentmindedly twiddling his cigarette between his fingers. "There's four of us left. I know I didn't do it. Mabel's too innocent and naïve to plan something so bad. That or she's the greatest liar on the face of the earth. I have my reasons to doubt that Johanna's behind the deaths. That leaves you."

"I saved your life!"

"Yeah, you did," Leon stated objectively, still fiddling with his smoke. "Then again, if you walked out that door and saw me bleeding and didn't do nothing, that would've been a lot more suspicious. I already know you can kill. There's clearly a side of you you're not showing."

"Killing Demiese was probably one of the most unpleasant things I've ever done in my life. I never want to do anything like that ever again."

Leon looked straight at me, visibly stunned. "*What?* You feel *bad* you killed that genocidal general?"

"I had other options," I confessed. "I let my emotions get the better of me, and I regret it."

Leon let out a dry chuckle. "Unbelievable. Un-freaking-believable. Leave it to Davy Prince to mourn the loss of our dearly departed General Demiese. I'm sure if you killed freaking Osama bin Hitler, you'd be the first one in line at the funeral. Davy, can I ask you something real personal?"

"Yeah?"

"What are you doing here?"

"Pardon?"

"You're the top agent at Eastway, adored by Weiss. As the infiltrator, you get the missions written around you, you carry a gun most of the time, yet when you kill one of our targets in borderline *self-defense*, you sound like you just put down a puppy."

"Dunno, just felt wrong when I did it. It still feels wrong now."

"Guys like you don't belong at the Academy, I swear." Leon shook his head disapprovingly. "You and Pryce are weak. Too afraid to pull the trigger when it counts."

"I'm sorry, but since when were you so high and mighty?"

"Since my life depends on how well you do your job," Leon stated bluntly. All the warmth and relaxation was gone from his face, and now I was staring down cold eyes, just like Johanna's. "I have an opportunity here. It's the only thing I've got in life. It's my only chance to do something real, something worthwhile. I never had that before."

"Even before, when you were in real school?" I asked, cautiously prodding for answers. Talking to Leon about his past was very tricky.

"I was top of my class," Leon let his cigarette butt slip out of his fingers and proceeded to stamp it on the ground. "That wasn't good enough. Not to get out of my town. Maybe I was friends with some of the wrong people who didn't always make the right choices. It's enough for most schools to reject me, regardless of my grades." The large boy looked away, cringing at a painful memory. "Then I get a chance to come here. A chance to make everything right."

"I don't believe it," I said. Rebuking Leon was a dangerous endeavor, but I was caught up in the heat of the moment. "I *refuse* to believe that Eastway was your only chance."

"So friggin' naïve," Leon grunted quickly, under his breath. "You know *nothing* of what I had to go through to get here. You may have lost a lot, Davy, but I never had a lot of that stuff to begin with. If you want any proof that I'm not the traitor, figure that Eastway is the only sure thing I've got. If it's gone, I've got nothing to live for."

"Huh," I let out a slow sigh. I thought about what would happen if I had nothing. I remembered the agony I felt after Charlie's death, and I imagined if that pain never existed. I imagined if he had never existed in my life, and there was no pain or rage.

"What, you pity me?"

"More like envy," I scowled. "If all you care about is Eastway, you're lucky. You don't have to care about your friends, or what happens to them. You don't have to care about other people in general, do you? All you have to worry about is Eastway and yourself. You wanna trade places? Cuz that sounds like a pretty easy life."

Sudden fury ignited in Leon's eyes. He lashed out toward me, grabbing my exercise shirt and pulling me close. "My life ain't easy," he growled, "and I got the scars to prove it. Wanna trade places, bro? Fine. I'll take your broken ribs, and you can have my gunshots. Parents? I'd like to think of 'em being murdered instead of committing suicide."

I gasped, dumbfounded. "Your parents . . . they . . . ?"

Leon let go of me, coughing to the side. "We ain't having this conversation. Not now. Sorry, I lost my cool there."

"Sorry I ticked you off like that," I said. I meant it, too. "Um, you wanna start walking again? I'm enjoying the sunshine."

"Had enough of it in San Pablo," Leon remarked. He wasn't smiling, but his tone of voice lowered, and he looked to be calming down.

Just as we began to resume our walk, the glass door behind us slid open. Professor Weiss burst outside, his face beet red. "You two, get inside, now!" he demanded. It was one of those rare moments where he had raised his typically calm and collected tone, and the product sounded almost unnatural.

"Something wrong, Professor?"

"Johanna," Weiss called. "She's gone."

CHAPTER EIGHTEEN

A small crowd had gathered around Johanna's room when we arrived. There were doctors, suspicious men in black suits, and police officers talking amongst themselves. "When I came to check on her," Weiss explained as we walked, "I found her window had been smashed and her attending nurse unconscious. My help claims that they couldn't hear anything from outside the room, but I find that hard to believe, don't you?"

"By 'your help,' you mean those guys, right?" I asked, pointing to one of the finely dressed men.

"Part of a local company I've got some buddies in. Their price is steep, but they can handle social environments and blend in, if need be. When it comes to support, no other organization is firmer. Guess they're like human sports bras, if you know what I'm saying."

"Please never use that analogy again, sir," I muttered, quite disturbed. "Why exactly do you need so much . . . *support*?" Leon flashed me an exasperated look and I realize that I shouldn't have said that.

"Well, with an apparent saboteur and two dead students on my hands, one can't be too careful," Weiss said, in his usual voice. "Of course, Johanna's disappearance throws a wrench into any sense of stabilization I wanted for you children." The professor motioned for us to follow him through the growing crowd. We slipped our way inside the door at the center of all the commotion. Inside, a man in a loose black topcoat was hunched over a shattered window while three police officers to his right were talking to a nurse with a bandage over her eye. "Detective Penney," Weiss called out, waving to the man in the coat, "I'm back, with some friends. Any news?"

Penney shook his head, scowling. "We've got patrols going up and down the highway, and dogs in the woods," he explained. "We'll keep looking, though. Don't see how a girl can keep us looking too long."

Weiss shrugged absentmindedly. "These woods are dense. Slow progress is forgivable. I wouldn't worry about Johanna, though. Deep down, she's a very sweet girl and I know she'll come around."

I couldn't help but smile at Weiss's painfully incorrect comment. Behind me, I could hear Leon begin to crack up, drawing the attention of the adults. "Are you alright, son?" the detective asked, his eyes studying the large boy behind me.

"Yeah," Leon responded, subconsciously touching the dressings on his throat. "Just got in a little baseball accident."

"Baseball?" the detective asked, surprised. His reaction was weird. Rather than mere shock at the audacity of the comment, he almost seemed angry, too. He looked like an actor getting angry at another actor for messing up their lines. "I wasn't aware Eastway had a team."

"Actually, we were undefeated last season," Weiss said, cleanly covering Leon's mistake. "Haven't lost a single game."

That's because we haven't played any. "Sir," I interjected, attempting to put the conversation back on track, "you sound pretty certain that Johanna ran away."

"It's been verified by the nurse over there," Penney divulged. "You can talk to her if you like. Given how no heavy objects have been moved from the room, we believe it's pretty safe to assume that your student used her briefcase to break the window, once she realized that it was locked."

"Briefcase?" Weiss said, now frowning. "They allowed her to keep her briefcase? Do you know how much that thing weighs? They essentially gave a hospitalized girl a blunt weapon. Ridiculous! No wonder American hospitals are failing—this is ridiculous!"

"Professor," the detective intervened in a hushing voice, "the staff claims they allowed her to keep it because they found nothing threatening inside. There were just a few magazines and a laptop. It's not like she required medical attention or anything, either. She was more or less waiting for your other students to recover from . . . from . . ." Penney scratched his head, probably realizing he had no idea why the Academy's students were in the hospital.

"A freak baseball accident," Weiss reminded the befuddled officer. "Spring training can be very dangerous, you know." Penney's comment on Johanna's briefcase interested me. As I recalled, the only magazines in there were the ones you loaded into a rifle. *Where did her weapons go?*

"We'll be waiting for you outside, Detective," one of the officers said, walking out with the other two and the nurse.

"Right, I'll be just a second," Penney beamed at the two, only to scowl back at Leon and Weiss. "A *baseball accident*? Seriously, kid? This guy better not be your infiltrator, Auric."

"He's not, Tom," Weiss assured. "That's Davy over here."

He extended his hand. "A pleasure."

"Detective Penney knows about us?"

The two men laughed. "Thomas Penney, graduate of the Thirteenth Academy," Weiss informed me. "You honestly thought that Eastway could keep its secrets without a little help from the outside?"

"It's alright," Penney said. "I was just like that when I was his age. Always figured the less I knew about how things ran behind the scenes, the better."

The idea surprised me, however. I always thought that once I left the Academy, I would get as far away as possible. I couldn't imagine why people would want to stay and protect it.

We were politely escorted out of the room by the detective, who stated that he had to review evidence. Once in the hallway, the professor gave a small nod to one of the black-suited men before continuing down the hallway with his students. Reaching my hallway, the professor more or less shooed me away, wishing to talk to Leon alone. This was troubling, as I knew Weiss must have had some suspicion of me. "Collect your things," he ordered. "The limousine will be arriving within the hour, hopefully."

"Limousine?" I asked, unfamiliar with the singular form of that word.

"Of course!" Weiss informed, matter-of-factly, "With Johanna unaccounted for, there's only three of you. I think the rule is three students to a car, correct?"

"Oh, right," I responded, as the realization of just how small our team had become washed over me. Walking alone the remainder of the hall, I fathomed the new discomfort I felt and realized that I was indeed worried about Johanna. She was unsettling to say the least, and had a special way of angering those she didn't freak out, but she also was the smartest person remaining in our group, and (if she wasn't the traitor) might have had something of a grasp on the dangers ahead. I feared for her almost as much as I feared her.

I found Mabel in her bed, avidly reading something. "Another tome, I assume?"

"Quiet, I'm almost done," Mabel looked up from her work, frowning and annoyed. Although her eyes were wide, dark circles still surrounded them, and it was clear that her previous night's sleep wasn't very pleasant. Despite her poor appearance, I couldn't help but smile as I watched the girl do what she enjoyed, recovering from the events of the previous week. "And yes, it's another big book," she responded. "I know there's a lot of words and no pictures to follow along to, but some of us enjoy this heavy reading." Mabel was never particularly the sarcastic type, and any dry wit was usually a product of spending too much time with either Charlie or me.

"We're leaving soon," I said. "And Johanna's gone missing."

"They told me," Mabel said, sighing. "And then there were three. Why do you think she ran?"

"Either she's the traitor running away from Weiss or she's innocent and running away from the traitor. Either way, she's running, and they're not gonna find her."

"That'll make good car conversation," Mabel remarked strangely, before pointing to her book. "And so will this."

I smirked, remembering the written conversation we had the previous day. "Leon will be in the car with us. I'm not entirely sure he's a fan of ancient history."

Mabel pondered for a second, and then quietly spoke, "We can trust him. We can't keep what we know a secret just between us two. There's only three of us now, and we gotta stick together . . . you know, for the good of ancient history!"

• • •

"What?" Leon shouted, so loudly I was afraid our driver could hear. "You gotta be kidding me!"

"Calm down, bro," I said, clutching his bulging shoulders as he sprang up from his seat. Mabel and I had just informed him of what really occurred during Ozzy's death.

"So Chuck was innocent this entire time?" Leon grimaced, his face full of guilt.

"Well, no," I informed him. "Before he died, he told me he gave away our position to the LLA. The artillery strike just never came."

"Why?"

"I . . . I don't know," I confessed, frustrated that I didn't have all the answers. "But I'm pretty certain he's not the traitor, given how the next sabotage resulted in his death."

Leon's eyes narrowed, "How can I trust you, Prince?"

"Please, Leon," Mabel chimed in, struggling with her seatbelt to get closer to the conversation. "You know it would be borderline impossible for them to shoot us down at such a distance. A bomb on the plane under Ozzy's seat makes too much sense to be ignored."

Leon fell silent for a few moments. He stared down Mabel and then looked back to me. "If what you're saying is true then, Prince, the traitor was initially trying to kill you."

A chill ran down my spine. "What?"

"Ozzy sat where you usually sit for our plane rides," Leon explained in a methodical tone of voice. "Charlie moved you to the left of the cabin, perhaps believing there would be an artillery strike or something. Had you sat there, you wouldn't have had a chance of surviving."

My thoughts raced, trying to keep up with Leon's logic. It never struck me how smart Leon was. Under his bulging muscles and rash attitude, there was a competent mind. "That could have just been a coincidence," I countered, partially out of fear. "Maybe the bomb could have been stowed under any seat, and it didn't matter which."

"Why bother putting it under a seat at all, then? If you wanna crash a plane and leave no survivors, why not put a bomb in the engine or on one of the wings? Why not get a bomb with a bigger charge on it to eviscerate us?"

"Well, obviously the bomber wanted the plane to have survivors," Mabel remarked. "I mean, assuming they were on the plane as well."

"This is all ridiculous," Leon commented, scowling. He turned once again to glare at me. "Why didn't you tell me this earlier? Like, back on San Pablo?"

"Oh, sorry," I reproached, "I think we were a bit too busy fighting an army bent on killing us!"

"How about we get some rest?" Mabel offered. "We've still got a little bit of a drive ahead of us. Leon, you know getting angry isn't good for your condition. Stop yelling or you'll mess up those bandages again."

"Yes, Mother," the boy chided, gently shutting his eyes and leaning toward the window.

Mabel leaned close to me and whispered, "Something weird happened to me last night in bed."

The mere phrasing of the sentence turned my cheeks red. "Um, what?"

"When I fell asleep, my book was under my pillow," she explained softly. "I woke up in the middle of the night and realized that it was gone. I wanted to go out and look for it, but there were men outside our room."

"Men in black suits," I added. "They were hired by Weiss to watch over us."

"I figured. So I went back to sleep, and when I woke up this morning, it was back under my pillow, as if it had never left."

"Maybe the tooth fairy took it," Leon interjected. It initially shocked me that he could hear Mabel's whisper, for they were on opposing sides of the car.

"This doesn't concern you," Mabel shot at Leon. She turned back to me, "It was . . . just a weird occurrence."

Someone could have read our conversation in the book, I realized. "Are you sure you weren't dreaming, Mabes? Maybe you just weren't in the right state of mind."

"Maybe . . ." the girl accepted, still with a bewildered look on her face. I felt very uncomfortable with the idea of Weiss or Johanna finding out what we had written.

"Let's, um, change the subject," I suggested, still wishing to talk to Mabel for just a little bit longer.

"Yeah," Mabel said, letting out a big yawn. "I could hardly sleep last night to begin with. You snore really loudly, y'know."

"Gee, thanks," I grumbled.

"Like, *really* loudly. Couldn't get back to sleep till—"

"Thank you, Mabel!" I shouted, silencing her. I was very insecure about my sleeping habits. Charlie once told me that he could hear me through the walls and claimed that the easiest way for him to pull an all-nighter for him was just to allow me to fall asleep before he did, and he would be kept awake by my incessant "nighttime snoring."

After Mabel's remarks, the limousine became truly silent. I believe Leon went to sleep, although it was difficult to tell. Mabel quickly fell unconscious as well, as evidenced by her mouth hanging open and the destruction of her posture, the latter of which led to her head resting on my shoulder. Her weight pressing against me was uncomfortable and probably prevented me from getting any shut-eye. It was also, though, strangely gratifying to be so close to Mabel. For a moment, enraptured by the quiet, I felt oddly at peace with myself and the world around me. "Everything's gonna work out in the end," I whispered. Whether I was talking to myself or a latent Mabel, or whether I knew I was lying, I couldn't remember. "I think we're gonna be okay . . ."

CHAPTER NINETEEN

My hand felt strangely clammy as I clutched on to my gun. This wasn't like me. Even in the disgusting, sticky heat of San Pablo, my palms were one of the last parts of me to remain dry. The only reason my hands would get anything close to clammy is if I were nervous, and I wasn't nervous. I was alone in the school shooting range, an indoor, concrete palace of learning how to kill.

I tried my best to focus, raised the gun, and fired three successive shots at a poster shaped like a body on the far side of the room. The poster didn't sway or even budge, like it usually did when bullets hit it. Considering it to be a fluke, I fired another round of ammunition, this time holding the gun with both hands. Once again, I couldn't see any movement on the poster. Baffled, I pressed a green button on the wall and the poster slowly sailed toward me. My fears had been confirmed: the outline of the human torso was free of bullet holes. In fact, the poster as a whole seemed unscathed. I had missed.

But I never miss, I realized. The first and last time I didn't hit the poster was on my second day of school, when I didn't even know how to fire the gun properly. My hands ran over the print, making sure I wasn't mistaken. I feverishly checked my gun, making sure everything was still in order. Angrily, I fired at the hanging target, releasing the remaining bullets in my cartridge. Even at point-blank range, they still weren't straight. The closest thing to a good shot was a bullet hole that grazed the target's shoulder.

Putting my pistol away, I tore down the poster in anger, throwing it on the ground. Something was messing with my shooting; a feeling I could not identify, something that made me lose my concentration when I pull the trigger. I was ready to set up another target, perhaps much larger, but the loudspeaker in the corner of the room blared. *"Attention,"* the voice said, belonging to Professor Weiss. *"David Prince, please report to the office."*

That can't be good. Cautiously, I put my gun away and walked outside. The weather had gradually worsened throughout the day and now, in the mid-afternoon, a foreboding gray overcast hung above me, bringing the promise of wet, miserable weather. While we were away, there must have been a brutal cold snap, as all the green that had begun to blossom in the trees had retreated, and the trees looked eerily twisted and gray. A light mist floated over Lake Pavus, which was nothing more than a dark sinkhole with no light to shine on it. As I walked, and the Central Building came into view, a chilly breeze swept under my legs. I looked up at the windows on the second floor, imagining the professor up there, watching me as I walked. In fact, since arriving back at Eastway, I couldn't shake the feeling that I was being watched. As usual, I kept a knife hidden in my sleeve for emergencies, and with every passing hour I felt more and more inclined to brandish it. If someone was stalking me, I wanted them to at least know I was armed.

The door of the Central Building opened with an ominous creak. The entire first floor was completely dark, adding to my uneasiness. Ascending the stairs, I could hear Weiss's voice. He was talking to someone, but I couldn't tell who. Opening his office door, I found him on the phone, shifting left to right in his swivel chair.

"The senator is still our friend, m'lady. With the right persuasion, he'll get over his brother's incredibly suspicious death, I guarantee you." He paused for a second, listening to the speaker on the phone. "Yes, I am aware of this new boy you speak of. How did his family die again? Train crash? Ugh, messy. Hope he isn't too traumatized. With Ozzy gone and Johanna missing, we'll need all the field agents we can get. Huh, what?" Weiss looked up, gave me a polite smile, and motioned for me to sit down. Speaking back into the phone, he said, "Yes, actually he's right here. Oh, I'll tell him you said that. I must hang up, m'lady. Yes, the pleasure's all mine." Weiss turned off his phone and gently placed it back in its holder. We stared at each other for a few awkward seconds before I realized he was expecting me to speak.

"'M'lady,' huh?" I commented. "Sounds pretty fancy. Who were you talking to?"

"Ms. Scott," the professor answered. "She's been calling frequently lately, no doubt worried about the situation that's unfolding here."

"Does she have a right to be worried?"

"The Academy's been through worse," the professor said, his voice as colorless as the sky outside. "She has no right to fear the deaths of two students. I'm pretty sure Johanna's little disappearing act has got her more riled up than anything."

"I can understand that. So . . . why am I down here again?"

"Right!" Weiss beamed, realizing my purpose. "Speaking of your dead friends, I need you to go clean out Ozzy's room for me."

"What?" I said, my mouth hanging open. "Do we have to do this today? Do *I* have to do it?"

Weiss shrugged innocently. "What's the problem? Ozzy was a neat boy. Neater than Charlie was, at least. I cleaned up his room this morning before I visited you at the hospital. The reading material I found under his bed wasn't as . . . desirable as what Mabel reads. In fact, why couldn't have Mabel been bumped off instead of Mr. Parker? It'd be so much less of a hassle to clean out her quarters."

As usual, I had to swallow my complete disgust for the words that came out of the professor's mouth. "Just seems a little too . . . morbid for me, sir. Can I just have a few days to settle back on campus?"

"I already forced Leon to write a letter to Charlie's Aunt Torta," Weiss reasoned. "It's only fair you do your part today."

"He wrote her a letter? What kind?" Tragic thoughts entered my mind. I imagined Charlie's aunt, his only family, preparing for her summer with him, reading about his death.

"It was a letter where he was pretending to be Charlie, talking about how enthusiastic he was for the summer," the professor debriefed nonchalantly. "What other kind of letter is there?"

"You're kidding," I said, trying to restrain my fury in the face of Weiss's cold expression. "She's gotta find out what happened to her nephew."

"Oh, she will," the professor waved his hand dismissively. "We'll tell her later, when things settle down. The last thing we need right now is a wealthy, distraught family member ordering an investigation."

"It sounds like this Scott lady has a lot of power," I pressed. "I don't think legal investigations would weigh you guys down too much."

"Which reminds me," Weiss said, subtly changing the subject with the snap of his fingers. "Ms. Scott sends you her regards. She's very relieved that you made a recovery and looks forward to your future activities."

"How kind of her," I responded flatly. I wasn't in the mood to be complimented, especially by Weiss's boss.

"Don't brush her off like that," the professor scolded, leaning on his desk. "She's taken special interest in you, child. More so than any other student who's ever attended this Academy."

This comment struck me. I was used to Weiss remarking on my "potential" and "untouched capabilities." I've rarely ever been called extraordinary by Academy standards, and when I was, it usually had something to do with dumb luck. "That's a very . . . generous thing to say," I said, now shocked. "Why so much interest?"

"Well, I guess you're going to have to find out eventually," Weiss said, probably talking to himself. "Allow me to answer your question by telling you a funny little story."

"What?"

"A while back," Weiss began, "Eastway had an exceptionally strong agent. This was in the early age of the Academy, back when nobody really knew what they were doing. Students dropped dead like flies, faculty had to be fired and quickly silenced, but through it all, he survived. There was a very small margin of error with him and thus, a huge profit margin for the Academy. After he left, Eastway more or less existed to find his successor. Someone who could be just as decisive, backed up by a more professional, elite team. They were—and still are—looking for someone with his . . . qualities."

"What do you mean by 'qualities'?" I asked, feeling further drawn into the conversation.

"He was like a human machine, I'll tell you," Weiss said. He tilted his head forward, keeping his eyes firmly planted on me. "He never objected to any order, no matter the danger. He strategized, improvised, and deceived perfectly. Every shot he fired hit its mark."

"This guy doesn't sound human," I remarked, trying to decide whether to believe in Weiss's tale.

"The Academy has been trying to replicate him for quite some time," Weiss continued, ignoring my comment.

"So she thinks I could be the new . . . super-agent guy?" I said, skeptical. "What makes me so special?"

"My higher-ups have used many methods over the years to create a new perfect assassin. Most centered around the Academy, and some were a bit . . . unorthodox," Weiss's icy blue eyes gave me a sad look, almost out of pity. "They've been watching you for a very long time, kid."

I knew what he was suggesting. A chill ran down my spine. "How long?"

"I don't think you really want to know," the professor muttered. Now he looked genuinely upset. "Just know that you mean a lot to her. Right now, you're everything the Academy stands for. You're the closest thing we've gotten to *him* in a very long time."

Disgusted and somewhat complimented that Weiss was comparing me to a fearless psychopath, I decided to delve deeper, recalling conversations I had earlier that day. "Sir, if there is a traitor on campus . . . would I be a good target?"

"Don't talk like that, Davy," Weiss scolded. His eyes began to wander, and it struck me that the cool, calm, and collected professor himself was growing uncomfortable with the conversation. "To put it in blunt terms, yes. If this traitor was well-informed enough. There are hardly any students here that know about Ms. Scott's preferences, probably only you and . . . " The professor's voice trailed off.

"Who else? What other student?"

Professor Weiss studied me very carefully. He sat forward in his chair, his jaw clenched, and his eyes narrow. I had never seen him so tense in my entire life. "Johanna. If you must know, it was Johanna. She's the only other person who could possibly know."

"Sir, I'm not comfortable with her being missing and knowing that," I stated firmly, keeping my cool as the revelations piled on top of me. "I don't want to be the next victim."

"I understand," the professor whispered in a hollow voice. He sat back in his chair like a president about to make the biggest decision of his term. "Never in the history of Eastway has one student intentionally harmed another. I understand that many may get frustrated, but almost all come to realize that this is an opportunity for them. An opportunity that they were entitled to by their hard work and intelligence. Johanna . . . Johanna was always a special case."

"She thinks you guys killed her parents," I responded, softly. "Is that true?"

"No." Weiss reclined in his chair, wincing at a painful memory. "The fire that killed her family was not the Academy's doing. Being the clever girl she was, she escaped very quickly. Once she found out her parents were still inside, she ran back. When they found her, she was perfectly calm, half her body scorched, trying to drag her parents' corpses out."

"Oh my gosh . . ."

"She didn't leave willingly, they said. Firefighters had to incapacitate her before she let go of the bodies. I remember when I first saw her in the hospital . . . half her face was bandaged up, and she could only see me through one eye. I'll never forget it," Weiss was speaking quietly now. The air and sound seemed to have been sucked out of the room. "I saw pure evil. I hate to use such simple words, but I don't know how else to describe it. I've been to war zones before, Prince. I've seen entire villages wiped out by plagues and famines. What I saw in that girl's eye made me feel the same way. Never thought she'd benefit Eastway, only bring us pain and deception."

"You sound like you've made up your mind on who the traitor is."

"I always had my suspicions," the professor asserted. "Mabel has a lot of faith in you. She told me that she had no doubts that you are not the traitor. I see no reason to distrust her word."

"Sir . . ." I began, unsure of what to say. Weiss was very forward in his judgment of Johanna, but any suspicion not placed on the sniper would be pinned on me instead.

Just then, a small red light on the professor's desk began blinking.

"What's that?" I asked.

"It alerts me when someone is at the gates."

"You don't think that's . . . ?"

"We can't take any chances." Weiss seemed to shuffle through his desk before pulling something out. "Take care of it." What he held in his hand was six-cylinder revolver, with a shiny barrel and an ivory handle.

"Sir! You don't expect me to . . . ?"

"Good grief, use your words, kid," Weiss growled, leaning over to hand me the gun.

"You want me to kill Johanna?"

"If it is her," he said, "I expect you to do what's necessary. Can I count on you?"

I begrudgingly took the pistol. The ivory felt very cool to my touch. Making my way to the door, I turned around, remembering one question that was bothering me. "That guy you were talking about, what was his name?"

The professor bit down on his lip as though he were debating telling me. "Angelo King."

"*King?*" I repeated to myself, unsure of what to make of it. "Is he dead?"

"Very. Now," Weiss looked back down on his desk and began to shuffle papers. "Now, I trust you can deal with our unexpected visitor."

The gates of the Academy are black and automatically open with sensors. These sensors are rarely on, as Eastway isn't exactly too friendly to outsiders. The black iron gate that protects us wraps around only half the campus, and the other half is protected only by the thick New York woodland. It was difficult to navigate, but if one truly wanted to get in, all they had to do was make their way through the forest and around the gate. Johanna was fully capable of this, which is why it was very strange that she would just be standing by the entrance. I suspected it was a trap, but it was too late to walk back now.

Halfway down the trail from the Central Building to the parking lot, the gates came into view. There indeed was a figure standing behind the metal bars, but from the first glimpse I could tell that it wasn't Johanna. This person was shorter and wore a beige dress. I'm pretty sure that Johanna would rather die a dozen times than wear a dress. The girl had her hands on the gate and hadn't seemed to notice me. "Hey!" I called, picking up my pace.

The girl released her hands from the gate, startled. She began to back up, but I called for her to wait, now at the gate myself. She was quite frightened, but she squinted her eyes and got a good look at me between the bars. "Wait a sec . . . I remember you."

Do I know this girl? I went through all the faces I could recall from town. One in particular stood out. She was a fresh face; someone new I had only recently encountered. "You're Ozzy's friend!" I realized, making the connection in my brain. *What was her name?* I knew it was something old-sounding, beginning with a vowel. "I . . . Edith?"

"*Ida*," she said, now looking more insulted than frightened. "We talked a week ago in town."

"How you doin'?" I chirped. I didn't why, but I felt a lot better looking at her. Maybe it was because she wasn't Johanna, and I wouldn't have to use the gun in my pants. Maybe it was that she reminded me of a happier time, which now felt like centuries ago. "What are you doing all the way out here?"

"None of your business," she said, anguished. I realized that my chipper tone had been inappropriate.

My heart sank. I knew why she was here. "Are you looking for Ozzy?"

She said nothing.

"If you're looking for Oz," I said, trying to think of an adequate lie. "He—"

"Save it. I know."

"Know what?" I said. "You really shouldn't be out around here."

"I know he's dead," she said.

• • •

As it turned out, Ida really did walk all the way out from town. Traversing the miles-long secluded road made little sense to me, but I was too busy trying to figure out other things to notice. I asked her if she wanted me to drive her back. She didn't say anything, but followed me to the parking lot, which was as good a confirmation as anything.

When I sat in the car seat, I realized that I was sitting on my gun, still tucked away in my pants. I certainly didn't want to pull it out in front of Ida, but the gun was an old revolver and didn't have a safety. Every single bump in the road had me worried. The gun misfiring wouldn't kill me, but if it were to hit the place I thought it would, I would wish I were dead. All the while, I was trying to get information from Ida. "How did you—"

"Me and him used to talk a lot," she said, slouching in the passenger's seat. She was completely composed, sounding more bitter than upset. "I couldn't meet him in person all the time, of course, but we talked online, playing games."

"I could see that," I said, giving her positive feedback in the hopes that she would continue talking. Ozzy was a big gamer, and so was Charlie. I liked to think that I was decent. I could beat Leon, who hardly bothered with the "childish nonsense," but when I went against the other two boys I would usually panic and resort to mashing buttons.

"He told me you guys were going away for something, but he wouldn't elaborate," Ida explained. "Said he'd be back in a few days, and that there was nothing to worry about."

"You were worried?"

"No, but he kept assuring me anyway for some reason. Guess I now know why."

Did everyone know how dangerous this mission was except me? Ida's statement made me ponder just how far out of the loop I was. I needed to find out how much she truly knew about the Academy. "What do you think happened to him?"

Ida probably figured what I was trying to know, because she said, "I'm not quite sure what you guys do over there, but I know you're not a school. He would always get so nervous when he talked about what went on there. What he did tell me, though, was kind of weird."

"Weird how?"

"He told me that he went to see one of his instructors one day, and he found him pacing around in his office on the phone, talking to his wife."

Weiss has a spouse? "Are you sure it was his wife?"

"Ozzy wasn't quite sure," Ida said. She then paused, clearly struggling to remember parts of the story. "He thought it was his wife. Kept calling her by her first name, 'Henrietta,' so that's the conclusion he came to, I guess. When he stepped in, the instructor got really angry and started screaming at him. After he said this, he got really quiet. Then, a couple weeks later . . ." Her voice weakened and trailed off.

"Yeah?"

"We were supposed to go on a quest together in a game. He didn't show up online though. Then I saw that his account got terminated. I knew something was wrong. He wouldn't just terminate his game without telling me! That's the only way we get to talk to each other."

"So, you think he's dead?"

"I know it seems like a stretch," Ida admitted, her words becoming more jumbled as she defended her shaky conclusion, "but if Ozzy had to go away, he'd tell me. Even if he never wanted to see me again, he'd *tell* me. He's not the kind of person to just disappear. And . . . and the look on your face when I said that to you, and you haven't denied it, have you? So it's true, right?" I could hear a note of reluctance under the superficial pleas of her voice. She *wanted* to be proven wrong, I knew. She *wanted* to think he was still alive.

"Ozzy liked you a lot," I said, focusing on the road ahead. We were almost to town. "I can see why." Words were stuck in my throat. I wanted to lie. I wanted to lie *really* bad, but couldn't. I couldn't tell the truth, either. That would ruin the girl and possibly put her life in danger. "I'm sorry, I can't say anymore."

"Ugh," Ida sighed. Her reaction made me think that she knew I was going to say that.

"I'm sorry," I said. Town was in sight. The buildings were getting larger. In a few seconds, I would never have to see Ida again. I hated to think like this, but it was probably for the best, for both of us. "If you want, I can—"

Before I could finish, there was an explosive *pop* and I heard Ida scream. The car shook wildly and swerved, doing a one-eighty on the road. While I tried to regain control of the vehicle, what had happened was soon evident. "What's going on?" she asked, panicked.

"Someone just blew our tire out," I explained, frantically looking around at the surrounding wood.

"They blew it out? With what?"

My body seemed to figure it out faster than my head did. I grabbed Ida and pushed her down, before sliding down myself, under the wheel. A second later, there was a crashing sound. A small hole was created in the window, surrounded by a web of cracked glass. "A bullet," I replied, not sure how to break the news. "Someone's trying to snipe us."

Ida turned ghost white. As I clutched her hand, I realized that she was shaking. Figuring that it was now appropriate, I pulled out Weiss's revolver. With my other hand, I cautiously clicked open my door.

"I'm going," I whispered. "I know who's out there. They're after me, not you. The second you hear another one of those cracking sounds, I want you to run to town. Don't stay on the road and don't stop until you see other people. Do you hear me?"

"B-but if you go out there . . ." Ida stuttered.

"I'll be fine. I know what I'm doing," I assured her. It was a lie, but it didn't matter. I'd rather have the sniper go after me than her.

With a twinge of reluctance, Ida nodded. I pressed my weight against the door and made my way out, slamming it hard behind me. My brain throbbed with fear and adrenaline as I scanned the nearby brush. I cocked my gun, but I didn't raise it. If the sniper perceived a threat, they'd be more eager to fire.

To strike the tire where it did, I figured, the sniper couldn't have been shooting from the trees. The angle would have been too difficult, especially with a moving target. I couldn't figure out which way the bullet had struck my window, but it seemed entirely plausible that she was lying on the ground. I treaded lightly, further into the forest, now focusing more on the ground. "You want me?" I shouted, mustering my confidence. "Here I am."

I looked for movement—any movement—on the forest floor. My opportunity came when a branch snapped to my right. I turned to see an upright figure, wrapped in the forest's shadows, pointing a sniper rifle at me. The gun must have been longer than her arm, and reached more than halfway between us. I couldn't see all her features, but I could hear her voice. A perfectly calm, cold voice carrying some small bit of decency. It was like a killer cordially acknowledging their next victim.

"Prince."

"Johanna," I replied.

CHAPTER TWENTY

We were both silent. In the distance, I could hear a small bird call out, accompanied by the gentle shaking of trees.

Johanna's twisted, deformed face twitched. She was smiling. She was happy. She began giggling. I felt a chill run down my spine, the likes of which lingered in my back and in the soles of my feet. This wasn't her cold, mocking laugh I had heard before. She was giggling like a schoolgirl half her age, causing the barrel of her rifle to shake. It was as if it was nodding in my face.

"What's so funny?"

"Hate to be anticlimactic," the sniper stated, trying to restrain her chortles, "but this gun isn't loaded. I'm outta ammo."

"What?"

"You can just fire away," Johanna reiterated. Something was very off in her voice. Her typical unemotional demeanor was completely gone, just as eerily unnatural as her laugh. "I'm defenseless."

Around this time *my* gun started shaking, but obviously not for the same reasons as Johanna's. Something was very wrong—that much was evident. I couldn't even begin to decipher Johanna's batty behavior as she pointed an apparently empty gun at my face.

"What's with the hesitation?" Johanna said, cocking her head. "Weiss wants you to kill me, right? Go ahead, your opponent's unarmed." To prove her point, she dropped her gun. It fell to the forest floor with a soft rattle.

"If you're goading me to kill you, why did you attack me in the first place?" I asked. The tension I felt within was evident in my voice; I was speaking much higher than usual.

Johann's face tensed, for some reason frustrated by my questioning. "I tried to kill you, Prince! That second shot was supposed to go through your head. Go on. Do what the professor wants and take down the traitor."

"Back on the beach, you told me that you were not the traitor," I said, trying to get a grasp on the situation. "I believed you back then. I don't believe you now, Johanna. I'm turning you over to Weiss."

Once again, Johanna began laughing. "And what do you think he's gonna do to me? Even after you've beaten a man to death *with his own cane*, you're still afraid of pulling that trigger, aren't you? Always willing to let someone else take the shot."

"Quiet," I interjected. Even though she was acting unusual, she still managed to get under my skin. "Unless you want me to take you back to the Academy, how about you try to be honest for once? Or do you really want to die?"

"It isn't a matter of what I *want*," Johanna took a step forward. I took a step back. "It's a matter of what *will* happen. The question is, who's gonna be the one to drag me down?"

Then, she leapt at me, swiping at my throat and reaching for my gun. Her sudden force caused me to topple backward.

On the forest floor, I desperately tried to keep my hands on the gun, while Johanna alternated between hitting my face and chest and pulling for the weapon. In the midst of the struggle, the gun misfired, narrowly missing Johanna's head.

Taking a big risk, I took one hand away from the grip and began hitting Johanna back. Blindly striking at her, I got a lucky shot in her jaw, causing her to temporarily ease up on her attacks to focus on getting my fist away. I took advantage, pushing her off and steadying my gun. Jumping toward her, I gave a swift kick to her side to keep her off balance before closing in. The tip of Weiss's revolver pressed against her chin, and Johanna froze. The fight was over. "Stupid Prince," she said, with a hint of resignation in her voice. "You're not supposed to hit girls."

"Well, you're not supposed to be off-the-wall crazy!" I countered. My voice was high and tense. Once again, I had had a close brush with death, this time coming from a familiar face, and the situation was only now sinking in. "We're gonna go to town, you and I. We're gonna find some place to sit down, and you're gonna tell me the truth for once. You need to tell me what's going on here. Why did you run away?"

Johanna looked at me, then down at my hand which was holding the gun, then out in the distance, past me. "You really want to know? Whatever. Just consider that I don't think you're gonna like everything you're gonna hear."

Keeping her at gunpoint, I helped her put away her rifle in the briefcase, and the two of us made our way back to the car. It was abandoned now, no doubt because Ida had heard the gunshot. I hoped she had made it to town okay. After a quick tire change, we drove the small distance to town before Johanna pointed out where we could talk: a small café on the edge of town.

I was in no sense of the word a coffee drinker, but now wasn't the right time to object. Johanna, smug senior turned self-destructive assailant, was finally coming clean. I followed her in, hastily putting away my weapon. A small bell chimed when Johanna opened the door. Just as she promised, the place was almost empty, save for a rather fashionable pair of men sipping coffee in a nearby booth. Johanna walked up to the barista and ordered a black coffee. She turned to me and asked me what I wanted.

"A mocha-chocolate frappe with two shots of vanilla, please," I said. Johanna shot me a funny look. "What?" I said defensively.

The sniper merely rolled her eyes and we waited in silence for our drinks to arrive. I took a sip of mine as I followed Johanna to a booth. After a few moments of silence, I decided to initiate the conversation with some small talk. "I think there's only one shot of vanilla in mine," I growled. "This stinks. Mocha's gonna be too strong now, y'know?"

"Shut up, you entitled brat," Johanna spat, taking a sip of her coffee and sitting down as she placed her much-treasured briefcase under the table. "Why are you drinking that filth? How can you even live with yourself?"

"Um, sorry," I said, burying my face in my drink. I found it very hard to make contact with Johanna's angry, exhausted eyes. "So . . . moving on from my drink preferences, um, what's up?"

"*What's up?*" the possible traitor commented, taking a deep sip of her drink. "I run away and try to blow your brains out in the forest and all you have for me is 'what's up?'"

"Well, sorry!" I muttered. If I wasn't overwhelmed with the audacity of the situation and desperate for info, I'd probably laugh at the fact that I was apologizing to my would-be killer for being too awkward. "Can you, uh, tell me what happened before San Pablo?"

"It's quite simple," Johanna informed me, the tension in her voice decreasing somewhat. "I had a plan. Weiss foiled it. Now I have no plan, and I'm running and hiding like a head with its chicken cut off!"

"Don't you mean—"

"I know what I mean!"

There was another moment of silence, followed by my realization that she was done speaking. "That's it? Can you . . . go into any details? What was your plan?"

"Ugh, so persistent," Johanna took another sip of her bitter drink. "My plan was little more than a fetus, growing in the fertile womb of my mind, when it was aborted by Weiss. Flushed out!"

"Um, how about something besides an uncomfortable metaphor . . . please?" I frantically looked around the café, hoping that Johanna's shouting wasn't attracting too much attention.

"It was more like an idea. A manifesto! An adherence to my creed. I kill Weiss before I graduate. Slay the slayer of my family. Remove the bars of the gilded cage that binds us. I thought that that would solve all my problems and end the guilt that I have embedded in my heart. I convinced Leon to join, saying it would be for the good of the Academy. I also presented the idea to Charlie. I could kill Weiss by myself, but if I wanted to escape afterward I would need people in the loop to cover for me."

"Why not go it alone? Why risk more people knowing?"

The sniper reached across the table and covered my mouth with her hand. "Don't interrupt me!" she snapped, reluctantly removing her arm as I started to struggle. "How was I supposed to know that anyone would trust Weiss over me?"

"Of course," I said tentatively, waiting to be shut up again. The sound of the sniper's gunshots in the forest were still fresh in my ears. "That's silly, someone wouldn't trust you."

"So I got those two boys on board, but there were complications almost immediately. You see, Charlie didn't fully trust the plan, thinking it was too dangerous. Took forever to get him on board, and even then I guess it was all a ruse. He went to Weiss and told him what was going on. Weiss made him his informant, and when the time came, Charlie foiled my scheme by crashing the plane."

"Charlie told me your scheme was to escape after we were done with the mission."

"Well, Charlie was a lying, double-crossing little dirtbag, so I'm not surprised he fed you false information," she continued, angrily. "Probably wanted to keep as many people out of the loop as possible, maybe to make things easier to manage."

I didn't doubt that Charlie lied to me, but I couldn't accept that he had the black intentions Johanna was suggesting. Despite the continually unhinged look in Johanna's eye, I continued to press her. "How did that foil your plan?" I asked, tentatively.

"Oh, I shouldn't have trusted that coward to begin with!" Johanna exploded, garnering attention from the barista and the other occupied table in the café. The elder girl now looked visibly distraught, wiping her eyes. "Oh, Davy, it's awful! I've waited five years for the perfect moment to have vengeance and everything falls out of place. Charlie told me to wait for the San Pablo mission. I knew he was feeding me lies. I should have trusted you instead of that wimp. You're . . . you're the only one on this team I have faith in now!" Johanna hid her face in her hands and began to sob quietly. I had never seen her do anything like this before. It baffled, amazed, and continued to terrify me.

"It's . . . it's okay . . ." I comforted, not entirely sure what to do, considering that she tried to kill me minutes before. Johanna's arm once again lashed out from across the table and covered my mouth.

"Did I tell you to speak?" she whispered, her jaw tense. "I'm having a crisis here, Davy! I need you to listen to me."

"Okay, okay!" I pleaded. For someone who didn't want to talk, she seemed to like the sound of her own voice.

"Chucky crashed our jet," Johanna continued bitterly, "and I always had the idea that it was him, from the second we escaped from the plane. I wanted to string him up just like Demiese did after he betrayed us. Cuz you see, if the mission was successful, I was gonna be the one to report to Weiss. The delay between me and the rest of the team was the most important thing here. Alone in his office before anyone else arrived on campus, I could kill him right then and there and run off into the night. None of you guys would face any retribution for it, since you'd all have alibis. If worse came to worst and they were gonna kill you anyway for some reason, Leon would step in and sacrifice himself and let the rest of you escape. Kid can soak up a lot of bullets before he goes down, y'know? Of course, after our plane crashed for a second freaking time, there was no hope for a regular meeting. The plan was effectively foiled. I didn't realize it at the time, but eventually I knew that I was ruined."

As I listened to Johanna's failed plan, I realized the simple genius of it. Had our plane not crashed, she was very likely to have succeeded, especially if she was alone on campus with Weiss. To see such a brilliant mind fall into an erratic state made me almost pity her. "Why didn't Weiss just confront you?"

"I think he had other motives when he was manipulating Charlie," Johanna stated, looking down at her drink. "Dark motives. Darker than the most bitter of mocha . . ."

"Johanna, please make sense," I begged. I didn't know whether or not to take her accusations against the professor seriously. "What motive does Weiss have to hurt us? Why would he sabotage our mission?"

"Ugh, questions, questions, questions!" Johanna screamed, rubbing her temple. "I think I'm starting to hemorrhage. Here's a question to answer yours. What happens when a Red Plan is initiated?"

"Easy. Every member of the team dies."

"Bzzzzzt! Wrong!" Johanna sounded off, mashing her teeth together. "All the *field agents* die. The planner—the party that initiates and oversees the Red Plan—is alive and well by the end of it."

"Where are you going with this?" I asked, now somewhat flustered myself.

"Oh my. So stupid. So dense," Johanna now started rubbing her head in wide motions, nearly toppling over her half-used cup of coffee. "That's it. You deserve to die. Weiss can kill you for all I care. I laid everything out for you, and you still don't understand! Nobody understands!"

"Please calm down!" I loudly scolded, beginning to lose my patience. I needed to change the subject, but I couldn't think of anything lighter to turn to. "Why did you attack me on the road?"

"Because I knew Weiss had sent you to kill me. Am I wrong?"

"Actually, he wanted to make sure—"

"No, I'm right," Johanna hissed. "Weiss wants to kill me."

I gave a half-laugh at the notion. "Why does he want that? *You* were the one that fled the hospital."

"Why do you think I did that? The night before I escaped, there was a figure by my bed, standing behind the curtains. It wasn't one of the nurses; I know that. It just stood there, breathing. I started screaming and yelled for help, and when the nurses arrived, that's when I decided to bolt. I knew that the shadow was gonna do something, so that's why I bolted the next day. If that shadow was the traitor, there's no way I would survive another night. I got my weapons from campus and have been in the forest since."

I shook my head, uncertain of what to believe from the unhinged psychopath. "So you think the professor was the shadow?"

"I know he was; I just know it."

"Can I have one last question, Johanna? If it's not too much trouble, of course."

"What?"

"I checked your rifle from our little standoff. It was loaded. You wanted me to shoot you back there, didn't you?"

The sniper slid back in her chair. "Even if I told you everything I know, Prince, there's stuff you'll never understand. I live for a purpose. I live for me and me alone. I hated the Academy, but it gave me *purpose*. Now there are no more plans, no more future. Nothing to look forward to. Just an unwanted past I could never get away from."

"You know what you need to do, right?" I said, softening my voice. "You have to go talk to Weiss. Bring a gun if you're scared. If you really think he's the demon that ruined you, go confront him. Find out the truth."

"What do you think, Prince?" Johanna cocked her head. "About Weiss. About my pathetic little story."

"I think you need closure," I said, taking one last sip of my drink. All that remained of it was whipped cream. "You're not gonna get that unless you go to his office and face him."

"Dodging the real questions. A typical Prince response." Johanna looked amused, but still resigned. "You were always the favorite, and I never understood why. Truthfully, I never thought you deserved it. Something's different about you, Davy. Something I can't see . . ." her voice flickered away, and she went back to staring at her dark coffee.

With no words left to exchange, I left Johanna and the café. As I opened the door to leave, I could've sworn I heard the faint sound of music playing somewhere on the radio. I instantly recognized the song as one of my least favorites. *"We could be dancing in the shades of crimson . . . dancing and dancing and dancing in a new shade of blue . . ."*

CHAPTER TWENTY-ONE

After a long and dreary afternoon, the light igniting the gray clouds reluctantly disappeared and night fell upon campus. I nervously paced my room, unsure of what to do with myself. I was still fiddling with my knife. I had given my gun back to Weiss, who looked even more concerned than earlier. I, of course, didn't tell him about Johanna, instead just telling him about Ida. He just seemed amused that Ozzy had a friend. I peeked outside frequently, observing a calm Lake Pavus as well as the Central Building to the far left. The professor was active, as I observed the familiar single light shining from his office. Leon returned to the dorm a little past eight, and after him I saw no other humans cross in front of the building. If she wanted to reach the Central Building, Johanna would no doubt take a stealthy approach. I imagined her skipping across the trees with a mad glint in her eye, carrying her briefcase, now stocked with weapons.

Mulling over our conversation at the café, I found myself returning to her accusations of Weiss, and how she brought up the Red Plan. *How does that fit into anything?* I pondered.

Did Weiss want us to initiate the Red Plan back on San Pablo?
I created a story in my mind—a scenario of what was going
on behind the scenes. It was nothing more than a theory, but
the more I thought the more I found things to be connected.
My thoughts shifted between Johanna, the music, General
Demiese, and even the ill-fated Tenth Academy.

Then, a little past eight, my window shattered. Panicked,
I clutched my knife and held it out threateningly in the
direction of the noise. The atmosphere seemed to explode
as glass fell to the floor along with a large, heavy object,
which landed on my bed. Seeing that no human was trying
to break in, I cautiously approached the object that seemed
to have caused my window to shatter in the first place. It was
a brick, heavy and rectangular, with a tightly woven thread
around it and a note tied to one of its sides. Cutting the
thread, I released the small piece of paper. It read, *Things
haven't gone as planned. Find me in the arcade.*

Mabel burst into my room, panicked. "What's going on?
I heard glass!"

"Yeah, I'm a little baffled too," I said, keeping my voice
calm. I wanted to maintain a façade of serenity in front of
Mabel. As terrified as I was by Johanna's ominous note, I
knew an unnerved Mabel might easily complicate things.
I pointed to the glass on the floor, temporarily distracting
the girl as I stuffed the note in my pocket. "Listen to me,"
I whispered. "Eastway isn't safe anymore. I need you to get
a gun and take refuge somewhere you don't think people
could find you."

"You can't be serious . . ." Mabel murmured, shock
setting onto her face. She looked at my face for a second,
straightening out her own. "I . . . I understand. I'll get
changed and go to the girl's bathroom. Say something to tell
me it's you before you walk in. I . . . I can trust you."

It was with that last declaration that it occurred to me that Mabel didn't have to trust me. She could have naturally assumed that I was setting her up for a trap, or at least being somewhat dishonest (which I was, for the moment). Instead she ran to my room, fully assuming that I was trying to do the right thing. This faith gave me a new outlook on the situation: I had people counting on me now. "Do you need a gun?" I asked, regretting that I never taught her how to shoot.

"Nah, Leon gave me one of his shotguns in case something like this happened," she beamed sweetly. "So if I saw someone who's trying to hurt me I could splatter their brains on the wall behind them!"

"I love the mindset," I smirked, tucking away my own weapon. Against a gun, I'd be at a disadvantage, but there was always a chance that my opponent would underestimate me. Plus, if the combat was close quarters, I prefer a combat knife against something that you had to aim and shoot.

"Where are you going?" Mabel asked, now with concern rather than panic.

"The arcade," I said, deciding to entrust Mabel with the truth. "Johanna called me down there because apparently something went wrong."

"You've kept in contact with Johanna?"

"Well, kinda . . . not really, no," I said, trying to get the words out of my mouth as fast as possible, before Mabel could lose her faith in me. "Look, I've had a pretty weird day today. I'd love to explain the finer points of it, but there's seriously no time."

Before Mabel could respond, a loud shattering noise erupted from another room. "What was *that*?" Mabel asked, gasping.

"Sounded like it came from Leon's room," I observed. "We've gotta get out of here, now. Go upstairs and get your things. If you see Leon and he's carrying a gun, hide. Only approach him if you know he's friendly."

"Yessir," Mabel agreed, darting out of my room. Once she was out of my sight, I ran out into the hallway and down the stairs, practically sprinting from the dorm. Across the lake, I could see a single bright light shining. The arcade must have been switched on.

As appealing as the entertainment venues at Eastway were, I found that after the first two weeks I hardly ever visited them. Between training, missions, and Charlie's antics, I found that I hardly ever had time to go to the movie theater or arcade. The theater always had new movies, just as Weiss had promised, and the arcade had some genuinely fun games, although the video game consoles in the dorm tended to be higher quality. It was a deceptively plain building, with slightly larger windows than the others at Eastway. When the arcade was powered—as it suspiciously was that night—you could see a varying rainbow of colors flicker through the windows. Mostly the building just stayed dark. Since it took up so much power, and we were nowhere near a plant, you needed special permission from Weiss to "turn on" the building, and even then you could only play for an hour or two before it had to be switched off again. The power being switched off always seemed to happen at unwanted times for me, typically when I was about to beat *that one* high score.

Stepping inside, I was bombarded by more colorful light exploding off the screens of the arcade machines. Most of them had annoying music looping too. They were mainly retro tunes using electronic chimes, almost reminding me of the alternative music Johanna was fond of. "Jojo?" I called out, raising my voice over the noisy arcade, making sure that I could be heard.

No answer.

Fearfully, I drew my knife and began to silently skim the rows of arcade cabinets. Between the saturated colors, I could see that the aisles were vacant. "Johanna?" I called out again, choosing a row to walk through. Through the electronic beats and pings, I heard a different kind of electronic sound. It was a tinny voice, loudly repeating the same words over and over again: "Winner! Winner! Winner!"

I rushed toward the source of the noise, leading me to a large machine at the back of the arcade. I vaguely recognized it as a large shooting range game Weiss had installed the previous year. On either side of the machine there were small tunnels that yellow ducks with targets on their sides would swim in and out of. Using a toy gun, the objective was to shoot as many ducks as possible before time ran out. Sure enough, the machine was the source of the voice, which eminated from an old-looking pair of speakers. A sparkling and impressive sign was above the machine which read, *Shoot! Win!*

Confused for a moment, I saw a blinking red button near the base of the machine, next to the coin slot. In large, white letters, there were the words, *Try again?* I punched the button and immediately heard the machine begin to rumble and groan.

"Winner! Winner! Winner!" the tinny voice continued to announce. The machine began to groan and whirl. The conveyor belt on the machine moved, but no yellow ducks came out. Instead, I realized, the belt was glistening with blood.

"Johanna?" I asked one last time, before the horrifying truth rolled in front of me.

Johanna's body rolled forward, streaked with red. Her eyes were shut, and her hands were clasped together across her chest. She looked oddly serene. Her expressionless face seemed the most unsettling to me. A face that only a few hours before contained life, despair, and fury now contained nothing. I let out a horrible cry, unable to process what was before me. The colored lights in the room began to spin. My stomach heaved and I felt a sharp pain. In my ears, the words rang out louder than ever, "*Winner! Winner! Winner!*"

I pulled the body off the conveyor belt, examining it furiously. I felt Johanna's neck and wrist, looking for any sign of a pulse. Holding her in my shaking arms, I saw that her head was bent in a strange way. I felt a deep wound right below her head, where her spine began. Feeling the warm blood trickle through my fingers, it finally struck me: she was dead. My legs began to wobble and I had to stumble forward to regain my balance.

"What is going on?" a loud voice, deeper than mine, spoke up. I looked up to see Leon now standing in front of me, looking about as shocked as I felt. "What is this?"

"I found her like this," I explained. As I spoke I realized how dry my throat now was. "I don't know what happened."

Leon drew his shotgun, "No freaking way. Johanna warned me about you. Sent me a note saying you were after her. I can't believe it!"

That must have been the noise I heard, I realized. A brick must have shattered Leon's window, giving him this new, false information. "Leon, you have to believe me," I gently placed Johanna's corpse on the ground, preparing my knife to defend myself. I could tell by the look in his furious eyes that nothing could curb Leon's vengeful rage. "We're being manipulated. Someone's trying to turn us against each other."

"I've had enough of you and your lies," Leon leveled his gun and fired at me. Seeing the initial gesture, I dropped to the floor and felt the brief heat of the blast pass over me. Leon looked down at his gun—perhaps it had jammed— and I darted past him, running down one of the aisles, keeping my head tucked down. I turned to see Leon following suit, trying to get his bearings as the colors and lights shone around him. He was wincing, trying to keep his eyes focused on me. The arcade lights distracted me as well, although stabbing him would have been much easier than shooting him in the current conditions. Even if I did stab him, there was a good chance that Leon could still overpower me. Running wasn't an option; I may have been an overall better runner than him, but an infuriated Leon was an excellent sprinter. This had to be solved a different way. I hesitated before stopping midway down the aisle. Leon stopped also some distance away, still trying to line up his perfect shot. "There's no need for this!" I begged, symbolically throwing my gun to the ground. "We have to talk this through. We both know I can't fight you, Leon."

The enormous boy looked at me for a second, baffled by my gesture. He lowered his gun, and for a moment I thought I had finally gotten through to him. Then his face tensed up again, and he growled, "You're full of it. You're treating me just like our marks! I know your tricks!"

"No!" I called out in frustration, unsure of what to do. Leon let out a roar and began running toward me. I preferred this to facing a shotgun, but two hundred pounds of muscle charging toward you could be equally terrifying in the moment. I held out my arms and braced for him, hoping that he would fall on my knife. There was a brief moment of total contact, where all of Leon's weight pushed down on mine. I fell to the carpeted floor, feeling a new wave of pain burst inside. My weapon fell harmlessly out of my hands and on to my side. Leon stood over me, repositioning his shotgun. I stared down the barrel of it, knowing that my death was inside. "Never bring a knife to a gun fight, Davy."

What happened next happened so quickly that it took me a couple of moments to process. A bright light emitted from a machine next to Leon—brighter and hotter than the artificial light regularly produced by the machines. A wall of fire briefly consumed him before the force of the explosion toppled him to the ground. More loud crashing noises followed, with bright lights emitting not just from the other aisles of cabinets, but the beams supporting the ceiling as well. As I sat up, small bits of debris and heat struck me. Every explosion caused the building's foundation to shake. Then the fire alarm began to blare and water began to rain from the ceiling, but it was clear that the sprinklers would not be enough to vanquish the growing blaze. In the confusion and chaos, one thing in my mind became very clear to me: The arcade was now an inferno, and Leon and I were in the middle of it.

CHAPTER TWENTY-TWO

Using my hands, I pushed myself from the floor and sheathed my knife. Leon was still on the floor, unmoving and with smoke rising from his torso. Not knowing whether he was dead or alive, I made my choice to pick him up and carry him on my back. He weighed much more than I did, but my adrenaline-filled body didn't seem to notice. Another nearby cabinet burst, bursting with a strange fizzling sound. Sparks whizzed past me, and some connected with the wooden ceiling, which was turning an unnatural coal-black. Ignoring the throbbing in my head and the burning smell stinging my nostrils, I began to walk. With each successive step, I heard creaks and groans from above. It was only a matter of time before the roof collapsed, which would bury Leon and me under six hundred pounds of burning wood.

The last of the firebombs burst, and the room was now dark and relatively quiet. The sound of crackling fire began to grow louder, as well as the sound of the snapping of wood. I paused to try to catch my breath, only to gag on the toxic smoke and cough violently, almost dropping Leon in the process. My lungs had not felt such suffocating pain since my unfortunate first mission in Quebec. My vision began to dim. Things became either black or a fuzzy red in my eyes as the weight on my back seemed to increase. I could feel the warmth of the fire grow as it licked my legs. *It can't end like this*, I persisted, forcing my legs forward. *Three students were not going to wind up dead in the freaking arcade.* My will to live, as well as my pride, would not accept my body's submission.

Getting into a steady rhythm with my feet, I charged toward where I thought the door was. I made contact with nothing, and it was only after I tasted the cool evening air that I realized I had made it out alive. Now exhausted, I dropped Leon carelessly and collapsed. My ears picked up a great, resounding crash behind us as the roof caved in. "Guess I'm never gonna beat my old high score, eh?" I muttered between deep breaths. I received no answer from Leon, and then I remembered that he might be dead. Carefully, I placed two fingers by his neck. They were happily greeted by a pulse, and as my vision returned, I saw his partially burned chest move up and down. I let out a long sigh of relief, thankful that my effort hadn't been in vain.

In the dark of the night, I could not make out all of Leon's burns, but I saw some faint discoloration on his cheek, which looked relatively severe. If my speculation was correct, he would need serious surgery to fix the wounds. If they were sustained on a mission, Weiss would always pay for such surgery if necessary, as recognizable facial scars were the last thing any covert agent needed.

Professor Weiss. My mind shifted to new matters. After the fire and pain I faced within the arcade, everything became remarkably clear to me. I knew exactly where I had to go, and why I had to go there. I felt my face. Parts of it were strangely wet, but I couldn't tell if it was from sweat or blood. As I stood up, the only physical pain I felt was exhaustion in my legs, which was a good sign. I did a few brief stretches, watching what was left of the arcade behind me. Completely collapsed, all it was now was a black skeleton of beams and rubble, with a few red cinders still glowing in the charred heap. I knew Johanna's body was there, buried under the ash. As unsettling and infuriating as her murder was, I recalled the way she looked at the café, how tired and broken she looked. I prayed that maybe she could finally get the rest a violent soul like hers deserved.

As for me, I knew that my night was just beginning. "No rest for the weary, eh Leon?" I said. Leon didn't answer because he was still unconscious. I imagined him saying yes. As horrible as I felt leaving him there, I knew that there was no way I could bring him all the way back to the dorm and have strength to spare. Plus, something told me that the darkness of the outer forest might be a safer place for him than the warmth of the dorm, where anyone could find him. I rearranged his body to be in what I thought was the most comfortable position, checked again to make sure he was still alive, and then went on my way.

Much to my embarrassment, on the path to the Central Building, I had to stop and rest twice. Once was to merely lie down and catch my breath, as my legs were once again being uncooperative. The second was to drink the fresh lake water, which helped relieve my burning throat. As I walked, I tried my best to hug the outer rim of the path, by the trees. My thought process was that if someone was to look down at the path from the Central Building, I would be partially hidden by the darkness. The Central Building, to my surprise, now looked completely vacant. There was no more light coming from Weiss's office, making me fear that he wasn't there. *Has he fled campus?* I couldn't accept that. He had to be there, and I needed my answers.

Slipping inside the ornate door, I was greeted with a completely different atmosphere than the one I had encountered earlier that day. A musty smell hung in the air, and the rooms on either side of me were pitch black. If someone wished to sneak up and do away with me, it would have been an opportune time. Walking up the stairs, each step gave off its own distinct sound as the old wooden foundation underneath me moaned. The upstairs hallway was just as dark, and I found myself almost stumbling to reach the correct door.

It opened with a terrible screech. My stealthy approach toward the office had been ruined by unoiled hinges. With a sigh, I threw the door open and barged inside. The room was pitifully empty, save for an open laptop on Weiss's desk. Its screen illuminated the large window behind it, drawing me closer to the desk by sheer fascination. I rounded the bureau and sat in the seat, keeping one eye on the door and another on the laptop. On the screen there was a short, opened email:

> *Auric,*
> *Project Prince's new results are disappointing. If things do not improve by the next interim report, we're ready to pull the plug and restart.*
> *Here's to a better future,*
> *Scott*

Exploring the computer, I found that there was another screen behind the email containing a paused video. Focusing my vision, I realized that it was a feed of the office I was sitting in, taken from a high angle. I looked around for a second and sure enough, in a particularly dark corner, a shiny lens was staring down at me, accompanied by a small green light. It had never occurred to me that the professor recorded his own room, but I supposed it only made sense. The segment on the video, however, appeared to be recorded. Curious, I pressed the play button and turned up the volume, unprepared for what was about to appear.

● ● ●

Weiss was in the bottom corner, sitting at his desk alone, swirling a glass of wine in his hand. There was another glass, along with the bottle, on his table. He didn't drink; instead, he only looked at the liquid churning in his hand. A few seconds passed and the door opened. Johanna, alive and well, stepped inside, looking just as disturbed as I had seen her in the café. She dropped her briefcase onto the floor with a heavy smack, alerting the professor to her presence. "Good evening," I heard Weiss say through the laptop's speakers. "I expected you'd come sooner or later. Would you care for some wine? I was expecting a guest tonight . . ." He gestured to the glass on his table and the vacant chair in front of him.

"I know what you're doing," Johanna warned. Nevertheless, she took a seat, but not before taking out her revolver and putting it on her lap.

"Five seconds into a conversation and a lethal weapon is already drawn," Weiss said. I couldn't see his face well, but I imagined him rolling his eyes. "You, Jojo, always know how to spice up any encounter. That's a very nice forty-four Magnum. You haven't tried to shoot me yet; I suppose you want to talk first, correct?"

"I'm not in the mood for a pleasant chit chat," the sniper snapped. "You're gonna tell me what I want to know."

"Oh, the noble Johanna asking for my humble assistance," Weiss said, sarcasm bleeding from his voice. "I'm truly honored. I suppose it's a professor's job to provide his students with information, so how may I help you, Miss Wills?"

"Were you or were you not the planner of the Tenth Academy?" Johanna said in an empowered voice.

"Humph," Weiss clutched his chest, "right in my heart. You really know how to get down to it, don't you? What did you find that suggested such a noteworthy assumption?"

"Like all other past students, the names of the members of the Tenth are crossed out if you look at documents in the archives. Through my own methods, I've managed to uncover the names of all of the field students, but I couldn't find the name of a planner."

"Too difficult to uncover that name in the files?"

"Actually, it doesn't exist. Throughout the entirety of the archives, I could not find any mention of a planner belonging to the Tenth Academy. Every Academy is required to have at least one planner, yet the Tenth apparently didn't have any."

"Maybe that's why they all died," Weiss remarked, giving a dry, insincere chuckle. "A planner is the brains of any successful mission, and given how horribly screwed over they became, it's not out of the realm of possibility."

"If the Red Plan happened thirty years ago," Johanna continued, undeterred by the professor's vicious sarcasm, "you would have been fourteen or fifteen. I have no idea how our organization recruits people for your post, but I assume that they are former students."

"A fair assumption, I suppose . . ."

"Let me ask you again," Johanna said, in a determined voice. The more she spoke, the more comfortable she seemed. I saw less of the crazy girl from the diner and more of the cold, sharp girl I had known and hated for many years. "Were you or were you not the planner for the Tenth Academy?"

There was a long pause. Weiss let out a deep sigh and said in a still highly superficial tone, "I guessed that the cat would come out of the bag sooner or later. I mean, there's no secret I can hide from a genius like you, Johanna. Are you sure you don't want any wine? It's—"

"Therefore," Johanna loudly interrupted, "it's quite safe to assume that you are indeed the traitor, the one that sabotaged our mission to San Pablo, in order to spite the organization that killed your friends in the Tenth."

There was another terrible silence. I still couldn't see Weiss's face and couldn't see whether he was now angry, calm, or somewhere in between. I could, however, hear his voice answer soothingly, "I think you should have that drink now. Something to calm both our nerves, so we can have a nice, grown-up talk. Do you like red? I got it on a supervision job in Corsica a few years back. Good vineyards they have in Corsica, with nice hard workers . . ."

Johanna stood up and approached the desk, clutching her revolver tightly in her hands. She looked very ready to pull the trigger. "Answer my question, Professor," she insisted. "Are you the traitor?"

"Have a drink first," Weiss bluntly retorted. "I refuse to speak to anyone right now until they tell me if I made the right selection from my cellar." As the professor spoke, he stepped away from his own desk and looked out the window, absentmindedly placing his glass down. I could see half his face, and he looked just as I had suspected: calm and collected. There was also a hint of a smile on his lips, which bothered me deeply. Behind his back, Johanna rearranged the glasses so the one Weiss held was now in front of her. The professor turned back around and picked up the new glass in front of him. "To a bright future, eh?" the professor said. The two clinked their glasses and sipped their drinks. Parting his lips from the glass, he remarked, "You knew that

I had poisoned a glass and you switched them around, didn't you? Couldn't pass up the opportunity to kill your professor with his own trick?" A small grin appeared on Johanna's lips. After a few moments passed, however, that smile faded, and her face began to grow pale. "Unfortunately for you," Weiss continued, "as insidious as you are, you're also pitifully predictable."

Johanna grasped her throat and let out an angry cry, "You disgusting little—" She was unable to finish, however, and began to choke, collapsing to the floor.

"Sorry, didn't catch that last part. What was that?" Weiss began to laugh as his victim struggled, her white face now turning blue. "Oh my, this is precious. Of course, I would have been poisoned had you not switched the glasses, but I had faith in your spite toward me." The professor walked around his desk, kicking a writhing Johanna as he made his way to her briefcase, clicking it open. "You can relax. It's fast acting, but it's not lethal. A death so painless wouldn't suit you one bit, now would it?" He began to rummage through Johanna's things, haphazardly throwing objects on the floor. All the while, Johanna still lay on the floor, hacking violently. "You were so gifted that your talents nearly matched your arrogance. You did, however, have the special flaw of ticking off just about every person you met. You have no heart. You think of people as mere tools. It's only fitting that the way you die is by your own deception. You can relax, though, cuz the rest of the monsters in this place will soon be joining you."

The poisoned girl on the floor wormed her way toward Weiss, only to be kicked back. After going through its contents, Weiss shut the case and turned his full attention back to Johanna. Picking her up, he placed her facedown on his wide desk. Johanna was no longer making choking noises;

rather she appeared to be letting out demented wails, almost crying.

"Such a shame," Weiss picked up Johanna's metal briefcase and walked over toward her. "So much potential wasted by a corrupt mind. Don't worry; this is where you belong." Weiss raised the briefcase above his head and brought it down. Just as it was about to make contact with the back of her neck, Johanna managed to choke out a high-pitched screech, and the screen went dark.

•••

I clicked on the mouse for a couple of seconds, confused on why the video stopped. It then occurred to me that the power had somehow been manually switched off. "What the heck?" I muttered.

I heard a loud, mechanical noise behind me. *The cocking of a pistol.* Before I could turn around, I felt the familiar cold metal of a gun barrel press on the back of my head. "Good evening, Mr. Prince," a familiar voice rang out. "I see you've managed to survive the whole arcade ordeal. I could see the flames from here. Looked pretty terrifying."

"So it is true," I said, gulping. "You are the traitor. You're trying to kill us."

"*Trying?*" Weiss chuckled. "I think I'm doing a pretty good job of it, wouldn't you agree?"

"Are you gonna shoot me?"

"Oh, you sound so calm," Weiss muttered. "So familiar with death, I love it. Yes, you're going to die, but first, I think I have one last lesson to teach you."

CHAPTER TWENTY-THREE

All that rhetoric," I said, "all those talks about our bright futures and potential—they were all lies?"

"They were never my words," Weiss said, sighing. "It was never like I had a choice, Davy. Either I graduated early—where they would most likely kill me for my 'failure' to protect the team—or I worked within the organization, bringing it down from the inside."

"That makes sense," I said. I gave a slight nod, still very conscious of the terrible danger I was in.

"You don't sound very surprised," the professor noted.

"To tell you the truth, sir, I was suspicious of you," I confessed.

Weiss let out a hearty laugh, clearly still in the jovial mood he was in when killing Johanna. "You knew that I was the traitor and you still let poor Jojo go off on her own? Typical of you, I suppose. Always throwing others in harm's way to test out the waters for yourself. What gave me away?"

"The radio," I said with a gulp. I would have very much liked to turn around and look at Weiss face-to-face. I could see some of his reflection on the computer screen, but most—including his eyes, which I could've used to judge attitude and intentions—was hidden. "The radio back on San Pablo. It stuck out to me when I went up in the terminal. It was newer than the rest. Starting with that radio, the rest of your plan began to make sense."

"Oh, do tell," the professor said, clearly amused.

"Johanna was plotting to kill you. You were made aware of this by Charlie, who was reluctant to join in on it and was intimidated by its mastermind. You contacted General Demiese on the island, warning him about us and manipulating him into playing along in your game. You rigged a bomb to remotely blow under my seat in the plane after receiving a radio signal from Charlie, who was under the impression that it would be an artillery strike from the island. To further screw us over on the island, you gave Demiese the *MacVeagh*, which alerted him to our presence and killed the only member of the team that knew your secret. All the while, you played that weird song to confuse us and eventually place suspicion on Johanna. After we scattered the army and returned home, you used Johanna's erratic escape to your advantage, killing her and luring Leon and me—the only two field agents left—into an explosive trap."

"Impressive reasoning," Weiss complimented.

"What I can't understand, though," I added, "is why you even bothered keeping us alive for so long. The explosive in the plane could have been placed on the engine or on the wings, for instance."

"Where's the fun in that?" Weiss continued his chuckle. "I hate two things in this world, Mr. Prince. One is the Academy, naturally, and the other is General Demiese, Santana, and the LLA. They were, after all, directly responsible for what happened to the Tenth. I couldn't stand to watch them live on. So, I made a little game out of it. My team versus the murderers of my comrades—it was perfect! I was very capable of taking care of either side alone, so it really didn't matter who won."

"So I'm guessing you got wind that a coup d'état was going to take place in the LLA, and you wanted to take advantage of it."

"With every word you say I feel slightly guiltier about killing you," the professor said, sighing. "You've got a beautiful brain up there, Davy. Kind of a shame when I'll be wiping chunks of it off my desk. Once I was made professor, I had total control of you agents so that part of the plan only required me to bide my time and win over the trust Miss Scott and my other higher-ups."

Slowly, I reached for the laptop's mouse and exited out of the video, leaving the email. I needed to keep the professor talking. If he wasn't talking, he would likely shoot. "Did this 'Project Prince' thing have anything to do with me?"

"Looks like we've got a friggin' Einstein here," Weiss said, scoffing. "You were supposed to be the end. *You* were supposed to be the next Angelo King. You could handle the burdens he handled, and there'd be no need for Eastway anymore. The Sixteenth would be the last Academy. Imagine that! You were my biggest hope, Davy."

"I guess I disappointed you, then?"

"The moment you stepped into my office, Prince, I knew you were no Angelo. Ms. Scott wants to start over. How many more generations would it take, do you think? Two? Three? How many more kids were gonna have to die in the line of fire, trying to fill out contracts? That's when I realized I needed to end the Academy, and Demiese's coup gave me the perfect opportunity."

"That's it, though?" I said, still trying to maintain an unenthused monotone. Weiss couldn't figure out what I was thinking. If he knew how terrified or desperate I was,

I would quickly lose any chance of getting out of the chair alive. "You kill *us* to get revenge on Scott? Why not go for the lady herself?"

"Scott's untouchable," the professor explained, sounding frustrated. "You have no idea how powerful a woman like her is. The only way to end the Academy is to decimate it totally from the inside. Killing the others would be inconvenient. Killing you would be a setback. But if all of you were gone . . . that would send a message loud enough for her to hear."

I had to take the initiative. Before Weiss could react, I spun around on his swivel chair, careful not to press or move my head away from the pistol, which was now pointed at my forehead. "Sorry, this is more comfortable," I remarked. He glared at me, narrowing his eyes. I glared back. We had something of a staring contest, except instead of trying to get the other guy to blink, one of us was one finger twitch away from killing the other. In this new position, however, I felt more in charge of the situation. I could see Weiss's pale white face, understand the emotions coming out of it, and, if I got lucky, manipulate it. "You can't kill me, y'know," I stated, speaking as though I was trying to pull off a Jedi mind trick.

Weiss could have easily pulled the trigger right then and there. He had known me long enough to know how I operated. Perhaps it was his overconfidence in his understanding of me that kept me alive. No matter what words I said, he believed he would never be manipulated by them. "And why not?"

"Because Ms. Scott would get very angry at you," I replied. "I know you already know this, but she has quite the temper."

This time, Weiss's laugh didn't seem to end. So much so, I considered making a move to take advantage of the distracted professor. "How do you know Ms. Scott?" he asked, fancying my ridiculous comment.

"We've been in contact with each other," I continued, not entirely sure where my wild story was going. "She never had very much faith in you, Professor, and honestly, who can blame her? She asked me to keep an eye on you a few months back, and after the whole ordeal in San Pablo, I alerted her of my suspicions. If I was such a disappointment to her, why else would she visit me in the hospital, personally overseeing my surgery? She said she'd 'take care of you' if anything were to happen to me, her prized possession and the successor to Angelo King. Naturally something did, back in the arcade. After surviving the explosions, I contacted her, and she said she'd be here within a few minutes, with reinforcements she stationed in town just for me. If they find me dead, their first objective will be you, and you won't be able to escape."

Weiss looked at me in awe, and for a second it seemed as though he had actually bought what I said. "That was," he began, "the most glorious pile of BS I have ever heard in my life. Excellent! Was that rehearsed? When did you come up with that? Truly marvelous!"

"It's true," I insisted, in a very serious voice. "You don't have to believe me. Frankly, after everything you've done, I don't mind dying if it means you'll get what's coming to you."

"You don't know when to quit, do you? If you and Ms. Scott are so close, then," the professor inquired, "what's her first name?" The fact that he was asking such a question told me that he was at least acknowledging my tall tale, which was a minor win.

"Henrietta," I said, without missing a beat. I needed him to believe me. Just for a *second*. "Henrietta Scott. Has a nice ring to it, wouldn't you agree? Any other questions?"

For a brief second, I saw Weiss's jaw tense. *Bingo.* It was clear he had not expected me to answer correctly, and I could tell now that he was beginning to feel some form of pressure.

It was clear that Weiss wasn't sure what to do now, and fearful that he would do the obvious thing and shoot me, I became desperate. "I heard some voices when I was walking up here. They might be outside right now. You gonna take that chance? I can—" I was silenced when the professor withdrew the pistol from my forehead and instead shoved it in my mouth. My tongue tasted the open metal tip of the barrel.

"Enough," he said in a soft, uncomfortably soothing voice. He leaned in close, "Look me in the eyes." He began to judge me. We stared at each other deeply. I focused on the small fraction of light he had in his pupils, and he looked into mine. I was not afraid of what I was showing Weiss through my eyes. I wasn't afraid that he had a gun in my mouth. I was no longer afraid of what would happen to me in the long run, or to the Academy, to Leon, or to Mabel. All that mattered now was staying alive, just for a few more seconds. *Believe me. Let my lie influence you, just for a moment.*

After what felt like an eternity, Weiss looked up above me as if a sound had startled him. "There's no one out there . . ." he muttered, taking his gun out of my mouth and looking out his window.

Now it was my turn to act.

In a swift and terrible motion, I pushed Weiss's gun away from me and launched myself out of his seat, pushing him against his glass window. Turning around, I leapt over his desk and bolted toward the door, shutting it loudly behind me. A gunshot rang out, making me run faster down the hall, practically throwing myself on the stairs. I heard footsteps charging after me, as well as another gunshot. The gunfire didn't scare me as much, given that the bullets were being fired in the dark by a middle-aged guy trying to keep up with a teenager.

Now in the foyer, I ran, arms outstretched, to the main door. Furiously shaking the knob, I was horrified to find that it was locked. Back on the stairs, I heard heavy footsteps begin to descend. "Don't make this difficult, Davy," Professor Weiss called down, in a voice similar to a father calling his children. He wasn't scared. He had little to fear from me. Everything was according to his plan, and my shenanigans meant nothing.

With all my remaining strength, I pushed against the entrance. With every heave, the old wood seemed to give way until a crack formed by the knob. This fissure spread until the door itself gave way, and I was able to break free. More gunshots told me that Weiss was still close behind. I needed cover and I needed it fast. The Central Building had a wide terrace with ancient trees scattered across it. Getting a running start, I launched myself up the nearest one, reaching for the nearest branch and hoisting myself up until I was certain the leaves concealed me. I looked down to see that Weiss had made his way out of the building. He began shooting into the treetops. It was clear he couldn't see me, so I clutched hard onto the branch I was perched on and focused on staying perfectly silent.

Back in the office where I had just disarmed him, Weiss was in perfect stabbing range. I kicked myself thinking that I didn't take out the professor when I had the chance. *Was something still holding me back?*

"Seriously? Hide-and-seek?" Weiss called out. "You really want to do this the hard way, don't you? What's your plan now, to run away? Leave the campus? Go ahead. Leave with the knowledge that you let Mabel die. I know she hasn't left the grounds yet, so it's only a matter of time before I find her."

My fists tightened around the branch. I wasn't running away; I knew that. It was much too risky to try to kill him, though, as Weiss would shoot the second I made myself known. All that I could do was listen to the professor and his taunts.

"We doing this the hard way, Davy?" Weiss said, ranting up to the treetops. "Fine. Then lemme turn the clock back two years. I never understood why you were so antsy about that night. It's traumatic, sure, but I always figured the truth would come out one day. Then I thought of something: what if you knew what had happened all this time, and you were just hiding it from the lot of us? What if you *did* do something that night so unbelievable, so evil, that you were perfectly fine with the truth never coming to light? Isn't as much of a stretch as it seems. After all, you *are* a psychopath."

What? When Weiss said his last word, Johanna's face immediately came to mind. Her distorted, inhuman face. I could see it indifferently looking down as she tortured a crab or some small animal. I wasn't like that. I cared about those around me and looked out for them. How could I even be compared to a ruthless killer like Johanna? Then, other images surfaced in my mind. I saw Demiese's bloodied face and the heels of Beauregard's boots. There was Johanna's sickening arrogance at the beach, and what she said.

The professor, perhaps sensing my shock, followed up by saying, "Oh yes, you didn't figure it out? You boys always liked to poke fun at Miss Wills, and it's true that she was always a much more severe case, but one of the base qualifications to be accepted to Eastway is that you display psychopathic traits. All of you just imitate the good in society around you because you know that the alternative is unacceptable. Even Miss Pryce—poor, innocent Mabel—is a high-functioning psychopath."

Weiss must have been lying. He was trying to get me to blow my cover, and he was lying. Mabel wasn't psycho. The very idea seemed preposterous. I had doubts about myself, but Mabel was different. She was the most human out of all us.

"Engineering one of the deadliest plans in Academy history didn't ring any warning bells to you, then?" Weiss began pacing the lawn, continuing his one-sided questioning. I drew my knife, praying for an opportunity to close the distance between us. "What a tragedy! The girl's doomed. So afraid of becoming an emotionless agent, she doesn't realize that deep down inside she already is one!"

I couldn't take it anymore. I felt the same way I did back in the terminal. A frozen hate. This time, though, it felt justified. I needed to kill Weiss not just to protect myself, but for the others who depended on me. He was right under me with his gun as at his side. I wasn't gonna get another chance. I dove down knife-first toward him, feeling a rush of evening air. The edge of the razor was about to make contact.

Then the pain hit.

It was a viciously sharp sting, like a dozen needles shoved into you all at once. I held in my breath, but couldn't exhale. My knife was just an inch from his face, but Weiss looked perfectly calm. "You think you're the only one that keeps something up his sleeve?"

I looked down. His arm was holding me up in the air, holding something that was digging into my abdomen. Auric Weiss had stabbed me. He threw me down, allowing his knife to make a jagged exit wound as I dropped to the ground. The pain, at its worst when the knife left my body, was replaced with total numbness. I couldn't feel anything. I couldn't breathe, only watch as the dark spot grew under my shirt. I moved my hand in an attempt to cover it, but Weiss just kicked it away.

"Just let it flow out," he said, his million-watt grin illuminating the blurry darkness around us. "This is how it's meant to be, Davy. You're nothing but a monster. All you do is obey and kill, kill and obey. You were created to be a monster. You were trained to be the *perfect* monster. And now . . . now you can die the death you always deserved." He picked my knife up from my limp hand and tossed it, still keeping his bright eyes firmly planted on my dying ones. "If it's any compensation," he added, "the skies are clearing up outside. You can die thinking about how bright tomorrow will be without you."

I couldn't move anything anymore, and my vision went completely fuzzy. I watched a hazy Weiss step over me and disappear, leaving me alone on the terrace. Even though I could no longer control or feel my mouth, some stray words fell out of it, and I called out in a weak voice, "Y-you're wrong. I'm n-not . . . I d-didn't . . ."

CHAPTER TWENTY-FOUR

Where am I? What am I doing? What's going on?

The world around me shifted. I was in a long, dark hallway, similar to the upstairs of the Central Building. That, of course, was a place I didn't know yet. I was back in my house, approaching the kitchen. It smelled like leftovers, as well as a new, unknown scent. The voices that I had heard upstairs were still there. The same two male voices; the female voice—Mom—had fallen silent.

"You're being unreasonable," I heard my Dad say as I neared the door. "He's none of those things. He's just a boy. He doesn't want to hurt anyone."

I reached for the doorknob, but I quickly lost my courage when a new voice, a voice I had never heard before, spoke. "That's our main concern," he said. He sounded much calmer than Dad. "He's become too integrated into society here. He's not going down his intended path."

"All the more reason to keep him here," Dad pleaded. I'd never heard him sound so unnerved in my entire life. "He has emotions. He can be afraid, angry, happy . . . he's not the boy you're looking for. He'd never kill."

"He's the boy we gave to you!" the man snapped. "Don't make this more difficult than it has to be. The very code his body follows was taken from the greatest mind of our generation. That sort of genius doesn't belong here. He's nothing more than a loan we gave to you."

I eased open the door, carefully making sure that I wasn't making any noise. The image I found in that kitchen would be one that I would repress for the rest of my life. My mother lay face down on the hardwood floor near me. I couldn't see any blood, but she was clearly inactive, and a knife was by her hand, stained red. Unable to comprehend such a sight, I looked away, up at the two men conversing. One was, naturally, Dad. He looked the same way I saw him at dinner, except now he was clutching his left wrist. Looking closely I could see traces of crimson up and down his arm. "He's just a boy," he pleaded, repeating his previous argument. "He's nothing else. Taking him away will only bring you disappointment."

The other man smiled. He wore a very expensive black business suit. Despite being well-dressed, he had a grotesque mouth, with his two front teeth missing. "I believe Ms. Scott is disappointed enough as it is."

Ms. Scott. It was a name I would not hear again for another few years, and even then I would greet it with confusion. In my delirious, terrified state, I took my hands out of my sweatshirt and instinctively picked up the bloody kitchen knife off the floor, clutching the wet hilt with both of my quaking hands. I took a small step toward the two men.

Dad noticed this. He turned his head and said, "David?" Taking advantage of this moment of distraction, the other man advanced on my father and pushed something into him. I listened to my father take a short gasp of breath before getting pushed down to the floor, dead.

"Dad!" I screeched. I considered running toward him, but my legs refused to move, still under the influence of my terror.

The other man walked toward me, cocking his head. "Are you Mr. Prince? It's very nice to meet you." He spoke sweetly, as though he were talking to a little kid.

I staggered back, mortified, clutching the kitchen knife protectively to my chest.

The man looked down at the knife and shook his head. "No, no . . . that's not right." He reached out and forcefully took my arms, straightening them out so the blade was facing him. "There we go."

Then the killer leaned toward me. I pushed the knife forward, stabbing him under his tie. Crimson began dripping down from the blade and onto my hands. His body shuddered, but he didn't cry out. As I looked up at his face, he was, in fact, still smiling. "That's it," he said, as a small river of blood flowed out of the side of his mouth. He then whispered a single name, quite clearly: "Angelo . . ."

One more body dropped to the floor, dead.

The walls around me began to grow fuzzy and melt. Once everything became clear again, it was evident that I was still in the kitchen; the room hadn't changed. Three bodies were lifeless around me, with various amounts of blood around each. The blood I had gotten on my hands was gone. I was also no longer wearing my sweatshirt, but rather a comfortable dress shirt, the kind I typically wore at the Academy. It was dead silent, and at first I was unsure of what to do. Then, I heard a faint sniffling in the corner. I saw a kid in my sweatshirt, covered in crimson, hugging himself tightly. His eyes were paralyzed with fear, clearly unable to cope with what was around him. I recognized him as the kid who kept me company in my cell in San Pablo, the one who wore my sweatshirt, complained about the July weather, and had a kitchen knife to protect himself. We locked eyes. He knew me from somewhere, and I recalled him vaguely as well. We were accomplices who had been separated by a great distance.

Feeling obligated to say something, I slowly approached the boy, unsure whether to smile reassuringly or weep with him. I crouched down, maintaining eye contact. He had the most bloodshot eyes I had ever seen, which eerily matched the rest of his equally scarlet face. It was red in all the wrong ways, though. "Hey," I whispered in a hoarse voice.

"Hi," he responded. I was pretty sure he didn't know what to say, either. "It's been a while, huh?"

"Yeah," I nodded, somberly. "Didn't think I'd ever come back here. I really didn't want to." I couldn't help but quickly glance back at the bodies behind me. The young boy swallowed hard, and proceeded to softly weep again. "Hey, hey, hold up here," I cooed in a quiet voice. "Don't be like this. It's okay. Just try to calm down and relax."

"I'm scared," he whispered. I could tell that his eyes were shifting away from mine and were focused on the horror behind me.

Almost on reflex, I responded, "Yeah, I'm scared too." The words felt alien to me as they parted my lips. I was, after all, the great Davy Prince. I improvised, trusting in myself and in my instincts to get me out of even the most difficult situation. Only now, I didn't trust myself at all. I felt no better than him, and I wanted to join the kid I was staring at in the corner and cry about what happened to me years ago. Then I could cry about the horrors happening to me in the present day.

I couldn't, though. I knew that. Instead, I wrapped my arms around the boy and embraced him reassuringly.

He leaned close to me for support, burying his face in my shoulder. The bloody kitchen around us disappeared, and it was just us, floating alone in a void of darkness and uncertainty. The illusion and the terror around us was fading and soon, I knew, it would become just another tragic memory. It became something I lived beyond.

A faint light returned in the boy's eyes, and I couldn't help but give him a weak smile. Then he was gone.

• • •

"'Ere we go!" Leon proclaimed, stitching my wound.

I let out a terrible cry of anguish that would have put the thirteen-year-old version of myself to shame.

"Whoa!" the attending boy exclaimed, dropping his needle and backing away from me. "Holy crap! Davy, you're awake!"

"Where am I?" I cried out, still in a good deal of pain. The open wound under my bare chest made it hard to breath. I looked around at my surroundings. I was resting on a cushioned table, with white cabinets above and below me. The walls were white, as were the tiles on the floor. The room was also quite cold, but that was probably because I was shirtless.

"The infirmary," Leon stated, still looking rather shocked that I was awake. "Heard the gunshots and found you on the terrace, real bloodied up. It's a miracle you survived the trip over here." He carefully adjusted the dressing in his hands, "Hold still, I need to make sure I do this right."

"You went looking for me?" I said, surprised and pleased, albeit still in a good deal of pain.

"And I patched you up," Leon explained. "It's a miracle the knife didn't make it to your lungs. Guess the Sixteenth still has a little bit of luck with them." The boy said, resuming his stitching. The needle stung, but I pretended not to notice.

"I didn't know you could treat knife wounds," I observed.

"I guess when you've had so many yourself, you pick up on a few things. Johanna showed me a thing or two too. It's the least I can do for . . . y'know . . ."

"Trying to kill me?" I said with a smirk.

"Yeah," Leon blushed. "You sure you're okay? You almost died, man. Don't think now is the right time to smile like that."

"Given what's happened recently, I've gotten used to almost dying." My grin evaporated when Leon tugged hard, trying to close the open wound. I couldn't help but let out a hard grunt. "That," I panted, "that, I haven't gotten used to yet."

"Sorry," Leon muttered, haphazardly resuming his work. His stitching was sloppy, but I figured it was better than nothing.

"You run into the professor when you went looking for me?" I asked, using my question as a distraction from my mild agony.

"Nah, I hid in the woods when he approached the terrace. He seemed so calm that it made me think he didn't know what had happened. Think he was going in the direction of the arcade," he said, "So it was him, then? The professor?"

"Yeah," I nodded dumbly. "Had us all fooled. He was a member of the Tenth Academy, and now he wants revenge on his higher-ups and thinks if he gets rid of us all the program wouldn't be able to start back up again. Honestly, I really don't blame him. It's the trying to blow me up part I really don't like."

"You mean back in the arcade?" Leon pondered, absentmindedly rubbing his face. I realized that his burns could be very severe—I saw uneven skin on his wrists and cheek—but the way he acted and talked it seemed as though they weren't there.

"Yeah, and back on the plane, remember?" I elaborated, "The professor seems to have it out for all of us, but I'm at the top of his hit list. The higher-ups want me to become a perfect agent, and they've been watching me for a long time."

"How long are we talking here, months?"

"Years, I think," I said, distressed. "I saw something really weird when I was passed out."

"I can imagine that. When I was carrying you over here, you kept mumbling. I think you were talking to yourself."

I couldn't help but smirk at that comment. *Yeah, I was definitely talking to myself.* "I saw the night my parents died," I continued. "From what I saw, I wasn't the one who killed them."

"Who was it?"

"Dunno," I said, looking back. The memories no longer hurt as much to recall, but I could still feel a slight twinge. It was my subconscious telling me that nothing good can be found where I was looking back to. "He had no front teeth. Fine black suit—maybe Italian—creepy smile on his face. Told my Dad that I was just a 'loan' to them. It was weird . . ."

Leon put one last bandage on my torso, carefully making sure he wasn't touching one of my sensitive ribs. "Listen man, I'm really not in the mood to play investigator. If whatever acid trip you had made you feel better, I'm cool with that. Now, can you stand up?"

"Lemme try," I leaned on Leon for support as I slid off the infirmary bed. My legs shook for a second, then gradually steadied. My oldest gunshot wound—the one in my foot—burned once again. I assumed Leon had given me some painkillers, but I wanted more.

"Good, good," Leon began to slowly walk me around the room. His voice changed to an oddly sad tone as he said, "So . . . does that mean it's all over? The Academy, I mean."

"Yeah," I responded, a little too matter-of-factly. "We have to find Mabel and get out of here. You don't honestly want to stay on campus, do you?"

"No, of course not. Well . . ." Leon paused for a second, deep in thought. He let out a sigh and stared at me, "Is it okay if I let down some serious crap on you? Think you can handle it right now?"

"Um, sure," I said, shrugging indifferently. "What's wrong?"

"Eastway's our home, man," the large boy looked away from me, frowning bitterly. "If we make it out of here, what happens next? Where do we go? What do we do?"

"I don't know," I confessed. "Right now, I'm just focused on surviving the night."

"So freaking close," Leon shut his eyes in frustration. The arm he was using to support me tightened. "Get to go to whatever college I wanted. Get to choose my own path in life for a change. It was *right there*, Davy, I saw it. You know how much I had to put up with here to get a freaking chance?"

"I thought you didn't care about killing."

"Never said I enjoyed it," Leon growled. "It's just the facts of nature. Same way our destinies are chosen. I was never meant to have a bright one."

"What do you mean?"

"When my parents abandoned me," Leon proclaimed suddenly, his face stoic. Every word he said felt increasingly strained, like someone was sticking him with needles. "When they found their bodies, police thought it was just an accident, somehow. Then they came home and found the bills. And the drugs. And the notes. Then they knew. I was in third grade and they called me down to the principal's office. I thought they were gonna reward me for my grades or some crap. I'll never forget that day. I remember how each and every single person looked at me."

"Third grade?" I asked, shocked. "You can only come here when you turn thirteen. How did you—"

"I got by," Leon answered flatly. Something told me he had been asked that question many times before.

"I'm sorry that happened to you," I muttered quietly.

Leon sat me back on the table and opened one of the cabinets. "Don't be," he said, in the same tone of voice as his previous statement. "I've had enough pity thrown at me in my life. All it does is weigh me down. Wear this," he handed me a plain white t-shirt from one of the cabinets. "Isn't like that fancy black dress shirt you had on, but if you start bleeding again we can tell."

Pulling the new shirt over my head, I shivered as the cool fabric made contact with the burning skin around and below my chest. "Okay, I think we're good," I said, vaguely realizing that the conversation about Leon's past had been dropped. *Most likely, it was for the better.*

"Yeah," he nodded, "let's go find Mabel."

Most buildings had an emergency weapon hidden. Although I wish Leon could have found my knife, we still had a small, single shot handgun which the boy had found in one of the infirmary's many cabinets. Lifting the chair he had blocking the door, the two of us trekked out.

The infirmary was about halfway between the Central Building and the washrooms, which were by the dorm. After I divulged to Leon where I had told Mabel to hide, we walked in silence. I really didn't mind it very much, as it was shaping up to be a very nice night out. The mostly dark campus let the stars shine above, including hints of swirling galaxies and colored nebulas. The air seemed to have warmed up, albeit slightly, making the lakeside breeze we felt along the path all the nicer. Weiss was nowhere to be seen, probably for the best.

Reaching the bathrooms, I felt a touch of concern when I noticed that the lights were off. It was the smart thing to do, of course, because if they were on it would have been one of the first places Weiss would have gone to. There was also, though, the possibility that she never made it to the bathrooms to have the lights activate in the first place. I quickly dismissed this fear. *She had to be in there . . .*

Just about everyone hated the bathrooms on campus. It was just one small building with two adjacent rooms for the boys and the girls. The girls' room had four showers and four stalls, while the boys' had four showers, two stalls, and two urinals. I can't speak for the girls' room, but for some reason one of the showerheads in the boys' would always have ice-cold water come out of it. Worse yet, the cold-water showerhead seemed to alternate by day, so you never knew if you were safe until you turned the knob.

I lightly peeked around the corner and called out, "Mabes? You in here? It's Davy. You can come out now."

No answer. Cautiously, I stepped inside, triggering the light. Leon stepped inside after me, noting his surroundings. "So this is the girls' bathroom," he noted. "It smells much nicer than the boys' . . . cleaner too . . ."

"Focus," I scolded. Although admittedly, I was enthralled by the scent pervading the air. It was like unused soap with the finest hint of cinnamon.

"Hey, boys!" a female voice cheerily chirped. The bathroom stall furthest from us flew open. Astonished, I stumbled backwards while Leon pulled out his pistol and pointed it at the door. Mabel poked her head out of the stall, widened her eyes when she caught sight of Leon and his weapon, and then slid back in, no doubt terrified.

"Mabel, it's okay," I assured her. "Leon's not going to hurt you. I think we're all just a little high strung right now. Isn't that right, Leon?"

"Yeah," Leon nodded. He dropped the pistol to his side, but did not put it away.

Mabel reluctantly stepped out. Between what Leon and I had both gone through throughout the night, Mabel's electric presence was almost overwhelming. She had the brightest shine in her eyes and a full smile of white teeth gleaming in the light. She was so brilliant-looking that you could almost forget that she had a shotgun in her hand, holding it like a club. "Oh, you're alive! I was getting so worried! I've been waiting the longest time in that stall in the dark, and it was getting real scary. I almost fell asleep, but I'm pretty sure one of the worst things a person can do is have a snooze on the can, I mean—"

"Mabel, Mabel!" I called out, silencing her. Rubbing my forehead, I stated, "Can you please keep it down? It's been a pretty long night."

"Right . . . sorry," Mabel sighed. "Where's Johanna?"

"Dead," Leon informed, scowling. "Weiss killed her, before trying to kill me and Davy. The arcade exploded."

"The arcade did what now?"

"Exploded. Like, bombs," I pointed to the wounds on Leon's skin. "It did this. All this is Weiss's doing."

"Ugh, I should have figured that out," Mabel muttered, frustrated. "He was the planner for the Tenth Academy, right?"

"Yeah, how did you know that?"

Mabel absentmindedly rubbed her bottom. "When you've been sitting on the john for as long as I have you get a lot of time to think things through."

"Er . . . right," I said, trying to make sense of the words that came out of the female student's mouth.

Mabel looked at Leon and me carefully, "Oh my gosh Davy, you look terrible! It's like you lost a pint of blood."

"Try a couple quarts," Leon said. "Mabes, we're in real tough shape. Do you think you can come up with a plan to find and take down Weiss? He's armed."

"You want to kill the professor?" Mabel looked astonished.

"That a problem?" Leon said, giving his usual intimidating glare. "He's responsible for what happened to Ozzy and Charlie. He tried to kill us. He's *trying* to kill you. There's no way we're leaving this campus unless he's dead."

"Al-alright," Mabel nodded, uncomfortable with the vengeful notion. "Well, uh, we'll be down a gun, though." She pointed to her shotgun. "Tried testing this thing out. I think the trigger might be stuck or something."

"Safety's on," I blurted out quickly. I swiped the gun away from her. "See this button by the trigger guard? Push it to make the gun go boom."

"Just keep the darn thing," Mabel scowled, rubbing her hands on her shirt. Feeling the gun, I did indeed notice that it felt very sweaty. "It'll suit you more than me."

"How many shells you got in there?" Leon inquired, leaning over.

With a distinct click the gun barrel opened. Despite having two barrels, only one appeared to be occupied. "We've got one shot with this one."

"I could run inside and get more ammo," Mabel volunteered.

"Don't bother," Leon shook his head. "Weiss set the campus on lockdown a few minutes ago. None of the dorm doors will budge on the outside. We could smash one of the windows, but I'm guessing we don't have that sort of time to spare, do we?"

"No." The wheels in her head seemed to start turning as she said, "We'll have to make do with what we've got. Two guns, two bullets, and one target. I can work with that."

"Um, I hate to be a bother, but," I fearfully chimed in, "there's something I need to ask Weiss about. While he's alive, he needs to tell me something. Can that work?"

The girl grimaced, reluctantly saying, "Yes . . . if it's that important, I can give you a few seconds."

Leon stepped in between us. He had a new look on his face, one that reminded me of a professional actor walking on stage for his closing night. It was a confident sort of smirk, with acceptance bleeding from his eyes. What fate he had accepted though, I didn't know. "Alright, time for the final mission of the Sixteenth Academy," he declared, looking down at his gun. "This . . . this was the first thing Weiss ever gave to me on campus." As he spoke, a full, malicious smile grew on his face. "It's quite old, and I'm not entirely sure if it still works, but . . . a gun claims many men before it's done. Just . . . one . . . more . . ."

CHAPTER TWENTY-FIVE

Professor Weiss probably had the best car on campus. It was this vintage pearly white Corvette, parked in the closest space to campus. Due to its light shade and age (most school cars were no more than three years old and were replaced regularly) it stuck out like a sore thumb. I was quite relieved to see it parked. Upon further inspection, all the other cars were accounted for as well. It meant that either Weiss was fleeing on foot—which was a silly notion considering how much he had planned ahead—or he was still on campus, and Mabel's recently hatched plan could take effect.

Unarmed and alone, I leaned on Weiss's car and patiently waited. The bugs in the forest made noises and the trees quietly rustled. I was typically annoyed and distracted by such sounds, but that night I enjoyed them. When you brush with death you look at the little bits and pieces of life in a new light, including the sounds of nature. It had been a very long time since I had felt so relaxed. Even when I saw

Professor Weiss approaching me, my muscles did not tense. I greeted him casually.

"Good evening, Davy," Weiss said in an equally lax tone. "Are you enjoying the night atmosphere around you?"

"Surprisingly, yes, Professor. You were right about the skies clearing," I observed, grinning. He hadn't pulled out a gun and shot me to death yet, so my smile felt justified. "How about you, sir?"

"I'm a bit disappointed," Weiss sighed, shaking his head. "I figured stabbing you was enough to do you in. Guess I'm just not as handy with a knife as I used to be."

"It wasn't a total loss for you, sir," I countered. "You did manage to poke a hole in my favorite shirt. That got me mildly displeased."

Weiss chuckled at my remark. "I was just about to say you look very stupid in white. Did you know that? Anyway, how did you manage to patch yourself up so quickly?"

"Turns out I'm just like Tinker Bell," I said, maintaining the light air of the conversation. "I just had to believe hard enough, and I came back to life."

"How inspiring. Not even knife wounds can stop that illustrious tongue of yours from irritating my ears," the professor let out a sigh. "Now tell me, where is Mabel? I'd much rather have both of you in my sight."

"Close, but not too close, if you get my drift," I said, trying to sound suave.

Weiss only rolled his eyes, "I don't have time for this. What do you want to ask me?"

"Huh?"

"Mabel is hiding, and you're unarmed," Weiss elaborated. My guess is—since she hasn't made a move to kill me—you want some information, and you're willing to take a sizable risk to get it."

"Sure," I said, without missing a beat. Inside, I was astounded by Weiss's sense of logic, and knew that now was not the right time to mess around. He apparently had no intention of killing me—perhaps fearing retribution from Mabel—but that could all change in a heartbeat. "Remember when you almost stabbed me to death, like, a couple hours ago?"

"Yes, I remember the experience quite fondly. Would you like to try again?"

"When I was on the ground, bleeding to death, I saw my father's murder. I didn't do it. There was another guy in the room, and apparently he was taking orders from a 'Ms. Scott.'"

"Even at the threshold of death, you delude yourself," Weiss shook his head disapprovingly. He rubbed the trunk of his car, getting some of the dirt off. Even though he tried to keep it as lustrous as possible, the dirt at the Academy had a special way of sticking, tainting its perfect white paint job, much to Weiss's dismay. "There are no reports of a third person, if that's what you're wondering. All the records say is that there is some suspicion that you had a hand in their deaths, but that's about it. I'm speaking honestly, kid."

"Is there any chance," I insisted, "any chance the records could be wrong? Maybe they were changed in a cover-up?"

"A cover-up against the whole organization? Ridiculous . . ." Weiss's mocking voice tapered off, and he scratched his chin thoughtfully. "Well . . . it's possible. Possible for you, maybe. You always were a special case . . ."

"What does that mean?" I said, angrily. "What makes me so special?"

"I'd watch your tone of voice, kid," Weiss scolded, threateningly moving his hand to his holster. "Even before you were born, you were always in Ms. Scott's sights. To her, you *were* the next Angelo King. Even if she had her doubts, if you leave this campus alive you will be hunted down by them. Either you become what they expect of you or they make you disappear. You were never meant to leave this campus once you entered, you see. What awaits in your future . . . the pain you shall suffer, the darkness that will consume you . . . you'll be praying for death." He tapped on his belt, and I heard the distinct metallic clink of a guaranteed demise. "I can alleviate the pain for you. There doesn't have to be a dark future. There doesn't have to be any future. I can give you the gift of *sacrifice*." On that last word, Weiss released a creepy smile. It struck me that he must have calculated that we'd come face-to-face again, somehow. "With you dead, we could still defy Henrietta Scott. One final, bold move to prove you're not a part of this awful machine. Isn't that a worthy cause?"

"Alright," I groaned. Knowing that I wouldn't get any more information out of him, it was now my turn to roll my eyes. "I think you've officially lost it. Mabes, you can come out now. I think this nutcase needs to be taught a lesson."

There was a brief pause. Weiss, angry that I wouldn't be a good boy and choose to die, pulled out one of his pistols. But before he could fire, the door to his luxury Corvette flew open, smashing into him, and he toppled to the ground. Mabel, brandishing a pistol, stepped out of the car and threateningly pointed her weapon at the traitor.

The professor only laughed. "You gave Pryce a gun? That's hilarious!" He sprung to his feet and pushed back at an overwhelmed-looking Mabel, pistol-whipping her across the face before turning his attention back to me.

Fortunately, Mabel's plan accounted for her own ineptitude. On the other side of the parking lot, a black convertible roared to life, shining its high beams on a stunned Weiss. In the light, it was difficult to see that a very angry Leon was behind the wheel. On the radio, set to its highest volume, blared Electric Sheep in Wonderland's classic alternative hit "Shades of Ruby."

Much to my satisfaction, Weiss looked utterly unnerved, unprepared for the sudden turn of events. "You've gotta be freaking kidding—"

Before he could finish his sentence, the convertible roared toward him, and he let out a cry as he frantically jumped out of the way. The car sailed past him and smashed into his Corvette, breaking the driver's side windows. To my displeasure, Leon almost hit Mabel, who was still recovering by the driver's side door. The convertible, missing its bumper due to the impact, backed up and prepared for another run against its middle-aged target.

Weiss, taking less than a second to get back to his feet, leveled his gun and fired a few frantic shots at me. They missed, although I could have sworn the final one whizzed past my ear. The engine to Leon's car revved up once again, and I saw that he was gunning forward for another shot at Weiss. The professor anticipated this and held his ground, firing at the convertible's wheels. A loud popping noise exploded through the air and Leon's car swerved unexpectedly. Instead of the mangled front, Weiss was hit with the passenger's side door of the car, enough to make him lose his balance once more. The convertible grinded to a halt in its new, awkward position, just as Weiss slowly rose to his feet. With some slight hesitation, he broke into a dash out of the parking lot. Leon leapt out of his seat and screamed, "He's getting away!" along with a stream of swears. He pulled out his shotgun and aimed at the frantic Weiss. I heard him mumble something else under his breath, but I was unable to make it out.

Then, he fired. The crack of his shotgun seemed to be the only thing that made a sound in the air now, followed by a hard *thump*. I turned to see that Weiss's silhouette was no longer on the horizon.

"Did I get 'im?" Leon asked, his voice full of uncertainty. He motioned for me and Mabel to follow him to where the body went down. As we walked onto the grassy terrace by the entrance, a strange, bright-white body came into view. It was certainly Weiss, with red marks spotted over his pea coat from where the shotgun's pellets had struck him. Leon inquired, "That was a long shot. Is he dead?"

I cautiously approached the unmoving body. Weiss's chest didn't seem to be moving, but his face looked too calm. Just as I leaned over for a closer look, his eyes popped open and, in a lightning-quick motion, Weiss jumped to his feet, grabbed me by the throat, and held me to his chest, pointing a gun at my forehead. "Was that it?" the professor proclaimed arrogantly. "I expected more from you, Mabel. Such a shame."

I could see Leon tense up as he raised his gun at Weiss. "You disgusting freak!"

"And a very unimpressive insult to boot," Weiss pressed the gun closer to my head, as if he were trying to push it into my brains. "The Sixteenth Academy has become a great disappointment. It's no wonder none of you will graduate."

"Still three against one," I pointed out, daring to speak. I was certainly shocked by the turn of events, but the fact that I was getting a pistol pointed at me yet again made me numb to the terror. I wasn't going to be afraid, not now.

"It's also one bullet against sixty," Weiss countered. His minty fresh breath gave me shivers. "I'm pretty comfortable with those odds. How about you, Davy?"

Leon looked ready to make a move, but before he could, something caught him off guard. A new sound entered the atmosphere: the wailing of sirens. It was light at first, but as it got louder I knew that they were headed our way. "What is that?" Leon asked, still snarling at Weiss.

"Oh, I called the police," Weiss responded humorlessly. "Told Penney that you kids rebelled against me and that you should be shot on sight. It's technically true. I mean, he doesn't have to know the whole story, now does he?"

"You called the police on us?" Mabel asked, in shock. "Seriously?"

"Yeah!" the professor snapped, angrily. I couldn't see his face behind me, but I guessed he had quite a large, ugly smirk on his face. "Who would have thought that secret agents could get taken down by a few officers? Not exactly what I had planned at first, but it will suit my needs. At last, the Tenth's vengeance will come to fruition."

"The Tenth Academy," Mabel whispered to herself. She lowered her pistol, looking confused. "That's what this is all about, isn't it? Getting revenge on the people that caused your friends to die? But if you're the planner, wasn't that mission's failure totally *your* fault?"

A weird silence fell over the air. Even the sirens seemed to be muffled. "What?" Weiss said plainly, unable to comprehend Mabel's words.

"Yeah, it was your fault," the girl reinforced, raising her voice. "I read over that mission at least a hundred times. I could never understand it fully, though, since the planner's role was weirdly omitted. Now it all makes sense. The students of the Tenth did really erratic things during that mission, things that led to their unnecessary deaths. I think you kept trying to initiate a Yellow Plan, but you failed along the way and had to order a Red Plan."

"*What?*" Weiss screamed, this time much louder. His enraged voice almost blended in with the wailing sirens, now quickly approaching. "I didn't do anything! Demiese—"

"Demiese and Santana killed them, sure," Mabel said, shrugging. There was a strong gleam shining in her eyes now, and I knew that she was confident in every word that came out of her mouth. "But it was *your* sucky plan that put them in danger in the first place."

Weiss's fury and Mabel's words began to worry me. "Mabes!" I called out, trying to warn her. Before I could say any more, Weiss's gloved palm shut me up.

Mabel must have known what I was about to say, and gave me a quick nod. *She's got this*, I realized, *whatever she's doing, she's got this*. Despite my full attention staying on Mabel, I couldn't help but notice that red and blue lights were flashing farther down the street, nearing the gates with their loud sirens. "If you want to punish those responsible for your friend's deaths, how about you put that gun in your mouth?" the girl declared. "Maybe then the mighty Tenth can have their vengeance."

I listened to Weiss breath unevenly. Even without hearing his voice, I could tell that he was ready to burst with fury. "Listen to me, Prince," he whispered in my ear. His words sounded very shaky and unrefined, completely different from the lax professor I had known for many years. "I'm going to kill her now, and you're going to watch." With a violent jerk, he pulled the gun away from my head and pointed it at Mabel, who also boldly raised her pistol. I dropped to the grass, shutting my eyes. I didn't want to see how it would end.

A single, loud crack burst through the air.

Then, it became uncomfortably quiet. Even the screeching of sirens seemed to have gone away, if only for a second. I heard a loud thump and realized that it came from behind me. Reluctantly, I opened my eyes, only to see Mabel—wide-eyed and trembling—clutching my pistol in her hands. A small stream of smoke rose from the pistol, showing that it had been fired. Stunned, I turned around.

Auric Weiss lay dead in front of me. His eyes were bulging, and his mouth was terribly agape. In his final moment, he was, no doubt, surprised that a young, obnoxious little girl would have the audacity to slay a mighty genius of his caliber. Leon called out, running toward the body. "Right between the eyes! Nice shot, babe!"

I looked back toward Mabes. She was still in the same position, seemingly petrified. "Um, Mabes?" I quietly moved toward her.

Mabel said nothing, and only looked down at the body. The confident heroism she had when confronting Weiss was now gone, and I could see tears welling up in her eyes.

"It's okay," I comforted her, approaching the shaken girl with open arms. While we were close, I subtly took back my revolver. "It's okay, Mabes. You did the right thing."

"Hate to break up this lovefest," Leon called, with a degree of intensity still in his voice. "But we got big problems on our hands."

Mabel and I both turned to see that the police had arrived. Six or seven patrol cars, as well as one SWAT truck, passed through Eastway's open gates. Car doors began to open in the parking lot, and cops' screaming voices began to be heard. The three of us made a break for it. Mabel, the former track star, ran much faster than her two male counterparts, who both struggled with the injuries they had received over the night. When she reached the edge of the forest, Mabel turned around and screamed, "They're coming!"

Leon and I both looked behind us. A small legion of uniformed officers and SWAT team members were stalking us, firing bullets and screaming incomprehensible things. A huge spotlight shined on the two of us from the parking lot. The light stunned me for a second, almost causing me to trip. Leon grabbed me violently by the shoulder and screamed, "They're too fast! Keep running!"

"What?" I called back, panicked. To my shock and terror, Leon stopped sprinting with me and turned around, limping back toward the armed officers. "Leon!" I called out in distress, realizing what he was doing. The loud, tinny voices of police loudspeakers and sirens seemed to intensify as Leon approached the crowd, lifting up his empty shotgun threateningly.

"Like I said before," he called out to me, giving me one last smirk. I saw the same acceptance in his eyes that I had seen earlier, only now I knew exactly what it meant. "You don't belong on campus. I think I do." He turned back toward the cops, letting out a defiant yell before charging straight for them.

A thousand shots seemed to go off at once, and over my shoulder, I saw Leon stop dead in his tracks, convulsing as the bullets rained down on him. He shook like a prisoner on death row receiving a lethal volt before unceremoniously dropping to the ground, where a dozen police officers swarmed around him. The last image I saw of Leon was between a SWAT officer's legs, right before I entered the forest with Mabel. He was gone and I knew it. I let out a final cry of anguish, and didn't care if any of the men around Leon heard me. The man who had tried to kill me earlier just saved my life by slowing down a legion of police, stopping Weiss's last furious attack against us.

With true, unbridled fury coursing through my veins, I grasped onto Mabel's small hand as she ran, and the two of us darted deeper into the forest. We kept running until we could no longer see the blue and red lights or hear the sirens. We kept running until the trees blocked out the moon and the stars, and all we had was the blackness in front of us. Then, surrounded by darkness, we became nothing more than children stumbling blindly into the night.

EPILOGUE

A few hours later, on another side of the world, Henrietta
Scott woke up in a plush king-sized bed to the smell
of creamy Parisian coffee and cherry blossoms outside. Her
suite contained a magnificent view of the Champs-Élysées.
If work wasn't too busy, she intended to people watch, one
of her favorite pastimes. Just as she was having her lavish
breakfast in bed, she received a notification on her laptop—
a new high-powered model that had not been released to the
general public yet. Much to her dismay, Iras's ugly, scarred
face popped up on screen.

"M'lady," Iras said in his annoying, gruff voice. It was
annoying voices like Iras's which made her wish surgeries
could change vocal chords. As loyal and intelligent as he
was, he also had an appearance that could make a class of
kindergarteners cry. On top of that, he was delivering very
bad news. Henrietta's beautiful morning was almost ruined
at that very moment. "The Sixteenth Academy at Eastway
has fallen. We recovered the bodies of Johanna Wills, Leon
Andre, and Auric Weiss on the scene."

"Weiss?" Henrietta said, shocked. She nearly choked on her waffle.

"If records are to be believed, m'lady," Iras continued, "he was the main perpetrator that led to the deaths of the other two students during the San Pablo mission."

"Leave it to Auric to mess up our fun," Henrietta rolled her beautiful, violet eyes and scoffed. "So, who's left? These students seem to be dropping like flies."

"Well, there's Mabel Pryce," Iras said. As he spoke, a picture of a girl popped up on the screen. She was rather pretty, with a round, but very defined face and a bright smile. "We also have David Prince, of course," the subordinate continued. A gaunt, serious-looking boy popped up on screen. Despite his looks, Henrietta had to note that he did have very nice hair. "They fled campus approximately around the time local law enforcement came. Their current whereabouts are unknown. They seemed to have been able to outsmart Auric and overpower him."

"Ah, Davy!" Henrietta chirped cheerfully, staring at the picture of the boy. She had her doubts, but perhaps there was hope for him yet. "That's my second favorite Monkee, y'know."

"Very nice, m'lady," Iras said, not even bothering to feign enthusiasm. "We've got the campus secure for the most part, and local news outlets and eyewitnesses have been silenced about the matter. Some came more quietly than others."

"Oh, Auric," Henrietta sighed, taking another big bite out of her meal. "Always having to make things messy for us."

"Now, what should we do about the two survivors?"

"Well, we gotta get Davy, of course," Henrietta eyed the two profile pictures. "The boy may very well prove his worth after all. As for the girl . . . meh, she's cute, but expendable.

Our top priority is finding Prince by the quickest and most efficient means."

"What do you suggest?" Iras asked, intrigued by his boss's words.

A dangerous gleam flashed in Henrietta's ageless eyes. "Are they aware of the other Academy?"

"Er, no, m'lady," Iras said, shocked at the notion. "You can't honestly be suggesting—"

"Your students haven't had a very difficult mission in a while, now have they, Iras?" Henrietta smiled warmly. "Well, here are two juicy targets, ripe and ready for plucking. It'll give them good experience, wouldn't you agree?"

The muscles in Iras's face tensed up, causing his many scars to ripple. He knew that it was impossible to argue against Ms. Scott. "Y-yes, m'lady. I'll get my students prepared for action."

"Very good, Professor," Henrietta beamed, satisfied with the way the conversation ended. She put away her laptop and lounged in bed, carelessly finishing the rest of her waffles. Soon Davy Prince would be on the right path once more, and then she could bask in the success of decades of planning. But for now, Henrietta Scott was very content with resting in her bed, looking through her open window and welcoming a bright, new, glorious day.

DISCUSSION QUESTIONS

1. The agents of Eastway Academy have a prevailing sense of entitlement when it comes to their futures. The loss of the opportunity to have what they deemed to be a successful life is what drove many to join the sinister program. In the modern world, should someone who is intelligent and hardworking feel entitled to a successful and happy life?

2. Davy Prince is presented as a well-intentioned, but ineffective hero in *The 16th Academy*, largely due to the fact that he cannot confront his past and the circumstances that brought him to Eastway. By the end of the novel it is clear that he is on the path to personal redemption by reflecting on and accepting what happened in the past, as well as confronting Weiss with the truth he's uncovered. Which is more important to redeeming yourself: realizing and accepting your own faults or taking real action to right wrongs?

3. Compare and contrast the methods, actions, and personality traits of Davy Prince with the more traditional dashing, heroic spy archetype.

4. Loss of identity is a major theme in *The 16th Academy*. Mabel Pryce voices her frustration with the internal pressures of the Academy system, but Davy assures her that she is in charge of her own personality and nature. Weiss claims that all of Eastway's students displayed psychopathic tendencies before the Academy, implying that the program merely unlocked a devious nature already present in the students. Is there any evidence to suggest that Davy's viewpoint is true? Is there any evidence to suggest that the professor is right?

5. All agents in *The 16th Academy* have different opinions on killing and death during missions. What do you make of Davy's aversion to killing? What about Johanna's complete acceptance of it? Ozzy's desire to do it? Charlie's fear of it? Leon's indifference to it?

6. Johanna calls out Davy for his attitude against killing, despite the fact that he openly allows her to kill enemies on missions. If you permit such killing to happen, should you be judged in the same light as the one pulling the trigger? Compare this idea of responsibility to Mabel's plan on San Pablo, which resulted in the deaths of hundreds.

ABOUT THE AUTHOR

Spencer Yacos is proud to be publishing his debut novel at Cedar Fort. He has been writing on the local level, as well as for magazines such as *Teen Ink*. Spencer was also accepted into the Emerging Writers Institute at Brown University over the summer of 2015. He looks forward to continuing with the *16th Academy* series as he heads off to study in college.

SCAN to visit

www.spenceryacos.com